SETTING THE RECORD STRAIGHT

THE TRUE STORY OF HOW I STOPPED A
MURDEROUS TYRANT AND SAVED THE WORLD
FROM NUCLEAR WAR

V.W. SHURTIFF

Illustrations by
BILL SHURTLIFF

FIFTH
AVENUE
PRESS

Setting the Record Straight

Copyright © 2018 by V.W. Shurtiff

THIS IS A WORK OF FICTION

Fifth Avenue Press is a locally focused and publicly owned publishing imprint of the Ann Arbor District Library. It is dedicated to supporting the local writing community by promoting the production of original fiction, non-fiction and poetry written for children, teens and adults.

Printed in the United States of America

First Printing, 2018

ISBN: 978-1-947989-23-8 (ebook), 978-1-947989-22-1 (paperback)

Fifth Avenue Press

343 S Fifth Ave, Ann Arbor, MI 48104

www.fifthavenue.press

Cover and Layout Design by AADL

To my children, who will someday tell of their own adventures of living in the city of Ann Arbor.

CONTENTS

PROLOGUE

THE LADY TALKING to the bus driver got pretty much everything wrong. It was frustrating to hear. We *are* talking about the most important events in modern history. But after being annoyed, I realized that it is not really her fault. Pretty much everyone has heard some version of the story, but I would guess not one in a hundred has even a basic understanding of what really happened. That is my fault. I kept waiting for Veronica to tell it – she has always been the better storyteller. But for whatever reason, she has not yet. And it has been more than six years. So I decided that I have waited long enough, and for the sake of history, I would write it down. After all, I was there for all of it. Here goes...

CHAPTER ONE

Normal does not exist anymore. Back then, I was a normal kid, with normal parents, a normal dog, and a normal house. Like almost all kids back then, I spent my non-school hours playing video games online with friends. That may sound strange today, but it was normal back then. That world is no more. The person I was does not exist anymore. The house I lived in does not exist anymore. The country I lived in does not exist anymore. Normal does not exist anymore.

This whole story starts with my crazy dog, Elmo. Elmo got his name because he looked like Elmo of Sesame Street as a puppy, and I was just a kid when I named him. But he had become a huge animal (Clifford might be more appropriate).

He woke me from a deep sleep. I had been dreaming that I forgot to come to school on exam day (which, by the way, is a horrible dream), and suddenly I felt my jean leg being pulled.

I opened my eyes a little. It was still dark. My leg was jerked toward the edge of the bed. Confusion. My leg jerked further. Then I heard a grunt.

"Elmo?" I groaned, "What are you doing? Leave me alone. It's still dark!" I pulled my leg away from the edge of the bed and rolled over. Out of Elmo's reach. Back to my dream. Back to school. I was running through the halls now. Trying to get to class. And I forgot to wear a shirt. Girls were laughing at me. Why did I forget my shirt? Why did mom let me go to school this way? No time, I was late for my exam. I entered the room in front of my whole class without a shirt.

"Grrrr!" said the girl in the front row. I looked at her. That was a weird thing for her to say. Then she bit my leg. Hard.

I opened my eyes in pain. I was back in my bedroom, and Elmo was on my bed with his mouth on my leg. The clouds in my mind evaporated as I tried to figure out what was going on. Elmo removed his mouth from my leg and barked at me.

"What are you doing Elmo?" I asked as I sat up.

Elmo was frantic. He was jumping on and off the bed, grabbing my pant leg and barking the whole time. I got up and put on a shirt. Not going to forget my shirt today. It was still dark out. I looked at the clock, and it was 6:00 am – too early for a Saturday.

My parents like their sleep and would probably be as annoyed by Elmo's barking as I was. He probably had to go outside. I opened the door as Elmo continued barking. I shushed him without effect. I was sure he was going to wake up mom and dad. As I stepped into the upstairs family room, there was a strange stillness. All that noise and no one was up. I shushed Elmo again, and it seemed to have the opposite effect. He continued barking even louder than before. Then he got behind me, and with his giant horse head, he started to push me. I lurched forward almost falling.

"What are you doing Elmo?" I said in a barely whispered voice. But he continued to push. We got to the stairs, and I noticed something strange. My parent's room, directly to the right of the stairs, had the door open. That was strange for two reasons. First, they always slept with the door closed. Second, why had Elmo not awakened them yet?

I turned to look in their bedroom. Then I felt weightless for a moment. Then pain in my ribs. Then pain in my knee. Then my head. The wind exited my lungs, and I tried and failed to breathe. Elmo had just pushed me down the stairs. I had fallen to the landing. Not a far fall but also not the sort of fall you want to take on your head.

So, I am not a dumb kid. Sure, I was failing Spanish, but other than that, I was getting straight Bs. Maybe I was a little slow from the sleep, but I still could not figure out what Elmo was doing: Elmo, sensing danger, was trying to save me. But not realizing this, I just laid there. I was sure that my fall would wake my parents. I wanted them to come and feel sorry for me. Maybe I could stay home from school today. Maybe they would drop Elmo off at the dog pound.

But, to Elmo's credit, he didn't just leave me. I felt him clamp down on my ankle again. Then, to my horror, I felt my knee start to slide off the second flight of stairs. He was going to drag me down the rest of the way! That would be quite a bit more painful than the fall to the first landing.

"Ok, Elmo!" I cried out in fear. "Stop, I am getting up!" He paused as though he understood me. I got up and limped down the rest of the stairs holding the railing and fearing another push from Elmo. But I forgot all about him when I reached the bottom.

When I had said goodnight to my parents the night before, my house was your typical house. Lamps were upright. Couches were on their legs. Chairs were not smashed or broken. Doors were hung properly. Tables were not pushed clumsily against the walls. Windows were not broken. And rain stayed on the outside of the house.

That was not the downstairs I now observed. In the shine of the waning moon that blended with the glow of the street light in front of my house, I saw what looked like the deck of a shipwreck. Every piece of furniture was overturned. Papers were strewn all over. Things smelled of smoke. The water was, strangely, running in the kitchen sink. The doors were off their hinges, and the windows were broken. Rain from the newly accessible windows added to the soggy effect.

"Run...," a hoarse and wheezing voice said.

I turned around and saw an old man laying on his side next to the tipped over and torn up couch. His legs were twisted in ways that legs are not built to twist. In the moonlight, I could see that he lay in a pool of dark liquid. His asthmatic breathing continued although he did not repeat himself.

I don't know if you have ever come to the realization that someone who was not supposed to be in your house is in your house (maybe when it is dark, and your parents are gone), but it is pretty panic-inducing. My body locked up and my vision tunneled as I turned to face the sound of the voice.

Who was there? Was this still a dream? What was going on? Where were my parents? What should I do? Dial 911? Go to help him or run away from him?

But the state of my mental shock ended abruptly. I felt a sharp pinch in my rear pants pocket. I turned, and Elmo had sunk his teeth into my hind end and was growling. I had been standing in open-mouthed shock, but Elmo had not changed his focus.

"Ow! Elmo, you stupid dog!"

"Run!" said the same voice with the same whispered and rasped liquid tone but louder and more urgent. I turned and faced him. I could just barely see his silhouette in the shadows of the overturned couch.

"Who are you?"

"You have five minutes," the man said as he rolled over and squared his twisted body in my direction. "Get to Ann Arbor. Find Jacob...," his voice trailed off.

I recognized those names. Ann Arbor was where my dad traveled once a month. He told me that he had business there. And Jacob was my uncle, my father's brother. But Jacob did not live in Ann Arbor. Maybe he meant another Jacob?

"I have no idea what you are talking about, but I am calling the police."

"The police will kill you," his voice seemed to be growing stronger, and I could see the paling sky shining in his eyes as he stared at me.

My eyes were adjusting, and I could see him more clearly now. He had dark skin and curly gray hair. His beard may have also been gray, but it appeared dark with the liquid that dripped from it as he raised his head.

"What are you talking about? Where are my parents?" I think this was the first time I had come to realize that my parents were not home. There was no way that all this happened without them waking. Too much falling down stairs, too much barking, too much chaos.

"Get to Ann Arbor, and you will find your answers. But you must leave now." He put his head back down, and his cheek rested in the pool of burgundy liquid.

"Jacob who? My uncle? He doesn't live in Ann Arbor. He lives in Washington, D.C."

The man reached out his hand. I could see a chain

hanging from his closed fist. As he opened his palm, I could see the chain was connected to a key.

"I do not have enough heartbeats left to answer your questions," his voice was once again soft and tired. His head did not lift from the ground. "The safe might have your answers. Grab what is there… and run. You have three minutes now."

He closed his eyes, and his asthmatic breathing became slow and low.

Elmo had paused from his incessant barking as we had our conversation, but he became frantic again. He grabbed my pant leg and growled.

I knew what safe the old man was talking about. It was the safe that my parents had in their room. I had never known what was in there, but I recognized that key. It was my father's, and he wore it around his neck. The fact that this blood covered old man laying in my destroyed living room now held it in his hand was more than a little disturbing.

I grabbed the key and ran. Back up stairs. I had to run fast because Elmo was trying to catch me before I did. I was going the wrong way. I got to my parent's room. Their bed was made. They had not slept last night. I went to their closet. I opened the door. There in the corner was a black safe the size of a microwave. On the front of the safe, was stamped an American flag. The corners of the door were rusty. But the key easily fit into the lock. I turned the key. The hinges creaked as I swung the door open.

"Sit!" I yelled at Elmo hoping to get him to calm down. He ignored me and kept barking and grabbing my leg.

Inside the safe was a single large yellow envelope. I grabbed it, folded it, and crammed it in my front pocket. I shut the safe again, left the key in the door, and ran back down the stairs. Elmo bounded after me. I stopped at the bottom of the stairs. The old man was where I had left him. He was silent. No hoarse breathing. No breathing at all.

I again considered calling 911. "The police would kill me?" What was he talking about? But he knew things. He knew about the safe. He knew where my dad worked. He knew my uncle. Elmo didn't seem to mind him. Some part of me could not ignore his warning. I left the house.

It was early March and the chilled morning air made each raindrop sting as it hit my face and arms. I turned and ran toward the bus stop. For a while, I leaped over puddles, but soon my shoes were filled, and my socks were soaked, and I no longer bothered to avoid them. Elmo was much faster than me and would race ahead, stop and wait, and then race ahead again. The sky was not yet light, but there were signs of dawn, and a thin line of light started to appear on the reddening horizon.

The streets of my subdivision were empty, and the rain clouded my vision. But I knew the streets well. The two-story houses designed and built soon after World War II were all very similar. They were built of brick on the ground level and were white wood siding on the second story. The maple trees that lined the center of the boulevard were just starting to recognize the coming spring and were beginning to adorn themselves with buds and tiny leaves of bright green and red. The rain made their branches shake and shudder as it splashed onto the buds before falling into deep puddles on the grass. The houses cracked and sputtered as their flooded gutters worked to remove the water. As I ran the half mile to the bus stop, early-risers were leaving their houses and getting in their cars and starting their morning commutes to work. Men and women dressed in suits covered by trench coats with upturned collars were exiting their houses huddled under umbrellas. As I ran, cars passed me. I wondered what they thought of the boy sprinting in the rain followed by a giant red dog. I wondered if I should flag one of them down and ask for help. They would probably call the police. And the dead man on my living room floor said the police would kill me. I kept running.

The bus stop that was my destination would take me downtown. From downtown, I could buy a bus ticket to Ann Arbor. Fortunately, I had slept in my jeans last night because I now had money. I had $100 cash in my front pocket. Yesterday was my fourteenth birthday. Grandma gave me $100! I was going to spend it on video games. Now I was going to buy a bus ticket. Woohoo.

As I approached the bus stop, I checked my step and almost tripped in my distraction. An enormous man dressed all in white stood in the rain staring at me. He turned and faced me as I ran but did not follow. His movements were too slow and steady. His face lacked expression. His hair was as white as his suit. His pale skin was almost translucent. And despite the rain, his eyes were wide open, and his brow was smooth. "That was super weird," I said to Elmo. Elmo seemed weirded out too. He softly growled as we kept running in the other direction. I glanced over my shoulder as we turned the corner, and the man in white was still facing us unmoved.

I got to the bus stop and looked for my phone to check the time. No phone. I must have left that on my nightstand. Of course. It turns out that was probably a good thing, but I was very unhappy at the time. I thought about running back to get it. But the idea of going back into a dark house with an old dead man was not something I was eager to do. And the old dying guy told me I only had five minutes. That time had come and gone.

The bus would be there soon. I knew the bus schedule because mom never gave me rides anywhere. "Take the bus," she would tell me, "that's why we bought you the pass." I rarely took the bus this early in the morning, but last summer I had basketball camp for a week and had to take the 6:19 ride to get there in time. It had to be about that time – if I didn't already miss it.

Explosions on TV always seem exciting and cool. And we all know that the coolest characters don't even look back as they walk away from big blasts. Well, I can tell you first hand that real explosions are a bit hard to ignore. My ears hurt from the sound. I was knocked back. Elmo and I stared in the direction of my house. Debris and smoke rose from that direction. I heard car alarms honking. I saw the lights in every house in the neighborhood turn on at almost the same time. A few moments later, I heard sirens. Firemen would be coming. Probably police. Police? Where was that bus?

The rain continued as the sirens grew louder. I could see that the entire neighborhood was awake now. People started to cautiously open their doors, umbrellas in hand, and walk down the street toward my house. The old man had been right to tell me to run. I had no idea what caused the explosion, but as I walked slightly away from the bus stop and looked down my street, I could clearly see the site of the blast, and there was not much left. In front of the blackened wreckage that had been my house was a small but growing crowd of spectators. The rain continued to fall.

Screaming sirens startled me. I saw a fire truck approaching, and it sped down my street without slowing. I turned to see another coming from the same direction. Behind it, I saw a police car. Where was the bus?

I moved closer to the sign for the bus stop. The stop had no shelter or bench, so there was nowhere to hide. I needed that bus to come. I wondered if I should give up and run or keep waiting. A second fire truck swung around the corner barely slowing.

Then I saw the police car. I turned around and faced the

other direction straining my eyes and praying for the bus. Relief flooded my veins as I saw it coming over the hill. Out of my peripheral vision, I saw the squad car approach and heard its tires squeal as it turned onto my street. The bus groaned and sputtered as it approached. It opened its door. I stepped onto the step and looked back. The police car was moving down my street slowly. They had not noticed me. I took a deep breath.

"Hello, Tommy! Elmo coming again today?" Mr. George's familiar voice surprised me. I turned and looked at him. Mr. George, the fat bus driver who always wore a Detroit Lions hat and an oversized red polo shirt, was a kind man who I had always liked. But I did not know who to trust at this point. The old dead man in my now destroyed living room had been right so far about everything. I was confident that I could not trust the police and was not about to start raising alarms with bus drivers at this point. He gave me a curious look noticing my soaked shirt and my soaked dog.

"Yes," I said, and I forced a smile. I quickly walked toward the seats hoping to avoid any more questions. Elmo followed, and I collapsed into a seat halfway back on the mostly empty bus leaving as much space between me and any other passengers as was possible.

The dark of the outside world and the light of the bus made the windows like mirrors. I looked at my face in the reflection. My normally light brown hair was darkened and soaked. Mom had been bothering me to get a haircut for weeks, and its normally cropped sides were long and hung over my ears and into my eyes. I combed it back with my fingers. My normally olive skin looked pale and white. My blue eyes were bloodshot. I looked like a refugee or... sort of like a scared kid that woke up to see his parents gone and a dead guy on his living room floor. Turning away from the window, I looked down at my clothes. My green polo shirt was soaked. My jeans were soaked. The small hole in the right knee had grown somehow and was large and torn. Mom would make me throw them out. If I ever saw her again. That thought caused a lump to grow in my throat. I was pulled out of these thoughts when I heard Mr. George make a loud and unintelligible exclamation. I looked up to see him pointing.

"What the heck is going on over there?" he managed to articulate as we drove past my street. There was a plume of smoke, and about 20 police cars and fire trucks were now blocking the road, and a large crowd of my neighbors surrounded the house.

"Uh... I'm not sure, fire?" I responded but probably not loud enough for him to hear.

I sighed and sat in silence as the bus rumbled toward the city center. How do you collect your thoughts after something like that? I had so many questions. Where were my parents? Who was that guy? Who blew up my house? Why would the police want to kill me? What is going on?

Elmo licked my face. It's hard to be too bummed out when you get a dog kiss. "Thanks, Elmo," I whispered. This dog had saved my life. And he had bitten me, sure, and I still felt the marks on my rear end, but I didn't mind.

The ride to downtown was normal which felt strange after all that had happened. Mr. George had his iPhone playing classical music, and the few other passengers on the bus kept to themselves. Most stared at their phones. Some stared out the window. I just tried to keep myself together. As the bus pulled into the downtown bus station, I got up, thanked Mr. George, and stepped off the bus with Elmo close behind.

I walked into the bus station and up to the counter. "I would like a ticket to Ann Arbor," I said. The man behind the counter looked like a college student or younger. He had earbuds in and was reading something on his phone. I was getting ready to repeat myself when he looked up. His bored expression changed. His eyes widened. He stood up, looked at me, then he looked at his phone and then looked at me again.

"Uh...," he stammered, "You stay there, I will be right back." And with that, he stood up and started to dial his phone.

Elmo, once again sensing danger, growled. I turned, and I ran.

CHAPTER TWO

As I RAN, I glanced back and saw the man yelling into his cell phone – something about "the boy from the house that blew up." How did he know that? I looked over at a woman sitting on a bench staring at her phone. On the phone, I saw my picture. I turned the other direction, and an overweight man was sitting on the sidewalk with a tablet that also had my picture on it. "Alert" was posted at the top of her screen. "Dangerous" was posted at the bottom.

My head was spinning. Why would they want me? To make sure I was safe? Somehow I doubted that. The police were involved. The police who, according to the dead old guy on the floor next to my couch, wanted to kill me. Who blew up the house? Maybe they think I did it? Who was "they"? The police? Why the police? Maybe they were working for someone? What was going on? How did I even get in this situation?

As I stepped out of the bus station, I turned left and ducked into the alley that led behind a restaurant. I needed to hide for a while, and an idea had come to me – Veronica's dad's apartment. She was with her mom this week, and I knew her dad was away on business in Shanghai. And it was close.

Emerging from the alley, I crossed the street and walked in the direction of his building. I cut across an empty parking lot, ducked through another alley, and emerged in front of the tall brick building. An old man was typing in the key code as I approached. As he let the door swing shut behind him, I quickened my steps and caught it right before it latched. The old man looked at me with a curious look, and I panicked a little. But fortunately, his look was not the sort of look you would give a boy who goes about blowing up houses. His look was one of disapproval toward my unkempt appearance. I looked in the reflection of the tinted window and saw my motley state again. Drenched. Muddy. With Clifford the Big Red Dog dripping all over the floor behind me.

"Uh, hello," I said. He paused, opened his mouth to speak, closed it again, and, to my great relief, walked down the hall away from the elevators.

I pressed the elevator button and waited for about two seconds. Then I pressed it again and again and again. Finally, the bell rang, and the doors opened. An old lady stepped off the elevator with a small poodle in her arms. She also gave us a look of disgust, and her poodle yapped at Elmo. But she forced a smile before walking away. Once on the elevator, I went to the fifth floor and made my way down the hall toward room 511.

Now came the tricky part. I had no key. I had no idea how to pick a lock. As I approached the room, I thought about my options. I could kick the door, but I have tried doing that before, and it hurt me more than the door. I could try to break off the handle, but that would make a lot of noise, and if there were a deadbolt, it would not get me in any way. I reached in my jeans pocket and felt my jackknife. All I could think of was poking around at the lock. Maybe I could spring it with the knife?

Sometimes things happen so fast that you do not know how they happened at all. This was one of those moments. I turned the corner and stopped. The door to room 511 was open. A cart full of cleaning supplies and laundry was in front of the room. The maid was in there.

As my slow brain came to grips with this unexpected event, I noticed a red blur enter my line of vision. Elmo was running. "Sit! Elmo, sit!" I hissed. He ignored me. Bounding forward, he entered room 511. I heard a maid yell, and then I saw Elmo come running back out at top speed. The maid, a huge old woman, came lumbering after him. She ran down the hall after him yelling in what sounded like a Russian accent. I slipped into the room.

She must have been close to being done because the room was clean. The bed was made. The vacuum cleaner cord was mostly rolled back up. I ducked into the coat closet and held my breath. A moment later, I saw through the slats in the closet door the red shape of Elmo come back into the apartment. Then, he flopped down in front of the closet door like he owned the place. About two minutes later, I heard heavy panting and gasping for air. I was worried someone was dying.

With my limited vision, I saw the dark blue of the woman's uniform. Through a crack, I could see her face. She looked very confused. She stared at the dog. She tipped her head sideways clearly thinking. "What are you doing here?" she said out loud. Elmo got up and walked over to the couch and flopped down on it. He rested his nose on its armrest. Next to the couch, on the lampstand, were photographs in frames. One of those photos was of Elmo, Veronica, her dad, and me. The maid lumbered over to him. She looked at Elmo and then she looked at the photo. "Oh...," she said in the unmistakable sound of someone solving a riddle. "You are Mr. Davis' dog? Why have I never seen you before? So... you belong in here?" She looked around. After pausing, she turned back toward the door, finished wrapping up the vacuum cord, emptied the trash by the door into her cart, paused one last time, and then left and closed the door behind her. I heard the lock click. I opened the closet and walked over to the couch. I sat down next to Elmo and patted his head.

After a few deep breaths, I thought back over the day. Elmo had awoken me. I was pushed down the stairs to see chaos and a dying man. That man's last words told me to get out of the house... and to get something from my parents' safe. The safe...the envelope! In all the rain, running, dodging, and hiding, I had completely forgotten the large envelope that was folded and wrinkled in my front pocket. I pulled it out and placed it on the coffee table. I tried to flatten it with my hands. There was black marker script across the back that, thanks to the rain, was runny and, at first, illegible. But looking closer, I was able to read some of it:

MY DEAR TOMMY, IF YOU HAVE THIS IN YOUR POSSESSION, IT PROBABLY MEANS WE ARE GONE. WE ARE SO SORRY. PLEASE FIND YOUR UNCLE JACOB AS SOON AS YOU CAN. HE WILL KNOW WHAT TO DO... DO NOT DELAY!

LOVE, MOM, AND DAD

UNCLE JACOB? He *was* involved. Once again, the dead, blown up guy in my living room (I really need to learn his name) was proved right.

I flipped the envelope over and undid the string that tied the seal closed. Using my finger, I opened the flap of the envelope and pulled.

"Tommy? What are you doing in here?" a soft voice right behind my ear said.

There have been a few times in my life when I have passed out. When I was five, I fell off my bike and hit my head, and I am told I was out for a short period of time. I fell down a ravine when we were on vacation when I was eight and bled so bad that, as my dad carried me back to the car, I passed out and did not wake up until I was in the backseat. I didn't pass out this time. But hearing a voice at that moment, with all that was going on, I almost did it. My heart skipped, and I slipped halfway out of my chair. And I let out that universal yell of fear that goes something like, "Aah!"

Elmo wagged his tail. I twisted around quickly and then recognized the source of the unexpected voice. "Veronica? Wow, you almost killed me sneaking up on me like that! What are you doing here?"

"What am I doing here? This is my apartment, remember? And I have a key. But I think I really should be the one asking the questions."

She was wearing her favorite Detroit Tigers t-shirt and an old pair of jeans. Her blond hair was tied back into a ponytail. She was smiling but she looked worried and her skin was paler than normal.

Elmo jumped off the couch, walked over to Veronica and rolled onto his back demanding a belly rub. She obliged him.

"I'm in trouble." I proceeded to tell her the story. As I spoke, Veronica kept interrupting with questions about who people were, what stuff meant, and why things happened. All the exact questions I had desperately been asking but had no answers to. When I got to the end of the story, we both sat there silently.

"You are a fugitive! That is sort of cool."

"Ok, now your turn. Why are you in your dad's apartment? He is gone this week, and you said you were staying with your mom?"

"Yeah... I have a little adventure of my own going on. Yesterday, Mom was supposed to pick me up from school, and she just didn't show. I thought maybe she just flaked out. I tried to call her but no answer. I could have stayed in the principal's office waiting for hours, but since this is pretty close, I just walked here to wait. That was yesterday. Nothing since then."

Veronica stopped petting Elmo's belly and looked at me. "Where do you think she is?"

I knew what she was thinking. Her parents and my parents were lifelong friends, and they all worked together. Her mother disappearing right after my parents disappeared (not to mention my house blowing up and a dead man in my living room) didn't seem like coincidences. "She's fine," I said, but both of us knew I had no way of knowing that and plenty of reasons why it was probably not true.

"Let's open that envelope," Veronica said.

We opened it. Inside were eleven pages of tiny type. Five-point font... maybe. No margins. Spaces between words were often missing. Every page was covered in tiny ink. In addition to the eleven pages, there was a small note card that also had the tiny type covering it. I squinted and read the card:

*WE WRITE **these eleven pages to detail the eleven control centers that we have identified, located, and diagrammed. After*** *reporting these centers to Homeland Security, we soon realized that the officials we were talking to were not only aware, but they were the very people running the centers. In what follows, we have typed out hard copies of these eleven pages. These centers are the greatest threat to our nation and humanity. Someone must destroy them, or they will destroy us.*

As I started to read the pages that followed, Elmo sat up. His ears perked up, and he turned his head to the door. He got up, walked to the door, sniffed, and turned wild-eyed back to us.

"Ok Elmo," I whispered, "we get it. Someone is coming."

Veronica ran to the door and looked out the peephole.

"No one," she whispered.

I followed her to the door, and she stepped to the side as I slowly unlocked it and opened it a crack. I peeked down the hallway and saw three men standing and talking by the elevators. One was wearing a police uniform. He was fat and old, and his face looked the color and texture of melted cheddar cheese. The second man was tall and handsome with a neatly cut beard, black hair that looked like he was ready for a movie, and a resting inviting smile. He wore fashionable jeans and a t-shirt covered by a sport coat. The third man looked pale and sickly. He was so thin that his clothes hung from him like clothes on a hanger. His head was completely bald, and his dark bloodshot eyes were framed with wire-rimmed glasses.

I closed the door. "They're by the elevators. No way out."

Veronica also ducked her head out before quickly closing the door. "Fire escape," she whispered pointing to the window.

I don't know how you feel about heights. Some people, I have found, do not mind being five stories high and standing on rusted stairs with a railing that was clearly just for show. Veronica was one of those people. Elmo appeared to be of the same mind. I, on the other hand, have a slightly different feeling when in that situation. My heart stops. Sweat pours out of me. My fists clench. My breathing stops. I get dizzy. And I move really slowly.

That last part was the problem. Veronica and Elmo would go down a flight. I would go down a stair. By the time they reached the ground and stood in the alley looking up, I was only to the third floor. The good news is that every step took me closer to the ground. As I reached the second floor, the panicked look on Veronica's face as she stared above me told me I was in trouble.

"Hurry," she yell-whispered. Elmo curled his lip and showed his teeth.

I heard shouting from over my head, and I knew that we had been spotted. As much as I fear heights, I feared those men in the hall more. I bit my lip and started running down the stairs. I got to the ground and joined Veronica and Elmo as they ran from the alley.

We looked toward the front of her building and saw a police car in front of the main entrance pulled up on the sidewalk with its lights on. A crowd was gathering. We turned the other way walking fast and trying to avoid attention. As we turned the corner at the end of the block, we started running. Veronica led the way.

She took us down an alley and then we ducked into a doorway that led into a Chinese restaurant. We walked down a hallway, and the smell of frying rice and soy sauce filled the air. We walked past the bathrooms and into the main dining area. The waitress looked at us as we passed toward the front door.

"We're going to my dad's garage," Veronica said to me ignoring the waitress and the diners as we walked.

"What is that dog doing in my restaurant?" the waitress yelled. We turned to see her standing next to an enormous

22

man with a cooking apron on and a shaved head. The veins on his neck were bulging, and he was heading our way.

"Let's go!" I said, and we ran out the front door and across Main Street.

As we ran, we heard the enormous man yelling in our direction. Elmo paused, turned and faced the man. He growled, curled his lip, and started moving in his direction. The man's eyes grew large, and he ducked back in his restaurant and held the door shut. Did I mention that Elmo is a giant dog? No one wants Elmo coming at them in anger. I swear it looked like Elmo was smiling when he trotted back to us.

Passing through a few more alleys, we came to the parking garage and ran up the stairwell. We got to her dad's old model black Lincoln, and Veronica pulled a key from her pocket and unlocked it. She jumped in the driver's seat and leaned over and unlocked the passenger door. I opened the back door for Elmo and then jumped in the front seat.

Up until this point, we had not talked about a plan. Going to her dad's car seemed like something to do, but I didn't really think about why we were going to his car. It suddenly dawned on me. She smiled, put the key in the ignition and turned it, and the car rumbled to life.

"You're not thinking...," my voice broke off. I knew that she was indeed thinking.

She gripped the steering wheel and said, "Let's get to Ann Arbor!"

CHAPTER THREE

Gradually, my fingers stopped digging into the armrest, and my heart stopped racing. Veronica had gotten us this far but not before doing some damage. In her defense, it is hard to reach the pedals when you are barely five feet tall. And there was that little fact that she had never driven before. With those facts in mind, it was understandable when she side-swiped that car on our way out of the parking garage. And it was also understandable when she had driven up on the curb and taken out the row of hedges in front of Westside apartments. Maybe you can give her a little blame for whooping out the window as we passed the Chinese restaurant when she saw the enormous owner standing by the door, but all things considered, she got us out of town, and we were now on our way to Ann Arbor. It was getting dark by the time we had reached the car. As we navigated through the traffic and out onto the highway, I calculated the distance from the glove compartment map and realized that we would be driving through the night.

Veronica talked the whole time, trying to keep awake, but grew silent as the morning grayed the world back to life. Elmo was sound asleep in the backseat. The rain Veronica had navigated through during the night was over, but the puddles remained. Our car splashed through them as we progressed toward our destination. When the rain had started, Veronica had no idea how to drive. Large puddles more than once almost caused us to spin out of control. But she learned with time, narrating to me as she learned, "slow the car by letting off the gas," "avoid the brakes when going through puddles" and "avoid over-correcting with the steering wheel."

As we drove, the traffic thickened by degrees, and trucks and early risers on the road increased as more and more people started making their way to school and work. Soon, cars crowded the road. I kept my head low and was glad that Elmo was asleep. I was worried that my face (now widely publicized as that of a criminal) might draw attention from the many passing drivers. I didn't think the giant dog (also widely publicized) would help things. But no one noticed us. Each person was in their own world, focused on the wet road.

I was not sure what we would do when we got to Ann Arbor. I had $100 in cash from my grandmother. Veronica had grabbed some cash from her dad's apartment before leaving, but put together we had less than $200. So best case, we had enough money for two nights in a hotel (presuming anyone would rent to a couple of kids and a dog). I didn't know where to find my uncle – and that was the sum total of our plan. I could see us getting there, sleeping in the car for a couple of nights, then coming back.

As we drove, I could not keep my eyes off the large branch; perhaps I should call it a tree, that was stuck to the front bumper from when Veronica hit that row of hedges as we left the city. It was blowing in the wind as we traveled down the highway. A glove compartment map helped us to navigate toward Ann Arbor. I finally had a moment to catch my breath, think, and pull out the envelope again from my pocket. What a day it had been. Who was that man in my living room? Why were the police trying to kill me? Why did everyone get an alert about me on their phones? Where were my parents? Why was I allowing a 13-year-old girl to drive me in a car going 70 miles an hour? Maybe the envelope had some answers.

I looked at the bent, once wet, now dry, folded and creased yellowish envelope in my hands. I read the front again. I read the notecard again. Then I turned to the body of the envelope. The eleven pages. As I scanned them, no light came to my clouded mind. The pages seemed to be describing buildings. They included building locations, sketches of floor plans, and a lot of tiny text that appeared to be nonsense describing things I did not understand.

I remember watching a TV show once that was supposed to tell a season-long mystery. Each episode added new clues, new characters who discovered new monsters, new secret codes, and new hideouts. I watched each episode taking note of each new clue. I was so excited to see how all the various seemingly disconnected pieces could possibly fit together to solve the mystery that had been built by the writers. Then came the final episode and I discovered that the writers had not planned the season out at all. They failed on almost every level to bring all the various pieces together.

I felt that way now. I had hoped that the blown up guy in my living room had been right when he told me that this envelope would have the answers. It provided no such satisfaction. In fact, after looking over those eleven pages, I was every bit as confused as I had been when things had started. No answers. No explanations. Just seemingly random maps, diagrams, and text that were completely meaningless to me.

"It is gibberish."

"What?"

"Gibberish! I have no clue what it means. It is a bunch of meaningless junk that I cannot figure out."

"Let me see!"

"No!"

"Why?"

"Because you are a 13-year-old first-time driver going 70 miles per hour and I am not ready to die."

"Ok read it to me."

"It is meaningless."

"Read it!"

"Ok."

For the next half hour, I read (or tried to read) every bit of text on in the envelope. I described the maps and diagrams in detail.

"That is gibberish!" said Veronica when I finished.

By my calculations using the scale on the map, we were about an hour from Ann Arbor. We had enough gas to get there without stopping. But I suddenly realized that I needed to go to the bathroom. We had stopped early on in our drive and loaded up on Mountain Dew and Red Bull, and I could hold it no longer.

"You have got to find a rest stop or gas station or something," I moaned.

"Seriously?" Veronica moaned back. "We have the whole

police force trying to kill you. You cannot hold it until we get there?"

"For the sake of your dad's car! Please just find a rest stop."

The sound of gravel and concrete became audible as we rolled into the rest stop. We pulled around the back of the old brown building with the poorly maintained lawn. Three trucks sat on the ramp leading back onto the expressway, but otherwise, the parking lot was empty of everything except weeds poking through the cracks in the pavement. As soon as we rolled to a stop, I jumped out and ran. Looking back, I saw Veronica supervising Elmo's own bathroom break nervously. "Hurry!" she yelled as I pulled open the glass door leading to a lobby empty of everything but a rack of travel pamphlets.

As I entered, I saw something strange out of the corner of my eye. Outside the window, a huge man in a white suit was standing on the grass near the parking lot. He was motionless, staring at something that I could not see. Strange. But I didn't look for too long. I had to go.

The small lobby contained a door on the left for women, and I turned to the right. A few moments later, I emerged much relieved and found myself face to face with Veronica and Elmo. I was going to tell her about the man in white, but before I did, she spoke. "They are out there," she said with eyes wide.

"Who is?"

"Remember those guys from my dad's apartment?"

I thought back to Veronica's apartment. Three men standing and talking by the elevators. There was the tall, fashionable man with the neatly cut beard and the movie star smile. And there was the pale, bald, sickly man with blood-shot eyes. And there was the fat policeman with the cheesy face.

"Where exactly…," I started to say, but my thoughts ended there. I felt a bee sting in my calf. Then another bee sting in my back pocket. The bees seemed to have a chemical bite to them. I turned, and as I did, the world spun. I felt nothing as I watched the sidewalk come up to meet my head. I felt the sidewalk jar my skull, but I did not feel what I can describe as pain. It was more like a bump. I saw red fluid pouring out around me. It was blood, I thought. My blood. The corners of my vision became black, and the blackness grew. Then there was nothing but black. Somewhere in the distance, I heard Elmo barking.

REMEMBER, when I said I didn't feel the pain? Well, the next thing I remember was a very different experience. I do not remember opening my eyes. I do not remember the first thing I saw. I do not remember the first thing I heard. But I do remember the pain. A screaming and overwhelming pain. More pain than I have ever felt in my life. My leg and back hurt so bad that I threw up. Then I screamed. Then I whimpered. Then I screamed some more.

"I am so sorry about the pain. Those tranquilizers of Isaac's are so very effective, but they hurt so very much." As I opened my eyes, I saw him place a glass on the table and step toward me.

"My friend," he said narrowing his eyes and looking into mine, "most things that most people say most of the time are completely unnecessary, and if not said, the world would be no different. But what I am about to say to you is actually important. And what happens to you depends very much on how you respond."

My mind was reeling. Who was this? What was going on? Why was I in so much pain? I whimpered again and looked around. I was in a second-story room with large windows that looked out over a city street. I saw cars driving below and people walking. I was on a bed by the window. My left wrist was handcuffed to a pipe on the wall.

"It has been two years since Gibion's plans were discovered. Everyone has been so scared. Except me... right now, things seem clear. Victory is not impossible. And even if it is, we are only given so much time on earth, and only cowards cling to life."

Where was Veronica? Where was Elmo? What was going on? The man paced as he spoke. He spoke in a rich tone and style similar to the actors in old World War II era movies – not a British accent but close. I recognized him but from where? My mind searched. It is hard to think when you are in so much pain. He was tall and handsome with a neatly cut beard, black hair that looked like he was ready for a movie, and a resting inviting smile.

He continued, "Before the war, had anyone asked me, I would have given lip service at best to the value of a good glass of wine, a classic work of literature, and a quiet night alone with nothing to do. But it has been years since I enjoyed those pleasures. Ask me now how valuable those blessings are. Ask me now." His voice trailed off.

I could not tell if he was drunk or crazy, but there was something different about him. I have seen drunks before. My mother's brother gets drunk every Thanksgiving. The old lady that lives next door gets drunk almost every weekend. There is a certain slowness of speech. A certain deliberation of behavior. Some of that matched his behavior. But some things did not match. He did not stagger when he walked, and his eyes were keen and alive. Maybe he was crazy.

He continued his monologue as he paced. He was wearing

a perfectly fitted suit jacket. A t-shirt. Brown polished shoes. He smelled of cologne.

"I have taste, but let me be clear – I am no aficionado. Isaac never cared for wine; he is a teetotaler." He paused and smiled. "That is a funny word, isn't it? It just means he drinks no alcoholic beverages. But I enjoy wine from time to time, and I lean toward a good port. Isaac reads only non-fiction, technical books. I, on the other hand, enjoy the classics. Dostoevsky is my favorite. And, to finish off my original point, Isaac never sat alone and relaxed (too much 'work ethic')," he said this with a certain disdain, "and I doubt if that would change if the war ended. When the war ends, that is all I will do. I will sit with a glass in my hand and a novel on my lap."

"What are you talking about?" I managed, biting back both fear and pain.

He turned as though I had awoken him. He muttered, "I speak nonsense in a nonsensical world." Then he smiled. Straightened his shoulders, fixed his tie, and tugged at his jacket nervously.

"Ah, you poor soul!" He spoke like I was an old friend. " I am so glad you are awake. You have been in and out of consciousness for days. I was quite worried about you. The tranquilizers were too much. Completely unnecessary. Isaac is always so hasty. That was a nasty fall you had after being hit. I can only imagine that between the pain of the darts and the huge knot on your head, you are suffering badly. Let me be the first to apologize on his behalf."

My head was spinning. So many words. So little sense.

"Tranquilizer? Where is Veronica?" I said through my teeth as the pain in my leg flared.

His pacing had stopped. He stood erect and smiling. But with my words, he winced ever so slightly but said nothing.

"Where is my dog?"

31

V.W. SHURTIFF

These words seemed to hurt him. He looked down and then out the window. His face contorted like he was going to cry. A long silence followed.

Anger overpowered my pain and fear.

"You didn't kill them did you?" I screamed.

These words brought him out of his silence. He squinted at me like I was crazy, and then his smile returned.

"Kill them? Why would we kill them?"

It sounded like a rhetorical question, and I waited for more explanation, but his continued gaze at me and his thoughtful smile finally caused me to realize it had been a legitimate question.

"Well, you shot me!"

A look of stunned disbelief came to his face. "With a tranquilizer. And I did not shoot you."

"You guys shot me."

"Isaac did. With a tranquilizer. Isaac stole a whole bunch of those from Gibion as we left. They're much more effective than trying to use a taser and nowhere near as deadly as using bullets. And Isaac thought the pain might scare you into talking."

"I think," I said trying to follow him but feeling like I had stepped into a conversation midway through, "using pain to get people to talk is called torture. Where is Veronica? Where is Elmo?"

"Elmo?"

"My dog."

His smile grew wide, and he almost laughed. "That is a fantastic name! How did you think of that?"

"Who cares? Where are they?"

"No, please tell me."

"After the Sesame Street character, ok?"

"Brilliant," he said, shaking his head as though I had revealed some groundbreaking scientific advancement.

"Yeah. Anyway, what happened to them?"

"To Veronica and Elmo?" he emphasized the name 'Elmo' as though he were making a witty joke. I nodded. "I have no idea. When the shooting started, everything became so crazy. I ducked behind the Coke machine, and when I came out, it was just you (bleeding from the head) and Isaac (standing over you, also bleeding)."

These words gave me hope but also were strangely confusing. The shooting? Up to this point, I had assumed that the only shooting was at me. I looked at the man and waited for more information. But no more came. The silence continued, and he looked out the window. After a long pause, he shook his head, chuckled, and whispered, "Elmo."

"Can you please explain things to me? From the beginning. You are talking like I know what you are talking about. I do not. I have no idea. I have been running and hiding since whenever this started." My eyes grew hot and wet as I spoke. "I woke up, and my parents were gone, and a dead guy was in my living room and..."

"That would be Sam... Isaac warned him not to go."

"What? You knew him?" I was starting to realize that this man had answers to questions that I had been desperately asking since all this craziness started. I adjusted my wrist, cuffed to a pipe on the wall, which had started to fall asleep. And at that moment, I was reminded that I was a prisoner. Who had been shot with a tranquilizer. By this guy's brother. Fear and pain returned. Mostly fear.

"Why am I in handcuffs?"

"Hand *cuff*."

"What?"

"There is only one of them. Your other hand is free."

"Okay, why am I in 'hand *cuff*'?"

"That was Isaac's idea. He can be rather paranoid. He is

not sure if you can be trusted. All your antics thus far have made him nervous."

At that moment, the door opened and in walked a man, pale and sickly, thin. His clothes hung loose. His head was bald, and he had dark bloodshot eyes. I had seen him before. He walked in with his eyes bouncing from me to his brother with a look of skepticism.

"David... hand *cuff*? I specifically said hand *cuffs*."

CHAPTER FOUR

Dᴀᴠɪᴅ sᴍɪʟᴇᴅ ʙʀᴏᴀᴅʟʏ, "Greetings Isaac! I wondered where you went off to."

"You have to be more careful, David."

"Did you buy cigarettes?"

"If he were to escape, can you imagine the opportunity we would waste?"

The well-dressed man, apparently named David, smiled broadly and then worked to put on a feigned scholarly expression and said in an artificially low voice, "Yes. Yes, I see. I am so sorry. I took a terrible risk." He could maintain this serious look no longer, and a full smile had returned. "But Isaac, fortunately, the boy did not escape." He turned and looked at me and pointed with both hands like a magician revealing the reappearance of an assistant, "There he is!"

Isaac's face did not change throughout this whole presentation. He stared blankly at me. His thick glasses made his stare disturbing.

"Has he said anything?" he said flatly.

"He said lots of things," David responded with a large smile.

"Did he tell you what he knows?"

David frowned, "Nothing about the parents if that is what you mean."

"What did he say?"

"He said…," David's eyes rolled up thoughtfully, "Do you remember Sesame Street?"

"What?"

"Remember Sesame Street? The PBS show we used to watch on Grandma's black and white TV in the basement?"

Isaac made some sort of noise, and his face was confusion.

"Remember Elmo? The little red guy?" He looked at Isaac as though he expected a response but none came. "Thomas says that red dog of his is named Elmo!"

"Get out, you drunk!" The color of Isaac's face had gone from white to red. He looked violent and deranged. He walked up to David, and it looked like he was going to strike him. David stepped backward. Smiled. Dramatically bowed. He disappeared through the door, and it closed behind him. I was alone with Isaac.

"My brother is a drunk and a fool," Isaac said almost to himself. "He once was valiant. He once was so courageous. Now look at him."

Isaac walked with a limp, but his shoulders were erect and proud.

"David is the reason there is still a resistance," He said this with import. And then he paused and looked at me with his eyebrows raised. Waiting for my reaction.

I would have loved to give the appropriate reaction. But I had no idea what he was talking about. I did not know what was going on. It was all so confusing. This whole situation was like some crazy dream.

There was a long somewhat awkward pause. Isaac staring at me. Me staring at Isaac. No one saying anything.

"I am sorry," I finally said, "I have no idea what you are talking about or what is going on. All I know is that I am in handcuffs, and I am in pain."

"Cuff."

"I am in hand *cuff*," I conceded.

"How is the pain?" He asked, but the question sounded like that of a detached scientist asking about the condition of a lab rat.

"Horrible."

"Regrettable that that happened," again he spoke with complete disinterest. "War causes such terrible things to happen."

"What are you talking about!" Throughout the conversation with David and now the conversation with Isaac, I had the feeling that I started reading a book midway through. Both of them were assuming I knew way more than I did, and both of them were talking about things I knew nothing about. "I know nothing about any war, and I know nothing about you. I know nothing about your drunken brother. I know nothing!"

Isaac stared at me. His eyes were locked on me. Slowly his lip curled into a sneer.

"You may be just a boy, but please stop lying to me. We found these on your person," he raised the envelope with his left hand and with his right he pulled the papers inside halfway out so that I could see. "You are a liar and a traitor and you are lucky I only shot you with a tranquilizer!" As he spoke, he grew angrier and walked step by step closer to me. His right hand pointed at me accusingly, and his left held the envelope tight. "I would have had every right to execute you before you and your worthless family destroy this country…" His voice trailed off, and he stopped shouting.

"And the world…," he concluded with a sad intonation as he turned to look out the window. After a brief pause, he turned and walked out of the room. As he shut the door, he said without turning around, "I will be back, and you will tell us everything you know. If you do not, I can no longer protect you." The door slammed behind him.

Up until this point, I had been strangely calm for a kid who had just been tranquilized and kidnapped. Now I panicked. Tears came to my eyes, and I groaned as I pulled as hard as I could at the handcuff. I placed both of my feet on the pipe next to the bed and pulled until my wrist bled. But the handcuff did not budge. The pipe did not budge. Nothing budged but my skin that now bled out onto the bed. I climbed off the bed and pushed it away from the wall to get more leverage. I winced as once again I pulled against the cuff. My arm throbbed. More blood. But no movement.

I could hear arguing out in the hall. David and Isaac were talking with a third voice. I was not sure what they were saying, but I hoped that they would stay out for a while longer. I needed to get out. I could not stay here. I was almost hyperventilating at this point. Grunting and squealing and crying all at the same time. Pausing, I looked out the window. Down on the street, I saw cars passing. Children playing. Birds flying. People walking. Everything was so normal out there. In here, madness. Blood. Kidnapping. Crazy talk. War? I had to get out there.

As I stared, I saw something in the window of the hardware store across the street. I could not believe it. The store was closed (possibly out of business given that it was closed in the middle of a busy day). The lights were out, and the neon 'open' sign that hung on the front door was dark. Two large windows filled with displays of lawn mowers, leaf blowers, and rakes were to the right and the left of the door. In the left window, I could see two shapes crouching and barely visible in the dark of the hardware store and the glare of the outdoor light. There was a part of me that wondered if it was just my rattled mind playing tricks on me. But as I stared, I saw movement, and with that movement, I became more confident. One shape was small, with a long ponytail. The other was the silhouette of a large dog. Veronica. Elmo!

My excitement was tempered as I heard the arguing outside the door come to an end. I heard footsteps coming my way. Panic returned, and I once again pulled at the cuff, trying to break loose. The door handle turned. And the door started to creak open. I heard a long low whistle. Then a clucking of a tongue.

"Oh dear," the voice belonged to David. "Oh dear. Oh dear!" He said louder, taking in the scene in front of him. I looked around. The bed was pushed away from the wall, the mattress was off the bed, and I was covered in blood.

"I told Isaac that handcuff was enough to hold you," he said with a wry smile, "but you sure tested it." He stepped closer and grabbed my arm just below the elbow. His grip was tight and strong. I tried to twist away from him, but I could not move. He held up my bloody wrist and examined it. He winced. The permanent smile that was on his face gone.

"I never signed up for this," he said to himself softly and let go of my arm.

I said nothing. My heart was pounding. My breathing was

heavy. And my arm ached as blood dripped to the floor. The two dart wounds in my leg were screaming again.

"I do recognize that I am an imperfect man," David conceded as though to avoid argument, "but I am not a liar nor am I someone that goes around shooting kids with tranquilizer darts. I spent five years with him. I know what I am talking about. Things are moving more quickly now," he waved his hand high above his head into a circling motion, "everything is happening so fast now."

"Isaac would have liked to dismiss this fact. He is still convinced that total war can be avoided. But Isaac is not stupid. He knows that I am the reason we have survived this far. He knows that I know what I know."

He started to leave and then hesitated. Looked at me and narrowed his eyes. He reached into his pocket and pulled out a small key. His smile returned, and he raised his eyebrows and looked at the handcuff. He walked to the bed and sat down next to me. He took the pipe end of the handcuff and unlocked it without saying anything. He whispered in my ear. "I will get you out of here. Follow me." He handed me the key and nodded for me to unlock myself. He looked at my bloody wrist and gave another wince. Despite the unbelievable pain, I was able to hold still long enough to release the other end of the handcuff and drop them on the bed.

David walked to the door, looked out and then ducked back in. "Coast is clear. We are going to walk directly down the hall to the fire escape and then down and out. You know how to get down fire escapes don't you?" he delivered this last line with a smirk and a wink.

I didn't know what to think at this point. Nothing had made sense since I came into this man's presence, and nothing was making sense now. But between him and Isaac and the mystery third voice in the hall, I thought I liked him the best. And he was the only person who seemed truly bothered by the fact that I had been shot, my head was bashed in from the fall, and that I had almost ripped off my wrist.

I stood up to follow him. The pain in my head, leg, and wrist all screamed. The room grew dark, and I felt the sensation of falling. Then I felt nothing.

CHAPTER FIVE

THE PAIN WOKE ME. My head, leg, and wrist all vied for attention. I felt cool air and heard the noises of a busy city street. I opened my eyes and saw the street three stories below me. I am ashamed of this, but my first reaction was to let out a scream that started off low and slowly got louder and higher. It seemed like it was coming from someone other than me, but unfortunately, it was all me.

"I would not recommend screaming, Thomas. Silence is most likely the wiser approach at the moment."

The voice was David's. It came from below me. As I became more aware and more awake, I realized I was being carried on his shoulder. He was half running and half walking down the fire escape. I stopped screaming.

"Much better," David said when I had grown silent, "I am doing something rather stupid right now, and I am doing it for you. And it will be very stupid indeed if we both die because you scream like a girl."

David came to the final landing of the fire escape and released the last flight. The rusty hinges creaked as it swung to the ground. He quickly stepped down it.

"Where are you taking me?"

"I am not sure yet," he said simply and continued walking. As I stared down David's back at the sidewalk below me, I heard the sound of the noises of the street. Cars. Air conditioners. Honking. Dogs barking. Then I heard another scream. I placed my hand over my mouth to confirm it was not me. It was not.

"Oh, my! Is he ok?" came the voice of an old woman. I twisted my head to see an old lady holding a very small dog in her arms and looking at us with her mouth wide open. Her free hand was pointing at me. The little dog yipped.

"Is who okay?" David said, looking around, and then, following the direction of her finger he looked at me, "Him? Oh, yes, he is fine. But thank you so much for your concern." When the woman continued to stare in alarm, David offered a bit more explanation, "He has been shot with a tranquilizer, and he tried to rip his hand off, but other than that, he is doing very well. And how are you doing?" From the corner of my eye, I could see David smiling broadly and looking at the old woman with a thoughtful squint.

The woman stammered, said something about being fine, and then slowly walked away. David turned and continued down the sidewalk. We made our way down the street, and when we came to a blue two-tone 1984 Ford Escort, we stopped. David opened the unlocked door and set me down in the passenger's seat. He walked around to the driver's side door, opened it, paused, sighed, and sat down next to me. He closed the door. He looked at me for a long time. He looked at my bloody arm. He looked at my scabby head. He winced sympathetically. He turned the key, and the low rumble of the unmufflered exhaust broke the silence.

"If you move, I will chop your head off," said a high female voice that I recognized. I turned and saw a young girl with a large ax (borrowed from the hardware store) leaning into the open driver side window. Her hands were choked up high on the ax handle with it cocked and ready to strike. There was a giant red dog behind her.

"Veronica?" I groaned.

"And Elmo!" David added with a wide grin.

"Veronica, he is helping us escape. Get in." I said those words and realized as they left my mouth that I had no idea if they were true. I had zero reasons why I should trust him.

Veronica gave me a curious look, lowered the ax, and climbed into the backseat of the car. Elmo climbed in as well. The Escort roared as David revved the engine. "We'll be there by dinnertime," he said with confidence and a broad smile. "Good dog," he added in a high voice, and patted Elmo on the head. Elmo curled his lip and growled in response.

The car pulled out into traffic, and I heard Veronica yell, "Oh, look out!" I looked up and saw Isaac and a fat policeman running out of the building with guns drawn. Bam! Bam! Bam! Three cracking noises and three holes in the back of the car.

The little Escort squealed its tires as we pulled onto the road, and David navigated around the confused and panicked drivers. He used the shoulder and the sidewalk to get around the corner, and 'bam!' another shot cried out, and we felt the unmistakable bumping of a flat tire. David accelerated anyway. For the next few minutes, the sound of the flapping rubber combined with the sound of a faulty muffler silenced any speech. David continued to weave through the traffic until Isaac and the fat policeman were well out of sight.

"Give me your phones," he said as soon as they were out of sight.

"I have no phone. Left it on the nightstand," I said with a tone of disappointment.

"That is a sensible place for it." He looked at Veronica and extended his hand. She reached into her pocket and gave him hers. But as soon as she did, she regretted it. She let out a gasp and then a cry as David rolled down the window and threw the phone out.

"What are you doing?" she yelled.

"Everyone will be looking for us now. We need to get off the grid. Nothing electronic. How do you think the whole world found you at that rest stop?"

After driving for blocks, the urban buildings became less frequent, and long stretches of green indicated that we had come to the edge of the city (that I now realized was Ann Arbor). David pulled the car onto the shoulder.

"Maybe dinner time was too optimistic," David said, turning to us and flashing a smile. He opened his door and walked to the back of the car, lifted the hatchback, and proceeded to pull out a small spare tire. Veronica and I sat in silence and watched as he worked with incredible speed and within a few minutes, he was back in the car. As he pulled out into the road, the thunder of the muffler was suddenly overwhelmed by the screams of jets flying low overhead.

We all looked up and watched them fly toward the city. David nodded knowingly to himself, narrowed his eyes, and tightened his grip on the steering wheel. He turned on the radio and fiddled with the dial. He stopped, and I recognized the song, "Street Fighting Man," by the Rolling Stones. He turned it up and silently mouthed the words.

My father was always a Stones fan and played them when he worked in the garage. The last time I had heard that song, I sat in a happy home. Mom was cooking. Dad's voice shouted the lyrics as he restored his 1973 MG Midget. Those were happy times. And they seem like ages past. Would I ever see my parents again? Would I ever see normal again?

As the song came to an end, David turned the volume down and began to speak, "Everything changed after *Enduring Freedom*." This sentence came out as though he was in the middle of a conversation that had been going on for some time. "After that, nothing was the same."

I knew that name. My parents had spoken of *Enduring Freedom*. It had something to do with the government's efforts to keep the country safe. Apparently, our government learned of a massive international conspiracy to destroy our nation. Everyone was involved. Almost every rogue state you can think of, every terrorist group, and even some countries we thought of as allies were involved. There was going to be a coordinated attack that would wipe out our nuclear capabilities and then execute a full overthrow of the government. The effort was stopped just in time, and our government was completely freaked out. Enter *Enduring Freed*om. My parents couldn't tell me the details, but our president made a public address, explaining that the program was "a wide sweeping, inter-agency information gathering effort designed to keep our country safe for future generations." There were a few news stories and reports at the time, but, with the exception of some fringe conspiracy theorists and privacy advocates, most people were not that interested, and the public mostly forgot about it within a few months. My parents worked on it for years. My dad was excited and happy to help at first. Then one day he came home and looked at my mother. They went into the spare bedroom, closed the door, and talked for two hours. When they came out, it looked like my mother had been crying. They never talked about *Enduring Freedom* again.

David continued his unprompted monologue, "Yes,

everything changed. It was not perfect before. No system is perfect, children. I am not saying that. But it was never this bad. And it is not even that I mind tyranny. I truly do not. But why can not tyrants be honest? Why can they not admit what they are? Why such a name? 'Enduring Freedom'? It is the dishonesty I object to."

As he spoke, he reached into his jacket pocket, pulled something out and handed it to me. I recognized it immediately as the envelope from my father's safe, "This belongs to you." He smiled broadly and added, "Don't tell anyone, but I stole that from Isaac."

"Thank you, but you could have kept it. It is gibberish."

David gave a knowing smile. He opened his mouth to speak, then clamped it shut. We sat listening to the noises of the road: wind, wheels, and gravel. We were making our way to the outskirts of the city. To my right, I could see the skyline. I turned around and looked at Veronica. She had been silent for so long I had almost forgotten she was there.

"How in the world did you find us, Veronica?"

Veronica grinned, looked out the window with a dramatic pause, and began to tell her story.

CHAPTER SIX

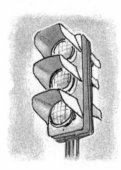

"WHEN THE SHOOTING started at that rest stop, there was a lot of craziness," Veronica began her story. "People were screaming. I was screaming. I jumped behind the trash cans and peaked out. That is when I realized you were down and bleeding. I was so freaked out. I would have helped you... but honestly, I was too scared. I just sat there. But Elmo didn't. He raced right at that other skinny bald guy. You should have seen it. He shot some sort of dart gun at him, missed, and then he ran like crazy. You have never seen someone that looked like a skeleton run so fast. If I were not so scared, I would have laughed.

"Then everything was quiet. I was about to crawl out when I saw a big guy dressed in white moving our direction. He had a gun in his hand. You were bleeding all over. I thought you were dead. Then he," she nodded at David, "jumped out from behind a coke machine. I heard you scream when he grabbed you. He ran toward the parking lot with you on his shoulder and put you in the old black Cadillac de Ville. The guy in white was running after you - like a robot. The Cadillac lurched into gear and starting speeding away.

"Remember when I said I was scared? Suddenly my fear was gone. I realized that if I didn't do something, I might not see you again. I saw an old pickup truck that had entered the lot right after all the craziness had died down was now pulling out right behind Cadillac. I did something crazy. I ran next to the truck, grabbed the top of the tailgate, stepped on the bumper and jumped in the back. As soon as I was in, I crouched down. As we started down the entrance ramp to get back on the highway, I saw Elmo coming back from chasing the man. And I could see him running on foot through the field at least a hundred yards away.

"I whistled; he looked up and saw me in the truck and started running. Just as the truck was starting to accelerate, he landed in the back of the truck and crouched down next to me. I was surprised the driver didn't notice anything, but I could hear he had his radio up. The Cadillac was so far ahead that I thought we had lost it, but suddenly the Cadillac screeched to a stop and let the man in the field jump in, and we were right behind them.

As we moved down the highway, I realized I had not thought my plan out very well. What were the chances that this truck and that Cadillac were going anywhere near the same direction? I knew what would happen next. Either the pickup truck would exit the highway and the Cadillac would not, or the Cadillac would exit the highway and the truck would not. Even if by some miracle they got off at the same exit, what was the chance that they would go the same direction from there? We were still tracking with the Cadillac for now, but it could not last long.

"Time passed. Every minute felt like an eternity. I kept peeking over the side of the truck bed, and I could still see the Cadillac up ahead. It was not speeding. I could see a lot of things going on in the car. I could see the driver somehow handing off the wheel to the man on the passenger side. The car swerved and slowed as they traded places. The man who had been driving now twisted around and was looking at you. He climbed into the backseat. I could see him tear some long white bandages with his teeth and I could see him yelling at the driver.

"Then, finally, the moment came. I saw the Cadillac slow and put its blinker on and begin to exit. Amazingly, our truck also started to slow as well. I looked into the cab of the truck, and I realized what was going on. The driver had also seen what was going on the back seat of the car and was interested. He was leaned forward and straining to see. He was an older man with a bald head, glasses, and a flannel shirt. His eyes were tightened and focused on the Cadillac.

"The Cadillac turned right as we exited the highway, and the truck followed. We were now on a two-lane highway, and there were farms on our right and left. I looked out and saw cows grazing in the fields. I was starting to get very cold at this point, and I hugged Elmo for warmth. The sky was overcast, and I hoped it was not going to rain. I saw that the driver of the truck was fiddling with his phone. He was probably trying to call the police, but based on the fact that he was also watching the Cadillac carefully while driving, he was having problems dialing. I saw him try two or three times before setting the phone down in frustration.

"The Cadillac started to accelerate. I peeked up again, and I could see... him," she nodded at David again, "looking out at the truck and then speaking to the driver. They passed a car on the two-lane highway and started to pull away from us. But the truck driver did not give up.

"I could feel him begin to accelerate, and he also started to pass the car in front of us. I looked ahead, and there was a huge truck coming head-on in our direction. It was at this point that I realized how unsafe this all was. The bed of the truck was rusted steel, there were no seatbelts, and I am pretty sure we were going a hundred miles per hour by now. The semi got closer, I screamed, Elmo barked, our driver glanced back in startled confusion just as he managed to pull back into the right lane, successfully passing the car and missing the semi. We were right behind the Cadillac again!

"The man was now looking at us as much as he was looking at the road. He opened the window and shouted, 'What in the world are you doing in my truck?' I shrugged. What could I say? But I credit that guy; he never slowed down. Imagine turning around and realizing you have a girl and a giant dog stowed away in the back of your truck. Didn't seem to faze this guy too much. He kept driving.

"We were actually catching up. But we were also getting closer to the city. A road sign said, 'Ann Arbor 6 miles' and there was increasingly more traffic. The farms became fewer, and we passed more buildings, gas stations, and warehouses. I saw a stop light up ahead. It was red. The Cadillac blew right through it (coming incredibly close to t-boning a commercial van in the process). We came up to the same light; I could see a steady wave of traffic coming the other way. And we were *not* slowing down!"

Veronica paused for dramatic effect. Then she added in a hushed voice, "We were going to die, Tommy."

"I heard brakes screech. Elmo and I got slammed into the front of the cab (I still have a lump on the top of my head from that). Then I heard someone (another driver) yelling. Then I felt the truck accelerate again. Without stopping for more than a moment, we were hunting the Cadillac again.

"We were truly in the city now. Large buildings lined the sides of the roads. I could smell the smells of pollution and restaurants blending. We passed a sign saying, 'Welcome to Ann Arbor.' The Cadillac went through red light after red light. My driver went through red light after red light. I wish they put seat belts in truck beds. I banged my head, my back, my elbow and every other part of my body. Poor Elmo looked like he was going to throw up.

"Then suddenly all the bouncing stopped. We were in the middle of the city. Old fashioned buildings lined each side of the street. I saw a young couple wearing flannel, dark-rimmed glasses and skinny jeans walking their dog. Elmo barked at them, and they stared until we passed from their view. After weaving through the old streets, we finally came to a screeching stop. Before I knew what was happening, my truck driver jumped out of the pickup and started shouting. The skeletal man got out of the Cadillac and walked calmly and directly into the alley and entered one of the buildings from a side door. Then the other man got out….," Veronica's voice trailed off, and she gave a knowing look at David, "and he was covered in blood. He stood next to the car, then bent back in and started lifting you out. Your head was wrapped in white bandages. There was also a bandage on your leg.

"The driver of my truck was speed walking up to the car. He was yelling and asking questions. He asked what was going on, who the boy was, and why his head was bleeding. The man in the suit…" Veronica again and nodded at David who turned and returned her nod with a broad smile, "seemed to be almost enjoying himself. After putting you back down on the seat, he introduced himself and explained that they were helping the boy. The boy had passed out and cracked his head on the sidewalk back at the rest stop. He reassuringly said that the man's concern was 'to be commended.' The truck driver said he was going to call the police and started to walk back to his car to find his phone. But the man in the suit stopped him, agreed that the police would be a great idea, and offered to call them himself. Putting his bloody hand in his pocket, he pulled out an old-fashioned flip phone and started dialing.

"His calm demeanor seemed to have a calming effect on the truck driver who was now talking in a more moderate tone. Elmo and I crossed the street to get a view of the events without being noticed. A crowd had gathered around to watch. A few moments later, a police car pulled onto the street with its lights on, but it was not racing as though it was in a hurry. It moved slowly down the street and rolled to a stop.

"The door opened, and out stepped a fat police officer. He had a thinning black hair cut short on the sides and back. He took a few steps toward the two men, stopped, turned around, and walked back to his car. He reached in and pulled out his hat and put it on his head. He stopped and looked at the growing crowd. I could see him clearly, and his face looked the color and texture of melted cheese. Remember that guy?" Veronica once again paused dramatically, raised her eyebrows and looked at me waiting for an answer.

"The one from the elevator?" I said.

Veronica gave a knowing nod. "The one from the elevator. When he looked at the crowd, I quickly ducked back behind everyone, and I do not think he saw me. As I peeked out again, I saw him walking slowly back to the scene. He said something softly, and I could not hear him. Then the truck driver spoke for a while. Then the three of them seemed to be arguing. Then the police officer turned half around and spoke loudly as though he was not only talking to the two men but also to the crowd. 'Well, we better get that boy to the hospital.' He pointed to the Cadillac. The three of them went back to the car and got you out. You had clean bandages on your leg and head. You whimpered a little, and it looked like you were not all that awake. The crowd gasped when they saw you bandaged and half unconscious like that, but I was a little relieved to see you alive.

"The three worked together to carry you to the police car and carefully stretched you out in the backseat. The policeman closed the door and again spoke loudly. 'I will get him to the hospital. Thank you, men, for helping the boy. A detective will be calling you to get your statement.' And with that, he got into the driver seat, turned his flashing lights on, slowly made a U-turn, and drove down the street at a pace one would not expect for a car getting a bloody kid to the hospital.

"At this point, I had no idea what to do. I had no way to follow you. I didn't really know where I was... I mean, I knew I was in Ann Arbor but nothing other than that. I watched as my driver walked back to his pickup scratching his head. He looked confused but also unsure of what had just happened. He turned and watched as the man in the suit coat walked into the building. Right before he got back in his truck, he stopped. He leaned over and looked in the back of it, then scanned the crowd looking for me. Once again, I ducked back behind the front row and pulled Elmo with me. He seemed like a nice man, but I didn't think he could help me, and I didn't want to answer any questions. After looking around for a few moments, he sat down in the driver seat, closed the door and turned the key. His truck rumbled to life, he turned the steering wheel, and slowly pulled out into the road. I watched as he turned out of sight. Elmo and I were alone again.

"The crowd slowly dissipated, and I found myself standing alone on the sidewalk. I looked around at the old brick buildings. There were shops and restaurants on both sides of the street. The bald skinny guy and the guy in the suit coat had walked into what looked like an old shoe store. There was a giant neon sign hanging above the door that was in the outline of a shoe, and various shoe brand logos were painted on the brick on both sides of it. The windows were now covered with newspapers, and the lights were out. I turned and looked around. There was a locksmith's shop behind me. It had a blinking open sign hanging on the door, and the window had a display of keys and safes. Next to the display lay a dog, a collie, sleeping. Elmo looked at the collie with interest, but he did not move or even growl. The next building to the east of the locksmith was an Italian restaurant. There was a life-sized statue of a traditional Italian waiter holding a pizza on the sidewalk beside the door, and delicious smells were coming from within. The smell reminded me of something. I had not eaten since breakfast, and the sun was now going down. I reached in my pocket, but I knew what would be there. Nothing. I had no money. If you remember, we had combined our money in the car and, of course, you had the wad in your pocket. I had no way to get food.

"I remember hearing a story about how a man once survived for twenty years without ever using money. They say that he became a scavenger. He found his food. One of the main ways he found it was digging in restaurant dumpsters. As horrible as that sounded when I first heard it, my growling stomach and lack of money convinced me to at least have a look. I walked down the alley between the locksmith and the restaurant. The big dumpster directly behind the restaurant was rusty and stinky. I immediately doubted I would find anything worth eating. I opened the dumpster and looked inside. I could see, right within reach, a pizza box that contained a half a pizza. It looked like it had not touched the trash - it actually looked good."

At this point, Veronica narrowed her eyes and looked at me. She said in a motherly tone, "Don't judge Tommy. I was starving!

"I reached for it but could not quite get to it. I needed a little more height. There was an old bucket on the side of the dumpster, and I flipped it over, stood on it, and leaned in. The dumpster smelled horrible, but the pizza looked good. I put my hand on the pizza. And then something pretty horrible happened. The bucket slid out from underneath me, and I tumbled into the dumpster. The lid closed and I was in complete dark and complete stink.

"I heard Elmo whining as I tried to get myself turned around. As I began to lift the lid, two men walked up. Embarrassed, I kept the lid low and waited for them to leave. They were talking. One said, 'I don't have my key with me, but I will leave the door unlocked for you.'

"The other answered, 'You sure it is safe leaving the door unlocked all week? I can't start painting until Tuesday at the earliest.'

"'I'm not too worried about it. Not much crime around here and nothing in there but a few old tools. Nothing anyone could steal that I would care much about. I messed up not bringing the spare key, but that's life. Thanks for your work painting the place. It has to be ready for the sale by the end of the month.' I watched through the mostly closed dumpster lid as they walked toward the back of the building, past the back door to the locksmith's shop, to the next building. They opened the unlocked door. Above it read, 'Acme

Hardware.' A few minutes after entering, they walked back out, walked out of the alley, and disappeared.

"I climbed out of the dumpster. I left the pizza – my appetite was gone. I longed for hand sanitizer. I longed for a nice warm bath. I walked out of the alley and back into the street in front of the shoe shop. The moment I stepped onto the sidewalk, I ducked back into the alley and pulled Elmo with me. A police car was coming back down the street. I saw a fat policeman with a face that looked like melted cheese behind the wheel.

"I crouched behind the trash bags in the alley and watched. The police car pulled up slowly and came to a stop. The policeman opened his door, stepped out, opened the door to the backseat, and pulled you out. He heaved you on his shoulder and carried you into the shoe shop.

"I was stunned. I am not sure why I was stunned (did I really think Cheeseface was going to take you to the hospital?), but I was stunned. I was not sure what to do. I could not call the cops. I could not help you. I could only watch. Cheeseface came back out a few minutes later without you. He got in his car and slowly pulled away again.

"You know me. You know I would never break into a building that was not mine. But what was I supposed to do in this situation? I had no shelter. I had no one to help me. And I had to stick by you... what choice did I have?

"I walked back down the alley with Elmo behind me. I walked up to the back door of the hardware store, opened the door and went in. I found an empty shop with an old fridge, a few tools, and a perfect view of the shoe shop out the front window.

"That hardware store was my home for the next four days. The fridge had about twenty frozen meals crammed in the freezer, and the old microwave next to it still worked. I feel bad about taking that food, but I was hungry. The next four days were rough. I was so bored. I sat there on the floor and read old magazines that were left in the bathroom. And I watched the shoe shop. Nothing happened. Every once in a while, I saw either the suit or the skinny guy come in or out but saw nothing of you for four days. Then, finally, I saw him…" she nodded at David, "coming down the fire escape with you on his shoulders. And you know the rest."

When she finished her story, the car grew quiet except for wind and road noise. Then I remembered a question that her story had not answered, "at that rest stop, any idea who the big guy in the white suit was?"

"I have no idea."

"I do," said David, "He is one of the reasons why we do not have cell phones, and he is the reason for the gunfire." He said nothing more, and the car grew silent again.

Then we heard thunder, which is a weird thing to hear when the sky is perfectly clear. The car started to shake. Elmo started to bark, and we all looked out the window and counted at least more jets flying overhead toward Ann Arbor.

CHAPTER SEVEN

THE CAR SLOWED as the sun set. The houses we passed had a chain link fences outlining overgrown lawns. Weeds grew in the potholes and cracks in the road. A large pit bull without a leash trotted alone down the street and crossed in front of us forcing David to slow. We pulled into the driveway of a one-story, white house with aluminum siding. The two large front windows were covered with plywood, and illegible graffiti was painted in red on the left window. We drove in the driveway to the large garage to the right and behind the house.

David got out of the car and looked around. He walked up to the garage, pulled a key from his pocket, reached down, unlocked it, and pulled up on the door. It did not move at first. David readjusted his grip and pulled harder. It moved a little, and as he exerted himself, it continued up slowly. He pushed up to get it open the whole way. He stopped and turned around, smiling at us as we sat watching him from the car. "It might need a bit of grease," he said in a raised voice.

He walked back to the car and slipped the still running vehicle into gear, pulling slowly forward into the garage. He shut off the car, got out, walked back to the garage door, and reaching up, pulled it down. It rumbled shut more quickly than we expected given how hard it was to get up. We were in the dark.

We climbed out of the car in the dark. The garage smelled of oil, dust, and dirt. It was a pleasant smell that reminded me of normal times doing normal things.

"What was the deal with those jets?" Veronica asked. David did not respond. As our eyes adjusted to the dark of the garage, we could make each other out, and I saw David walk over to a wooden table in the corner of the garage. He crouched down and fumbled around with a box underneath it and stood back up. He reached into his pocket and pulled out a match. He struck the match on the table, and in its glow, we saw that he held an old-fashioned oil lamp. He touched it with the match, and the garage become visible.

"The war is becoming more intense," David said as he blew out the match. His smile was gone. His laughing eyes were gone. For the first time since I met him, he seemed sad. There was a long silence.

I knew what I was thinking. I knew what Veronica was thinking. 'What war?' I wanted to ask. But up to this point, asking David anything was pretty worthless. I needed someone to explain everything from the beginning. I needed...

"Where is my Uncle Jacob?"

David opened his mouth to speak and then shut it. He did

not smile. He did not show any emotion. Then he smiled as though he had just thought of a good idea and said, "Yes, it is time for Jacob."

He walked, lamp in hand, to the wall of the garage. Previously hidden by the shadows was an old-fashioned rotary telephone. He picked it up. Psss. Rlllllll. His fingers pulled number by number as he held the receiver to his ear. After he had pulled seven numbers, he stopped and waited. Then he spoke.

"Jacob?" a large smile was on his face. "It is David here. How are you doing? Yes, things are a bit crazy right now. Yes, I saw the jets. No, I doubt I know any more than you do." He said everything calmly with a smile on his face and nonchalance as though he was talking about the weather. "Anyway, Jacob, I was not calling to talk about all that." He paused to listen. "No," he said. "No," he said again, this time more impatiently, "Jacob, I am calling because I am here with your nephew." He paused again to listen. "Thomas! Yes, you got the right one Yes, he is right here. I am sure he would love to talk to you on the telephone, but actually, we are going to need to have you in person... Yes, I know... yes, of course, they stopped monitoring land lines... Yes, I understand all that... Yes, I totally understand where you are coming from but... no... no... I... no, I cannot. I am so sorry, Jacob... I cannot. In person or no talk... Yes! He is alive... you are going to have to risk it... ok... ok... yes, you have guessed the correct location – I am impressed. Goodbye, Jacob!"

He hung up the phone smiling. "Your uncle is a wonderful man. And he has agreed to meet with us here."

Veronica looked at me and raised her eyebrows.

We heard more jets flying overhead.

"Listen to that," David said as though he were talking about the thunder in the distance.

"David..." I said. I wanted answers. I needed answers. I

had to try again. "David... I don't know if you think I know what is going on. I don't know if you think this is a game. But I need you to stop and to explain things. I know nothing. I don't know anything about what my uncle has to do with this. I do not know why there are fighter jets. I don't know who you are or who Isaac is or why he tranquilized me." I paused remembering that my leg had two holes in it from the darts and suddenly felt the pain. "Can you please just focus and tell me what is going on? From the beginning? Imagine you are talking to a normal person on the street because that is what I am. I know nothing. I was a normal kid. I woke up and... craziness. I have been running from pretty much everyone ever since."

David looked at me with concern. He opened his mouth to speak, raised a finger as though he was about to make a point, then he closed his mouth, sighed, and grew silent. The silence did not last long. We heard the sound of gravel being squeezed and kicked by car tires and could see out the small tinted windows of the garage door that someone had pulled into the driveway.

Out of the car stepped the first family I had seen since this craziness began, however many days it has been now. Dark hair, broad shoulders, a thick round face, and a large scar that ran down his left cheek. His face was unshaven, his clothes were disheveled, and he walked with a limp. But that was all normal for Uncle Jacob. He always looked like he had just woken up from sleeping outdoors. His eyes were as piercing and angry as ever, and his lips had the snarl that always had caused me to think he was scary. That was also normal.

Last Thanksgiving, Jacob stayed with us for a few days. The day after the holiday, he had almost been arrested when he jumped out of our car and had to be restrained before he could punch some guy who had given us the finger in a parking lot. He was the opposite of my always-calm father. And that is why my father was the only human I knew who liked him. My mother tolerated him. I was afraid of him. Most people hated him. My father genuinely liked him. My father is so calm and tended to defuse stressful situations. Jacob was a diplomatic challenge for my father. But he liked Jacob because Jacob, for all his spit and vinegar, was a man who could be trusted to do the right thing regardless of social pressure. Most people care what others think. Most people want the approval of others. This desire to please has caused many people to do wrong in the interest of getting along. Jacob never cared about getting along. And he always did the right thing even if it caused everyone to hate him.

There are few human beings on earth more intelligent and hardworking than Jacob Burke. He founded two tech companies that had billion-dollar IPOs. In the short period of time he worked for the government, he was recognized for almost single-handedly identifying and averting more than one imminent terror threat. You would think this would cause Jacob to have a lot of friends. He had none. Sooner or later everyone that tried to get close to Jacob would be offended or embarrassed by Jacob. Except for my father.

Jacob walked towards the garage. When he got to the door, he bent down and pulled on the handle. When it did not immediately open, he kicked the door and yelled, "Open it, David!"

David was resting against the table and chuckled as Jacob yelled, and he whispered, "Your uncle is a funny man, and he makes me laugh." He started to get up and then stopped. "Should we make him wait?" He asked with a huge grin as though he thought this was a prank that would be funny.

"No, please let him in!" I said pleadingly. I was so desperate to see someone I knew... someone who was sane.

Someone who might actually explain what was going on. Someone who might be able to tell me what happened to my parents.

"Oh alright," David said shrugging his shoulders with obvious disappointment.

He walked to the door, fiddled with the handle, bent over and pulled up. The rusty wheels and pulleys screamed as it opened. The light was blinding, and we all shielded our eyes. Into the light stepped the silhouette of Jacob Burke.

Jacob walked in and did not look at me. He did not look at Veronica. He did not look at Elmo. His eyes were fixed on David. He walked slowly and purposefully toward David. He stared at David with his fists clenched. David stared directly back with his hands at his sides and an easy lean to his composure.

Jacob reached backward without turning his head and closed the garage door behind him. The garage grew dark again.

"Jacob, welcome. Thank you so much for coming."

Jacob said nothing. A long silence followed. Jacob finally said, "I am trying to decide if I should kill you or not."

"Well, if you are asking for input, my vote is that you do not kill me," David said cheerfully and then turned to wink at Veronica and me.

"Do you think this is a joke?" Jacob said with barely suppressed rage.

"He thinks everything is a joke," I interjected.

"Thomas, never have words been less true. You are alive because of how seriously I take this all." David's smile was gone, and he had stopped slouching against the table and was standing firm. He did not turn to look at me but continued to meet Jacob's stare. This was the first time I thought I detected a hint of anger in David. But it only lasted a moment.

"Tommy, are you okay?" Jacob asked me without removing his eyes from David.

"I was shot twice in the leg with darts, and I busted my head on the concrete. It hurts, but I think I'm alright."

"Seriously? You shot a kid? How low will you go?" Jacob's anger was once again directed at David.

"I didn't shoot anyone. But I did save him from a man in white, provide him with medical care for his head and leg, and help him escape. I did take gunfire from my brother on his behalf. But don't worry; I certainly did not do it to get any sort of 'thank you' from you." As he finished saying this, he moved back toward the table and returned to his relaxed lean.

Jacob sighed, "Thank you," he mumbled.

"What was that?" David said with a huge smile on his face looking around in mock confusion. "I am not sure I heard what you just said. Veronica, did you hear him? Tommy? He said something and I missed it. What did he say?"

"I am leaving with the kids," Jacob said calmly as he stepped back into the stream of sunlight now entering the garage door window. "You can do whatever you want." He grabbed the handle and began to open it.

CHAPTER EIGHT

"Oh, Jacob," David said in the feigned voice of a parent chiding a misbehaving child, "you would abandon your country in her hour of need? What happened to the brave man I have heard so much about?"

"I am leaving. You should do the same. This building may not be here tomorrow."

"Jacob, you have to trust me."

"You are a drunken liar, and I have zero intention of

trusting you," he said as he turned the handle on the garage door.

"What sort of a man leaves without trying to save a life? You are supposed to be the righteous one," David said with disappointment.

Jacob stepped away from the door and took a deep breath. "I am not the liar. I know what I am talking about. The war is on. We are all in danger. It is time to lay low."

"Jacob, I know you want to dismiss me. Perhaps you only know me by my reputation as Isaac's drunken brother. But I think, deep down, you know that I am right. About everything. I was with Gibion. I know him better than you. I know what he is capable of."

"Let's say I did. What are you asking me to do?"

"We have to get to them. We need to start tonight."

"Impossible."

"Not impossible," David responded. He pulled a folded piece of paper from his pocket and started to spread it out on the table behind him. I immediately recognized it as a copy of one of the pages from the envelope. David pointed at a diagram on the center of the page as he spoke. "You are going to walk to South Gate at exactly 2:45 am. You are going to ask to see your brother. They will say 'no,' but you will ask. When they say no, you will turn back and walk to the car. Sit there and wait. Can you do that?"

Jacob looked with interest and sudden recognition at the paper.

David continued, "When you hear the sound, you will run to the line red line." He pointed to a mark he had made in red, "and then you will move this way and meet us back here."

Jacob did not say anything but leaned over to look closer at the marks that David had pointed to.

"I know you do not like the idea, Jacob."

"It is a death sentence."

"I hope not... but maybe. I hope the guards will be quite distracted before they reach you." David said that with seriousness on his face again. "But, Jacob, I remember the words that you once said to me that have always stuck with me. You said that the real skill in life is not learning to be successful but learning to fail. You said that real men are not afraid of failure."

Jacob's face grew sad. He stared forward. "You realize that this would put us in the middle of this war," he finally said in a voice that was close to a whisper.

Veronica interjected, "I need to use the bathroom." David and Jacob ignored her at first, and she repeated, "I *really* have to go!"

"In the house...," David finally answered, "the door should be unlocked. Make it quick please."

Veronica walked out the door, and the conversation continued. They argued about the plan, and they discussed the details. Jacob appeared to agree for a moment before backing out again. For the next few moments he and David debated the plan, and Jacob wavered as to whether he would be a part of it. Every few minutes Jacob would stop whatever was being discussed and ask, "You realized that this is an act of war?" After discussing and debating for a long time, the room grew quiet. Then Elmo started barking and would not stop despite our shushing.

It is at about that moment that we all realized that Veronica had been gone much too long. No one said anything directly, but you could see a nervousness slowly creeping into the room, and finally, Jacob said, "Where is she?" He opened the side door to the garage and immediately ducked back in and crouched down signaling us all to do the same.

David crawled on hands and feet to the garage door and

peeked out the window. I followed him doing the same. There standing by Jacob's car stood an enormous man dressed in a white suit with pale skin staring blankly and motionlessly at the car. As I watched, he walked robotically to the door of the car, reached out his arm, and pulled on the handle. The door, locked, did not open. Momentarily, he put his arm at his side, then he reached out again and, with one flowing motion, he put his hand through the window. The noise of breaking glass was followed by the honking of the car alarm as he unlocked the door.

"That son of a...," said Jacob through his teeth and he started to lift the door with clenched fists. David leaped toward Jacob and pulled him away. David hissed through his teeth, "Are you serious? You do realize that is a Gib-bot? Even 'Angry Jacob' cannot win that fight." As the two silently wrestled on the floor, David turned his head and smiled at me. Jacob twisted himself loose but stayed still on the floor. We all looked back out the window. The man in white was digging through the glove compartment, then the center console, then the back seat, then he walked to the driver's door, pushed a button, and the trunk popped open. From the trunk, he pulled a rifle and a metal box. He set the box on the ground and then stood up straight. He turned his head and looked from the house to the garage and then, without hesitation, he started walking to the house. When the side door did not open, he raised his foot and brought his heel down on it. It collapsed in front of him.

"Veronica!" I said no longer maintaining a whisper. David opened the door a crack, and they both slid under it. I followed, and Elmo somehow pushed through after us.

"I want you to take Elmo and go that way," Jacob said, pointing behind the house. "Get as far away as possible. We are probably going to die in there, and there is no point in you dying with us. Try getting as far away from Ann Arbor as you can. It will be a war zone by tomorrow."

I shook my head, but Jacob did not wait for my response. He yelled, "Go!" as he turned and ran to catch up with David. Now together, they moved quickly toward the house, David slowed, reached out and grabbed a cantaloupe-sized stone by the side of the driveway. Jacob, without slowing, reached his hand in his car's backseat and pulled out a baseball bat. Then they both disappeared through the newly broken side door.

Elmo and I stood for a moment. "Let's go, Elmo," I said. We turned, and we ran back into the house.

Have you ever been in a situation that seemed to be in slow motion? I remember when I was in first grade, I was hit in the temple by a baseball and, as I fell to the ground, the world slowed down. I saw the ground approaching, I thought about the girls in the stands who were watching and wondered what they would think. I even was able to think about the fact that I was passing out. It was weird. This felt like that.

I stepped into the door, and there was complete madness. The first thing I saw was the man in white. He was standing perfectly erect in what may have been the living room. The whole house smelled of stale cigarettes and cat pee. There were clothes and books spread all over the floor. The man in white held the rifle he had pulled from Jacob's car in his right arm. He held Veronica under his left. He was so still that he looked like he had been challenged to impersonate a manikin. The only thing that moved was the finger on his right hand, pulling the trigger of the rifle. The deafening sound of bullets ringing out in a small house was jarring. I heard screaming coming from somewhere down a hallway, and I could tell it was Jacob's voice. The man in white cocked the gun open, and shell casings fell to the floor, he pulled the gun into his armpit and used his now free hand to reach down into the metal box he had taken from Jacob's car to pull out more shells. He placed them in the gun and cocked it shut again. But before his finger moved again, I heard a thud and realized it was the sound of a large cantaloupe sized stone hitting him in the head. He staggered but did not fall. The sound of thunder rattled the room again as the rifle fired, but the bullet exploded into the wall above the doorway to the hall. The man in white turned, and I saw his face. The rock, thrown by David who was apparently hiding in what looked like a dingy bathroom, had done some damage. The man in white's face was bloody, and his left eye was destroyed. Nevertheless, he did not lose focus and remained deliberate in his motions. He bent down, placed Veronica on the floor and said in a loud police-like command, "Stop. Do not move!" With both hands free, he sprang at the bathroom door. David tried to close it shut, but the man in white easily pushed it open.

All of this seemed like slow motion, and it takes a long time to write down, but in reality, it happened just seconds after I opened the door. What happened next was a blur. Time ceased to be slow and became quite fast. Elmo growled and bolted to the bathroom. Veronica stood up and ran to me. I ran after Elmo. I opened the bathroom door that had swung shut behind the man in white and saw a beating going on. The man in white stood over David mercilessly beating him in the face. Elmo crouched and then sprung on the man in white's back. For the next few seconds, there was a blur of red and white rolling on the floor before the man in white had Elmo by the scruff of his neck like a puppy and threw him out of the bathroom. Elmo slid across the floor and hit a kitchen wall. The man in white stood, straightened his rumpled suit, bent down, picked up the rifle, and started to walk toward Veronica and me. We turned and ran.

We ran back through the destroyed door and toward the

back of the house. The man in white came out after us. He started to run, and his speed was superhuman. In a few steps, he was right behind us. He grabbed Veronica by the hood of her sweatshirt and pulled her to the ground. I twisted to face him. He reached out and grabbed my shoulder. His hands felt like steel clamps, and I screamed in pain. He lifted Veronica under his right arm and pulled me under his left. He turned and started walking back toward the house.

Thunder. Jets flying low. Rumbling above us. I flinched, but the man in white appeared not to notice. He continued without pausing. I twisted my neck around and watched as the jets flew toward the skyline of Ann Arbor. And then I saw flashing. Then fire and smoke. Three plumes. A moment later I heard them. Explosions. Three loud blasts. Ann Arbor was on fire.

At exactly that moment, the man in white abruptly stopped. He became perfectly still. The bouncing, struggling, and movement all stopped. Suddenly there was a strange quiet. I turned and looked at Veronica. She looked at me, and we both twisted to look at the man in white. He was frozen. Unmoving. Blood dripped from his eye where he had been hit by the cantaloupe-sized stone, but his face was emotionless and still.

I tried to twist free, but his grip was tight. "Hey!" I yelled at him, "Let us go!" He looked straight ahead without movement or acknowledgment of my yelling. I looked at Veronica again.

"Is he alive?" she asked. She reached out her hand and punched him. "Ow," she said, but the man in white did not react. I heard barking and turned to see Elmo running out of the house. I was glad to see him alive. He ran up to us and barked wildly at the man in white. The man in white did not move. Elmo jumped and attached his mouth to the man's arm. The man still did not move. Elmo pulled with his considerable weight, but the man's arm stayed wrapped around my waist without loosening its grip at all. As Elmo pulled, the man began to tip over. His right leg came off the ground, and he slowly leaned toward Elmo's pulling. And then he fell, remaining rigid even as he hit the ground. Both Veronica and I groaned as his weight landed on our backs, and we were left lying, still tucked under his arms, pinned to the ground.

Veronica was the first to wriggle free. Elmo had switched sides and was now barking, biting and pulling on the man in white's right arm. Veronica stood over me and tried to help me free. Eventually, I had to back out of his grip by removing my polo shirt, lifting my hands above my head and having both Veronica and Elmo pull on my legs.

Breathing hard, Veronica and I stood above the man in white and stared at him. His white suit was muddy, bloody and ripped. His arms were strangely looped as though he was still holding us, and his form was still in the exact shape it had been when he was standing with us under his arms.

"That is super weird," said Veronica looking down. "We better go back to the house."

In the struggle with the man in white, I had completely forgotten about the grisly scene we had left. Jacob and David were probably dead. I had heard Jacob get shot, and I saw that white monster smashing David's face.

We entered the house. The stink of cigarettes and cats was now overwhelmed by the smell of gunpowder and blood. Everything was smashed and turned over. I ran first to the hallway and found my uncle, unconscious and in a pool of blood in one of the bedrooms. I looked for the wound and found it on his shoulder. Blood was trickling out. I applied pressure and started yelling, "Jacob, Jacob, wake up."

Meanwhile, Veronica had gone to David. "Is he alive?" I

yelled down the hallway. I needed help. I was just a kid. I could not be doing this.

"I am for now," a confident male voice broke the silence. I looked up, and David was standing in the door above me. His nose was bleeding, and his eye was blackened and swollen. His normally perfect suit jacket and fashionable t-shirt were ripped and soiled with blood and dirt, and his shoulder and neck were visible and covered in blood. He was panting and gripping his left arm.

He crouched down and looked at Jacob. With his right hand, he felt his chest. He moved my hand away from the wound and looked at it before replacing my hand.

"Where is the Gib-bot?" he asked.

"You mean the man in white?" Veronica asked.

"Yes, the man in white."

"He is dead I think. He froze and is lying in the backyard."

David looked at her and raised his eyebrows.

"We need to get Jacob out of here. We all have to get out of here."

"We need a doctor!" Veronica said.

"We have one. I am a doctor," David said and smiled. I think he was trying to be his old self, but his mouth was bloody, and the smile looked very grisly, and he definitely lacked his normal charm.

"I don't think we should move him," Veronica said.

"Well, as a doctor, I would agree. But as a man on the run, I know that we had better move him or he will be dead. And, unless you are suggesting we leave him here alone, we will be dead as well."

Veronica and I both looked at each other.

"The timeline has not changed. If anything, those explosions tell me the timeline has accelerated. We have to get a long way away from here, and we have to do it soon."

David walked over to the bed and pulled off the

bedspread. It was nasty; a large yellow stain was in the middle, and its stuffing was coming out of a tear in the bottom of it. David folded it once and placed it on the floor next to Jacob. "Heave ho!" he said with mock enthusiasm as he stood up and lifted Jacob's lower half onto the folded blanket. He motioned that I should keep my hands on the wound as he gently lifted Jacob's shoulders onto the blanket. Jacob's face was becoming paler. His breathing was becoming more infrequent.

"Ok, medical team! We need to get this patient out to the car." David stood up and grabbed two of the corners of the old blanket. He winced as he was forced to use his hurting left arm to do it. "Hold on tight to the corners. Veronica, if you would be so kind, can you grab that corner of our gurney." He nodded at the corner opposite him at Jacob's feet. "And Thomas, you are going to have to take a brief break from the excellent pressure you are applying to that wound, to hold the gurney on that corner," he nodded at the corner on my right. "Excellent!" he said cheerfully when we were positioned as he asked. "On the count of three, we are going to lift and take him straight out to his vehicle."

He counted. We lifted. My corner was heavy, and I could see Veronica was struggling with her side as well. As we moved to the door with difficulty, David continued to encourage us cheerfully. Getting through the door required setting Jacob down and repositioning our grips so that we could edge him out by the ends of the blanket. With that, we came to the car. The car, a black 1988 Ford Thunderbird, looked big, but the interior was surprisingly small. David had Veronica and me climb into the car to help lift Jacob's feet in as he carried the bulk of his weight.

"Which one of you is the best driver?" I honestly did not know the answer to David's question. I had never driven before, and Veronica's last effort was more than a little frightening. But Veronica did not hesitate. She confidently said that she was an excellent driver. David pulled the keys out of Jacob's pocket, handed them to Veronica, and climbed into the back seat with Jacob. Veronica jumped in the driver seat. I sat down in the passenger seat and turned to look at Elmo. My giant dog that had barely fit the back seat of David's car now had to share the front seat with me. I groaned. Elmo, the giant red dog, jumped on my lap.

There is a famous roller coaster that travels indoors and in complete darkness. When I was on it, the most terrifying part was the fact that every turn was unanticipated and that I could prepare for none of the twists, loops, or drops. Every movement was a complete surprise. This car ride was very much like that. Instead of darkness, I saw only a giant red furry mass in front of my face. Veronica's driving was slightly better than last time but still a roller coaster. She didn't take out any hedges but did seem to be bouncing off the edges of the road and knocked over at least three garbage cans on her way out of the neighborhood. As David calmly told her to turn left and then right, she turned but did not slow before doing so.

Although I was pinned to my seat by a giant dog, I twisted my head to look over my shoulder. David had his knees on the floorboards, his feet curled behind my seat and was leaning over Jacob. He was working furiously and was covered in blood. He had successfully removed a bloody bullet from the shoulder and had pulled a needle and thread from his jacket pocket and began the process of closing the wound.

His directions shouted out without seeming even to look up were taking us out of Ann Arbor into the countryside to the south of the city. Cows and horses grazed in the fields as we passed farmland. I lost track of time, but it felt like an hour had passed when David leaned away from Jacob and said, "Well, that is all I can do. He is in God's hands now." Jacob looked dead. His skin was perfectly white, his mouth hung open, and his eyelids were cracked, but his eyes were rolled back so that only the white showed.

"Is he alive?"

"At the present," David said. No smile.

CHAPTER NINE

Nᴉɢʜᴛꜰᴀʟʟ ʜᴀᴅ ᴄᴏᴍᴇ, and still, we drove. Occasionally, David would mutter that Veronica should turn left or right. We seemed to be getting further and further into the middle of nowhere. The landscape had become hilly. I realized for the first time that I was extremely tired. The holes in my leg and the gash on my head were hurting again, and my wrist was now a mass of fresh scabs from the struggle with the handcuff, and it itched.

I was starting to drift off to sleep, but Veronica's voice broke the silence, "Who was that guy?"

"Who was who?" David asked, and he shook his head as though he had been dreaming.

"The guy in white."

"Specificity is the soul of narrative," David said smiling.

And then there was silence again, and he turned to stare out the window.

"Who was he?" Veronica said with an irritated voice.

"He was a Gib-bot."

"Ok, what does that mean?"

"It means that he was not really human. He was a cyborg – a combination of human and robot – originally designed as a peacekeeper intended to defuse dangerous standoffs for the government. Now they are pretty much kidnappers and thugs used by the Gibionites for their purposes."

"There are more than one of them?"

"Yes. I observed the manufacture of at least a hundred of them."

"Why didn't he kill us?" I interjected.

David looked at Jacob, nodded, and raised an eyebrow. "Yet," he added.

"Yet," I conceded.

"They rarely kill. They are programmed for monitoring and arresting. They kill only when absolutely required to complete a mission. I think that he came there to arrest you and Veronica. He doesn't know who I am. Or who Jacob is. Or he would have killed us both. "

"Why doesn't he know you?"

"No data in the system on either one of us. We were deleted."

"Deleted?"

"There is a database that has everything every human in this country has ever done in life. What foods you like. Who your second-grade teacher was. What sports teams you like. Everything. That was the result of 'Enduring Freedom.' But Gibion made a mistake when he invited me in on the project. I was loyal to Isaac and initially wanted to help. But you cannot ask me to sign up for a thing like that." David smiled when he said this. "Now he regrets it. And that is why they do not know Jacob or me."

"How did he find us at that house?" Veronica asked.

"They run algorithms on likely locations. They probably sent units to many places. I thought that location would be safe but I was wrong. Your uncle and father both knew of it and met there with Isaac and me about a year ago. Somewhere in the algorithm, the Gib-bots must have thought it was worth checking."

"What happened to him?" Veronica continued her questions.

David narrowed his eyes and tilted his head. "I was going to ask you that."

"He was walking with us back to the house and just completely froze. Like a statue. We were stuck under his arms. Elmo tipped him over…."

"Good old Elmo!" David muttered cheerfully.

"Elmo tipped him over," Veronica continued irritated by the interjection, "and he was still frozen. We had to squeeze out of his arms to get to you."

"Interesting," David said thoughtfully. "Did this happen before or after those jets bombed the city?"

"Right after."

"The Gib-bots are guided by the control centers. Each center is responsible for a certain number of Gibionite cyborgs. Centers are found in highly secret locations throughout the United States. Ann Arbor was always rumored to be one of the locations, given that it is where Gibion got his start, but I never thought he would be so dumb."

"So are all of them frozen?"

"I have no idea, but even if they are, I doubt they will be frozen long. There are ten other control centers from which they could operate. My guess is that they will be back up and running soon."

"Why do they call them 'Gib-bots'?" I asked.

David looked at me with squinted eyes and cocked his head, "You really don't know anything. Isaac was sure you were lying, and I assumed he was right. Did your parents really not tell you any of this?"

"Nothing," I said.

He looked to Veronica and gestured for a response.

"Nothing!" she said as though he were accusing her.

"They are named after Reginald Gibion, the man whose technology is behind most of this. He designed the software. He designed the cyborgs. He hired me. And he helped develop ADK-9."

"ADK-9?" Veronica questioned?

"ADK-9," David repeated.

"Ok...what is that?"

"Neutralizes nuclear reactions. You could set a nuclear bomb down in the middle of Ann Arbor right now, and nothing would happen. It is some sort of gas he developed, you spread it with an old-fashioned crop duster and once in place, somehow it degrades radioactive material and neutralizes the bombs. A small amount spread in the atmosphere above a city will act as a canopy for that city protecting it from incoming nuclear weapons – by sky, sea or land.

"Gibion was in the lab when the first successful test was done. He copied the formula by hand; then he destroyed all files electronic or otherwise. Naturally, he then killed the two other scientists working on the project – making him the only one alive that knew the formula. Don't ask me the science – if I knew that, we would be calling those cyborgs the 'Dave-bots,' and I would be the evil shadow emperor." David smiled at his own joke, but both Veronica and I sat with our mouths gaping open and eyes wide.

"Well, that is the greatest thing I have ever heard!"

Veronica exclaimed. "There will never be nuclear war again!" I felt the same way as Veronica. All my life, I had been told that nuclear war was one of the possible ways that humanity would destroy the world, and the idea that we could defuse every nuclear bomb and end that threat seemed fantastic to me.

"You missed the evil emperor part, didn't you? Did I forget to mention that the scary robots were named after him?" He paused for effect, tipped his head slightly as though he were thinking. "No. I am pretty sure I mentioned them."

"How is ending the threat of nuclear war a bad thing?" Veronica asked.

"Oh, there is plenty of threat of nuclear war," David replied. "In regione caecorum rex est luscus."

"What?"

"Latin. What do they teach kids in school these days?" David said clicking his tongue. "In the land of the blind, the one-eyed man is king."

"What does that even mean?"

"It means that if Gibion has the ability to disarm everyone else's nuclear bombs, he becomes almost infinitely powerful if he can get his hands on one."

Both Veronica and I silently processed this statement.

"Did he?" I finally asked.

"Did he what?" David responded.

"Get a bomb?"

David spoke more rapidly than I had ever seen him speak before. His calm was once again gone, and although he did not seem angry, he did seem agitated. His movements became jerky and quick. "What do you think I have been saying this whole time? Of course! This is precisely what is going on. This is the war we have been fighting. This is what your parents were working on. This is what all this is about!" He grabbed my envelope and held it up. "This is what Isaac and I have been working on. This is why your own govern-ment is now a full-blown tyranny. This is the problem. Gibion has at least one bomb and probably more. His power is growing. His wealth is growing, and the nations that once were the superpowers of the world are in danger of becoming powerless provinces in Gibion's global kingdom."

CHAPTER TEN

EFFORTS TO GET a fuller explanation from David proved fruitless. Our questions were met with a combination of half answers, enigmatic answers, and non-answers. Soon the car grew silent. Elmo had found a way to get his huge lower half on the floorboard between my legs, and his head was resting on my lap as he slept. I was able to get somewhat comfortable and stared out the window. We had been driving for hours, and despite all the day's excitement, a feeling of exhaustion began to overwhelm me. Our car, now far from the city, was driving down country roads. As we drove, I could feel the dirt road and taste the hot dry dust. The gravel hit the bottom of the car, and the warm wind flowed into the window. I was overwhelmed with worry and sadness when I thought of my parents and all that had been my former life. My thoughts returned to the fact that my house was now gone. Everything I owned. Nothing was the same. But, as I looked over and saw Veronica driving and glanced back and saw David sleeping against the window with Jacob's feet propped up on his lap, I also had another feeling. I had trouble identifying it at first, but the word came to me: adventure. I was on an adventure. It was unclear what my role was. It was unclear what exactly the adventure was. But despite my worry about my parents, my longing for home was gone. And although not a small amount of fear knotted in my stomach, there was a part of me that was excited… happy even.

Right before he fell asleep David had told Veronica to keep driving on this road for the next two hours. As we approached that time, Veronica said, "You better wake him up now." I twisted and pushed David's shoulder. He stirred but did not wake. I pushed again. Finally, he woke with a start.

"Are we there already?" he asked groggily.

"You said two hours. It has been two hours," Veronica said.

"Ah, so I did. Let me have a look around. What roads did we pass?"

Neither Veronica nor I had any idea. It was dark, and we had not been paying attention to road signs. We were deep in the countryside. Barns, corn fields, and the occasional farmhouse were all we could see in the now dark landscape. We had crossed into Ohio but had stayed off of main roads the whole way. David did not ask again and was scanning the landscape, clearly looking for something. "We are still a little ways out. I would say a few more miles."

A few minutes later, David directed Veronica to turn right onto a one-lane dirt road. The road was lined with large oak trees, and Veronica slowly guided the car forward. As we drove, I noticed a stone wall that ran behind the tree line on the right side of the car. Barely visible in the moonlight, it was ancient looking. It was tall, made of field stones, and on the top of it, there were short black spikes every few inches.

"Would you be so kind as to turn off your headlights, Veronica?"

Veronica turned off the headlights, and everything became black. Veronica slowed the car to a stop. After a few moments, our eyes adjusted, and the full moon provided enough light to see the road in front of us. David nodded, and Veronica moved the car forward again at a crawl. As we came around a bend in the road, we began to see light coming from the other side of the wall. At first, it was a just a glow, but as we moved forward, we began to be able to make out the shape of buildings and towers on the other side. Now we turned to the right and could see that in the distance there was a large gate on the side of the stone wall. The gate was well lit, and there was a small crowd of men holding guns next to an old pickup truck.

"That is far enough I think," David said cheerfully.

Although moving slowly, Veronica's slamming on the brakes caused the tires to slide on the dirt and gravel as we stopped. The car door creaked as it opened, and David stepped out. He looked at me and smiled. "It is times like this that a drink of whiskey would be nice," he whispered and winked. "Isaac would disapprove, of course." As he said this, for the first time I saw a likeness between him and his brother. In the silence of the night, the closing of the door seemed as loud as a gunshot. As he walked toward the back of the car, his steps thundered and crunched. He fiddled with the trunk, and it opened. I could not see, but I could hear him doing something back there before closing the trunk again. I could see that he had a baseball-sized object in his hand as he walked back toward us. "Jacob," he whispered into the back seat, "I was counting on you to have brought these, thank you. I will put it to good use." I had almost forgotten that Jacob was in the car. I turned to look, and he was still there – breathing but unconscious.

David looked at Veronica and smiled. "Veronica, you are an excellent driver! I appreciate you getting us this far. I plan to walk over there," he pointed toward the guards, "and chat with those nice men. There is a strong possibility that they will attempt to arrest me. Count to one hundred starting now. When you reach one hundred, drive away. Do not wait. If I can make it back to the car, I will. If not, go find a safe place."

"What about you?" I asked. The idea of being without David had never crossed my mind. We had no idea what we were doing. Suddenly being apart from him seemed unthinkable. Panic started to creep in.

"I plan to be back in 100 seconds," David said raising his eyebrows and giving a knowing nod. Then he stated again with emphasis, "but drive away even if I am not." David turned and walked briskly toward the gate. He walked out wide, across the gravel drive and then back toward the gate so that he was approaching the gate directly.

We could barely hear the voices, but as David got about 20 yards away, we faintly heard a guard yell, "Stop."

David yelled back, "I am here to talk to Reginald Gibion." He added, "I just need to talk to him."

Silence followed.

David stood... a statue.

"Come forward," the guard yelled.

I am not sure what was going through David's head, but he was the picture of calm. His arms rested at his side; his posture was relaxed and open. When he walked, he walked with an easy gait like one approaching an old friend.

The faint voices became fainter, but I thought I heard the guard ask, "What is your name?" as David moved closer. David's voice was a little clearer.

"David Rogers," he replied.

The guards all simultaneously jolted in surprise, and two of them backed away. The one in front stood firm and said loudly so that his fellow guards could hear, "I doubt it. But why don't you come with us?" He gestured toward the gate and reached for David's arm.

David stepped back, and I was sure that he was smiling although I could not quite make out his face, "That is quite okay. I will wait out here for him."

In that instant, chaos broke out. David reached back his hand and threw something toward the gate. The guards started yelling. And David started running.

"Thirty-Mississippi, Thirty-one-Mississippi…," I could hear Veronica whispering her count.

Two of the guards were chasing David. One of the guards had gone to inspect what David had thrown, and one of the guards looked right, then left, and then started running into the woods across the street from the gate.

I sighed, and fear fought its way through my body although I could see David smiling as he ran effortlessly toward us. The thunder of gunfire broke through the chaos, and my eyes focused on the guard who had been chasing. He had dropped to one knee and was firing his revolver at David. David crouched and started running in zigzags. Instead of running to us, he turned and ran into the woods. The guard rose and followed him into the woods.

"Sixty-Mississippi, Sixty one- Mississippi…."

As Veronica counted, I stared into the woods but saw nothing. In my peripheral vision, I could see the guards at the gate huddling together and talking. One of them was pointing. I could hear the rumble of the pickup truck being started and saw the headlights flash on. But my attention was on the woods, and there was no movement there.

"Eighty-five-Mississippi, eighty-six-Mississippi..."

"Where is he?" I yelled in exasperation. Elmo whined and sat up, mostly blocking my view. I tried to push him out of the way so that I could stare into the woods, but it did not matter. Nothing was happening.

"Ninety-six-Mississippi, ninety-seven-Mississippi, ninety-eight-Mississippi, ninety-nine-Mississippi...," Veronica stopped counting. Absolute silence. "Any sign of him?" she asked. I shook my head; the panic made speech impossible. "Should we go?" I shook my head again. We were not going to go on without him. I turned and looked at Jacob. Except for the breathing, he looked dead. I looked at Veronica. She was as scared as I was. "He said to go at one hundred! We have to go!"

"No... wait... just hold on!" I climbed out of the open window and sat on the door. I strained my eyes looking for any movement coming from the woods. Nothing. I climbed back in. "Go," I whispered.

Veronica turned the key, and we sat there and listened to the engine run. She shifted the car into reverse and began backing out. We turned around and started to make our way back down the oak-lined, one-lane drive that had brought us there. My eyes grew hot, and I had to sniff to keep my nose from running.

"Are you crying?" Veronica asked. "Don't cry. I'm not going to cry, and I am a girl. David will be ok. We just need to get away from here and find a place to sleep and..."

The explosion stopped her speech. The car rocked. The rear view window was pelted with debris. I have never felt such an explosion. A section of the wall, about a hundred yards away, evaporated. We heard a few gunshots like fire-crackers over radio static. The earth shook. The noise was so loud my ears were ringing, and I could barely hear. We could feel the heat from the fire before we turned around to see. The well-lit building that had been on the other side of the wall was now a fireball.

Veronica slammed on the accelerator, and my head was pressed back to the headrest. The car fishtailed as we made our way back to the end of the road. "What was that?" she yelled. Elmo howled. I turned around and had to squint in the bright light of the fire. The building inside the wall was gone, and nothing but fire remained.

"Uh, the building is gone."

Veronica slammed on the brakes, and I was slammed against Elmo whose giant head blocked me from hitting the windshield. Elmo whimpered. "Thanks, Elmo," I groaned, "you make a nice airbag." I pulled myself back upright and looked up. David stood in the middle of the road blocking our path. His right sleeve was ripped, and his face was filthy. But he was smiling. He walked toward the car.

His feet once again crunched on the gravel, and the door once again creaked open. He squeezed onto the front seat next to me further crowding the front seat and slammed the door. He looked at me without emotion. He politely asked Veronica to keep driving and, as she did, he climbed into the back seat, lifting Jacob's legs and collapsing. He directed us out onto the main road and gave Veronica some basic direc-tions on what way to go. As she drove, he started to try to straighten his appearance. He wiped his face with a rag. He pulled a needle and thread from his bag (maybe the same needle that he had used to stitch up Jacob) and started to stitch the arm of his jacket back together. A comb was pulled from the bag, and his hair was brought back into submission. He asked that I bring down the visor and open the mirror for him to see. Within a few minutes, he was something like his old self, and he sat back and sighed.

We were now driving through farm country again. We drove into the night heading north again. After some time, David took over for Veronica. She now sat in the front seat with Elmo. I was stuck in the back with my half dead uncle's feet on my lap.

A light fog was in the fields and woods. Pale outlines of barns, silos, and farmhouses started to pop up on both sides of the road. We were the only car on the long stretch of winding country highway, but the countryside seemed to be waking. As the graying brought detail to the world, we saw cows and horses walking to their fields to graze. Lights shone in the next farmhouse we passed, and as we drove, we began to see that every farmhouse was now lit.

"Jacob," David said, twisting around to talk to my still apparently unconscious uncle, "it worked well. Better than I expected." Then, although, we said nothing, he turned to us and spoke in a professorial way. "Jacob developed it. It harnesses the nearby energy to combust. The more lights and electricity the bigger the explosion. We probably should have counted to 50, not 100," he chuckled, "that was close."

Jacob stirred. His eyes fluttered. He twisted and groaned. His face was not as pale as it had been, and he didn't look as dead as he had the night before. As he twisted, he kicked my side but stopped when I protested. David turned to see what was going on and, raising his eyebrows, he said calmly, "Jacob, I highly recommend being as still as possible for as long as possible. I did all my work in the backseat of a car, and I cannot promise that it was done perfectly. Let us get to our destination, and I will double check my work."

Jacob moved his elbows under him and pushed himself up grimacing with pain as he did. His eyes were open and wild. He looked around at me, then at Veronica and Elmo, then at David. "David, what did you do?" A moment of silence followed. "You do realize that this is war right? You do realize that your action will be the shot heard round the world? If there is still a world when this is all done?"

David's face grew serious. He looked straight ahead as he drove. After what seemed like an eternity of Jacob staring at the back of his head, David nodded. "The war was already going on. I just joined the fray."

CHAPTER ELEVEN

OUR RIDE CAME to an abrupt end. After passing countless farms, we approached a village. The sign read, "Welcome to Grass Lake, Population 1,173" and below that, it said, "Cool City." After passing the sign, we were almost immediately in what appeared to be the downtown. Old shops lined a single block. We passed an old coffee shop, a boarded up ice cream shop, and a pizza place. There were two antique stores on the corner, and a moment later we were on the other edge of the town. Just as we approached the sign saying, "Thanks for visiting Grass Lake, Come Again!" we pulled into the driveway of a large white pole barn with a garage door.

Above the door, a sign read, "Excel Auto Repair." The door was rusty, and it looked like it had not been used for ages. David jumped out, walked to the door and lifted. It did not open. He walked around to the side of the building and a moment later the door slowly opened from the inside, and David was standing there. He walked briskly back to the car, put the car in gear, and rolled into the garage. As soon as the car was in, he jumped back out, pressed a button on the wall, and the door closed behind us.

It was dark but enough light came through the windows that we could see his outline. He walked to the wall, and the lights flickered to life. "Oh, my!" Veronica said, and her jaw hung open. I looked around, and I am sure I looked just as shocked. What had looked like an old pole barn in some village hours away from everything on the outside, now looked like the international space station on the inside. The walls were lined with monitors and computers. There were electronic devices of every variety in every direction we looked. The floor and every wall gleamed an immaculate white and the lights hanging from the ceiling were bright and brilliant.

We stepped out of the car. "This is awesome!" Veronica said. I was speechless. "This looks like a real spy hideout here! No more of this rickety old garage stuff. This looks like the Apple Store!"

David ignored her as he moved to a computer and started reading. For the next hour, he stared at a bunch of text on his computer while Veronica and I talked with Jacob. Jacob was only semi-lucid at this point and kept falling in and out of consciousness. Every time he was awake, he seemed angry. Then he would pass out, wake up, and be mad again. He kept talking about the war that David had started. David ignored him. He ignored us too. He was just staring at the screen. He got up and walked over to a small fridge that I had not noticed. He pulled out a bottle of beer, popped the top, and drank deeply. He turned and smiled at Veronica, Jacob, and me. "Thirsty!"

"Here we go," Jacob said with disgust.

"Thanks to our work tonight, there are just nine control centers left now," David spoke deliberately, "But nine is almost as bad as ten. And we have to figure out what to do next. Jacob is right that we are now firmly in the middle of this war. We were a nuisance before. They were not sure whose side we were on. But now we are enemies. I don't think they could have tracked us here, but they will be looking. I am pretty sure this place is safe. Pretty sure." As he spoke, his voice became quicker and more excited. He was enjoying this.

Jacob was lying down on a loveseat in the corner of the room. David and Jacob met eyes. Jacob's were filled with anger. David's were filled with a strange calm and cheer. Silence followed as the two stared at each other. Veronica and I waited.

A notice chimed on David's screen, and he turned around and started reading. Jacob tried to stand up. He fell back. He exhaled heavily and said through his grimacing teeth, "He is going to be the death of us." A cry broke from his mouth as he fought back pain attempting to sit up. His face was pale, and his jaw was set. Anger. His voice went from almost a whisper to a yell as he spoke. "David, if I could move, I would kill you. What are you doing? We are not even close to being ready for this. You are bringing everything to a head, and we have no organization, no weapons, and no plan. Are you *trying* to kill us all? Are you *working* for Gibion? What are you doing?"

David glanced at Jacob and smiled but remained silent as

he went back to his work. His fingers moved quickly on the keyboard, and he did not appear to give any thought to the words of my uncle.

Jacob used the arm of the couch to stand up, and he started to yell. But as soon as words started leaving his mouth his knees buckled and his body went limp. He collapsed onto the couch and passed out.

Veronica had been very quiet, but she now walked over to David and started questioning him. "What *is* going on?" David did not respond. "Seriously, what is going on? Why does Jacob think you are doing bad stuff? Tell me why Tommy and I should trust you? Is he right? Do you have a plan? Are you just messing things up?"

David stopped typing and turned to face Veronica. "Things are messed up, Veronica; I am not in a position to mess them up any worse. Jacob is wrong; I am not starting a war. War is started. Frankly, I am surprised at him. He usually is more willing to fight than I am. The fight is happening. The only question is: are we going to join in or sit on the sidelines? I do not love life so much that I would save it to avoid the fight." His smiles and flippancy were momentarily gone, and he spoke with a sincerity that was inspiring and convincing.

There are times when you do not know what to do in life. There are times when you do not know who to trust. There are times when nothing feels right. There are times when you want someone else to make the decision. But at this moment, I felt sure. I felt like I knew what to do. I felt like I knew who I had to trust. I felt like it was up to me to make this decision. I felt sure.

"David," I said softly but with confidence, "I trust you. And I agree. I will follow you into this war. And so will Elmo."

"And Veronica," Veronica added so softly that I almost could not hear.

"And Veronica!" David repeated with approval. "Well, thank you, Thomas, and Elmo... and Veronica. I appreciate your support. But I am afraid that in one important sense your uncle is quite right. We have started something that I have no idea how to finish. We are in a very bad position right now. Very bad. Thankfully, we have the best possible team in place. We have me, a doctor and someone that knows both the Gibionites and the U.S. government well. We have Thomas, a young man who has detailed plans for all eleven control centers neatly contained in a single yellow envelope. We have Veronica, who is an excellent driver and a brave warrior. We have Elmo, a big red dog with a very funny name. And we have Jacob, the closest thing in real life to the Incredible Hulk." He chuckled and shook his head. "He is an angry, angry man...," he took a deep breath, "And he is a genius who will figure out how to do this, assuming he stays alive." He looked over at the passed out Jacob and grimaced sympathetically. Then, almost as though he forgot that he had been talking, he turned back to his computer and started typing furiously.

Veronica turned to Jacob and took his pulse. "He is alive," she said in a reassuring tone.

"I know," I said, "I could see him breathing before you took his pulse."

"Ooh!" she said turning to Elmo and speaking in a mocking voice, "we have a future doctor here, Elmo!" She stood up. "Come on Elmo; I don't know when you ate the last time or took a bathroom break, but let's get you some food and then outside."

"No one goes outside!" David yelled from his computer without stopping his typing.

"Do you see how big this dog is?" Veronica said pointing

to the giant canine, "Do you really want to smell what comes out of him after a good meal?"

"I would prefer that to wrestling with cyborgs... you do remember the last time you went exploring, right?" He paused his typing to turn and flash Veronica a smile. Then he turned back to his computer and was back at work.

Veronica sighed in frustration and stood up to walk toward the corner of the warehouse that contained a mini-kitchen. It had a sink, cupboards, a microwave, and a micro-fridge. David had already told us there was human food there, but Veronica looked for something suitable for Elmo. Elmo had figured out that Veronica had intended to feed him and was acting like a puppy. He was circling her, wagging his tail furiously, and jumping in the air as she walked. I could not remember the last time Elmo had eaten. She found a can of beans and rice, opened it and poured it in a paper bowl on the floor. She then started looking for paper products that might function as a dog bathroom. She found some old newspapers that did the trick. After Elmo ate, he awkwardly used the bathroom on the newspapers, and Veronica and I turned our backs to give him privacy. We could smell when he was done. After the waste was disposed of (Veronica dry-heaved several times wrapping up the newspaper), the smell lessened, and I realized that I could not remember the last time I had eaten either.

I stood up, and my legs were wobbly from a lack of food. I made my way to the kitchen, and Veronica and I shared our first meal in as long as I could remember. Famished, both of us consumed massive quantities of various canned items. Our table manners were gone, and we ate directly from the cans with plastic forks.

We stayed in that garage for one full week. There were extra clothes stored in a plastic tub under the shelf and David was once again clean and fashionably attired. The bruises on his face faded as the days passed. On the third day, Jacob woke up and by the end of the week, he was moving around. He was still in pain but was much more mobile than he had been. With his health returning and time to spare, I was finally going to ask him questions I had been dying to ask.

CHAPTER TWELVE

THE TIME PASSED SLOWLY in our Apple Store hideout. David typed furiously almost the whole time. He said that he was trying to identify allies that might be willing to help us without tipping off our location to any of our enemies. But as the days passed he typed less, and it became clear that we were not going to get much help. Veronica and I sat there for the week fighting boredom. Then Jacob woke up.

When he was awake and alert, we were able to ask the questions we had been desperate to ask for so long. What he said changed the way I saw the world. Veronica says the same thing.

Ten years ago (before I woke up on that fateful morning

to find Elmo biting my leg, my parents gone, and a dying man in my smashed living room), Jacob had started working for a new government agency designed to bring permanent peace to the world by controlling all the data. The idea was that minor modifications to communications could take the most dangerous and violent messages and render them harmless. For example, you can make a dangerous situation safe by changing a text message from "meet me at 6 pm" to "meet me at 7 pm" – small changes that when detected later will be thought to be typos or miscommunications. It was decided that large control centers would be built to sort and manage all communications around the globe, and algorithms would detect potentially dangerous communications and then frustrate and confuse terrorists, foreign powers, and evil cabals with typos. Or something like that. You do not need to know the details. The only thing you need to remember is that the U.S. government, in an attempt at making world peace, decided that they should have the power to read and manipulate every communication that takes place anywhere in the world. Jacob helped them build that system. Maybe "help" is the wrong word. Jacob built that system. By himself. He built a system that could access, analyze, and modify every communication globally and make changes real time.

And it worked. Frustrated terrorists the world over failed to show up to critical meetings at the right time. They brought the wrong ingredients for bombs. They invited the wrong diplomats. They went to the wrong places. And the results were amazing. Incidents of terror dropped almost to zero. But even more than that, Jacob's system was accessing the databases of foreign nations and finding ways to decrease fighting between small warring states. An amazing world peace, never seen before, was achieved.

This was quite the moment for our government. They

had achieved success. This was a very frustrating moment for every terrorist and every foreign nation. But soon enemy forces realized that we were accessing, analyzing, and frustrating their communications. And that is when problems began.

A semi-secret council was held involving all the governments that were offended by our government's actions. And many were offended. Further, as that council was convening, terrorist groups from around the world asked to partake. And this league of offended nations and terror groups decided that only one response would be adequate: the complete destruction of the United States of America, all out war. But like our war on them, this war would be behind-the-scenes. They would take over IT systems, put secret operatives within our government, and buy off high-ranking officials. They would kill and destroy only as needed.

This counterstrike was performed with brilliance and speed. Our government had a much better offense than defense. And within weeks of setting up the effort, the enemy coalition was in position and ready to cause chaos if not destruction to the American way of life. One man figured out what was going on just in time. Care to guess who that might be? Yep. Jacob.

Jacob noticed that certain high-ranking officials from certain foreign nations had gone silent. Previously chatty officials and ambassadors were now increasingly offline. And there was a strong correlation between officials from nations that had gone silent and nations that had expressed outrage at the U.S. communications confusion efforts. Jacob found that suspicious. He started to investigate and found encoded messages that were used to unravel the plot. Our government was alerted, arrests were made, and catastrophe was avoided.

Jacob was just in time. They were just days away from

setting into motion a plan that officials conceded likely would have brought down the government. It was the closest our nation had ever come to being destroyed. Everyone was freaked out.

This was when 'Operation Enduring Freedom' was conceived. The idea was the ramp up our cyber defenses and domestic surveillance programs – to cover more systems, to control more communications, and to simultaneously be more hidden and less detectable. Jacob brought in my parents who were almost as talented as he was at building these sorts of data analyzing systems. As a team, they began to build the system that promised to do what Jacob's original system could not quite do, that is: bring true peace and lasting security to the entire world.

My parents were excited. They were given hundreds of staff members and an almost unlimited budget. The system that they built was, according to Jacob's description, "spectacular" and "genius." It was able to identify threats in a way that no system had ever been able to before, and everyone was very excited and confident. It was going to change the world for the better. And the efforts of my parents and my uncle were going to be the reason that war would be a thing of the past.

Then Jacob discovered Reginald Gibion. While Jacob was working to build his network, he realized that many of the things he was working on to investigate and monitor enemy powers and spies were also present in a shadow second system that he knew nothing about. In this system, Jacob's spy systems were also being used to spy on the citizens and officials of our own nation. Someone was building the domestic equivalent to what Jacob and my parents were building. As he investigated, the name "Reginald Gibion" kept coming up. They learned that Gibion was operating with the permission and authorization of the U.S. Government's homeland security agency.

But Jacob raised questions and objections. A nation that views its citizens as enemies, he argued, is no longer the good guy. A nation that spies on its citizens becomes one of the tyrant nations we fight against. My parents agreed. But they did not know what to do. It was clear that they had not been consulted, and objections were not likely to be taken seriously. For a while, they did nothing but stop working. Their projects stalled, and they provided bogus excuses when asked about the delays. Finally, after counting the costs, they decided that they had to fight.

They started to actively sabotage *Enduring Freedom*. They deleted certain whole individuals from the system (including Jacob, my parents, and several others) taking them "off the grid." They spent countless hours mapping the system to understand how it worked and how it could be brought down completely.

They were not sure exactly what to do, when to do it, or what the consequences would be. They had built a system that was pretty robust and to turn around and try to deconstruct it was almost impossible. As time passed and progress on developing the system had completely stopped, Jacob and my parents faced increasing questions about their lack of progress. This made their efforts even more difficult because they were getting attention and scrutiny.

One way they got around the scrutiny is that they brought two others into the cabal. Veronica's mother and father. They were old friends of my parents who had been invited to join from the beginning but had declined to take part because they suspected that the system would be abused. Now my parents went to them acknowledging that they were right and asked them to help fix it.

It was Veronica's parents who discovered something that

surprised and alarmed everyone. Gibion was not only working for the government; he was working to build his own power *independent* of the government. Veronica's parents detected early indications that Gibion had his own network of systems and employees that were outside of government oversight or control. It would still be a while before the full extent of Gibion's power would be discovered, but they now knew enough to realize that Gibion was even more dangerous than the government.

They started to research the man. According to public records, Gibion was just a very patriotic and brilliant computer scientist who had founded several cybersecurity firms. It was likely due to this profile that the government hired him in the first place. But as Jacob investigated, he found a different story. Gibion was no patriot. He was convinced that the U.S. was a bad presence in the world. He felt that if the U.S. could be dissolved, the world would be a better place.

One thing that was true was that he was brilliant. In addition to his accomplishments in computer science, he held a Ph.D. in economics, and had written several books (under a pseudonym) about business and politics. He was also rich. He had made many savvy investment decisions early in his career and by the time he was 40, was worth billions. So, he inserted himself in the center of government using personal charisma combined with bribery. From there, it was his passionate sincerity and belief in his own cause that truly made him able to gather people to his efforts. Quietly and quickly he did his work, and no one realized he had become the most powerful person on earth – until it was too late.

Then came a day that temporarily broke up the band. My parents broke with Jacob over tactics, and as a result, Veronica's parents left the effort entirely. My parents had decided that the only solution was to do the extreme. Originally, Gibion oversaw the building of twelve controls centers but one had been mysteriously destroyed and the remaining eleven control centers were used for both the domestic and international programs of *Enduring Freedom*. My parents planned to secure the locations and schematics of each location and then to figure out a way to destroy each of them physically.

Jacob strongly opposed the idea. Usually the hot-tempered one, he viewed this as a step too far. He thought it was crazy to attempt to physically damage properties that were still at least technically government buildings. But my parents were becoming more and more aware of Gibion's growing power. They knew what it took Jacob a bit longer to realize: Gibion could no longer be considered part of the government. The control centers were no longer government property. Far from attacking government property, the control centers were the single greatest threat to the government.

At the time, Jacob was not yet convinced of this and was uncomfortable with any such attack. And for a long time they argued. My parents gathered information. They secured the details for each of the eleven locations. They planned. They made contacts and built a network. But they held off on doing anything. They wanted Jacob to be on board. They needed him.

Jacob waited and could not decide. His whole life was about doing the right thing, but now he did not know what the right thing was. He went through several weeks of soul-searching, thinking and praying about the decision. Then one day he was walking home and looked up and saw a car with tinted windows following him from a distance. He turned down an alley, and as he came out the other side, he saw another car with tinted windows waiting for him at the other end. He knew that he was being watched. They were spying on him in the old-fashioned way – cloak and dagger. It was unnecessary of course (they could spy using security cameras, drones and satellites in a way that would make it impossible to notice). These spies were visible because they wanted to be visible. They wanted Jacob to know that they were watching. It was a threat. And in his weird way, Jacob loved being threatened. It clarified things for him. At that moment, it all came into crisp focus: with *Enduring Freedom*, everyone was being watched, all the time, just as those cars were watching him. That day Jacob decided that he would join my parents in their efforts to bring down the control centers and then work tirelessly to end *Enduring Freedom*.

But the situation soon became much more complicated. As they worked, they learned the true extent of Gibion's power. The emails of top-level generals now read like Gibion (not the president) was in charge. He had a growing number of loyal parties spread throughout the government. From soldiers to generals there were people who were willing to die for Gibion. He now had control over a large number of missiles and weapons systems. And one of the strangest things that Jacob found was that Gibion was using his huge government budget to build a cyborg army – human-like robots that were able to carry out complex orders with AI and minimal instruction. Hundreds of these "Gib-bots" (as the military referred to them) were being fabricated and deployed. But they were not being sent to enemy nations. They were being sent to work within our own nation. And his entire network (missiles, cyborgs, data monitoring, etc.) relied on the eleven control centers to operate. Gibion hid the locations of these centers throughout the Midwest and removed all traces of them from government records. They became invisible.

Jacob and my parents discussed all of this information as it was discovered. None of them knew how to start. My mother's idea (to get the locations and schematics of the eleven control centers with the purpose of some sort of physical destruction) was the goal. But the level of security and spying was much more complex than originally thought, and the first act of war would most likely bring a swift death to everyone involved.

It was then the war broke out. It was a silent war. The American people did not know about it. But it was a war. Bombs dropping. Tanks. Jets. Soldiers. Death. Destruction.

Gibion now had gathered a sizable majority of the American military that were loyal to him. And although some of this loyalty was gained through blackmail and bribes, by all accounts Gibion was a charismatic and inspiring leader who convinced his followers that the government was corrupt and that he could fix things.

It was during this silent war that Gibion developed his nuclear neutralizer, ADK-9. And everyone realized that this was a game changer. When President James was made aware, desperate attempts to find and kill Gibion were made without success. Both the president and Gibion now had military capability, and the dropping of bombs and the shelling continued. But throughout the hostilities, *Enduring Freedom* was used to manage press coverage. Unbelievably the war was kept hidden from the American public. Unless your house was actually bombed, you didn't hear at all the fact that bombs were being dropped. Every bomb that fell (whether that source was the U.S. government or the Gibions) was explained away on some local news website as a fire or terrible accident. The worst of the bombings were condemned as acts of terrorism by religious groups. News reports never showed a war – lots of weird isolated fires and explosions – but never a war. You might wonder how this is possible. You might say that people must have figured it out. But so much of what we knew in those days came from online news, social media, and television and the government controlled all of these. Whenever rumors of war would build, experts would be sent out to discuss the rumors and explain how mistaken they were. As unlikely as it may seem, I can assure you that it is true.

After the war began, my parents, Veronica's parents, and Jacob all tried to lay low. It was unclear what the war would do to their plans. Maybe now that the government was addressing Gibion, the whole situation would resolve itself somehow. But then, they learned that the whole the situation was even more complicated: they learned of another group, smaller and yet very powerful – a third party.

CHAPTER THIRTEEN

Isaac Rogers grew up with Reginald Gibion. They had been friends since childhood and had always shared a sense that the world would be a better place if there were more order and control. Isaac thought that democracy allowed stupid people to run things. If somehow the system could ensure that only the most educated and intelligent people could obtain power, the world would run efficiently and effectively. Reginald and Isaac started to discuss their political ideas in high school and continued to develop their ideas as college students at Harvard.

Both Isaac and Reginald made billions as inventors and as investors after leaving Harvard. When Reginald Gibion was brought into Homeland Security to help build the shadow system to utilize Jacob's security system against U.S. citizens, he did not have to think twice about bringing Isaac in with him. His old friend became his second in command, and soon Isaac was helping build *Enduring Freedom* – the domestic edition.

But the partnership only lasted for a few years. As Gibion gathered power, he expected complete allegiance – even from his old friend. But a prophet is never accepted in his hometown, and Isaac was unwilling to treat Gibion with the unyielding respect he expected. Soon there were fractures in the relationship. And then Isaac discovered a plot to kill him and fled. But not before mapping *Enduring Freedom* and learning its weaknesses and holes.

David Rogers had been hired soon after Isaac to work on the project. As a medical doctor, he was an important part of the effort to utilize medical histories as a method of tracking and monitoring. But almost immediately, David had ethical concerns about the program. And when Gibion sought to use these medical records as a way to kill political enemies (silently killing them in a way that would look consistent with whatever health issues they had), David decided he could no longer be a part. But before he could quit, Isaac and Reginald's relationship had completely collapsed. And Gibion, concerned that Isaac knew enough to be his biggest threat, focused every general, staff member, and cyborg on destroying him. And soon, he successfully tracked Isaac down.

Under a false name, Isaac made his hideout in a hotel just outside of Ann Arbor. As he paced alone in his second story room, he looked out the window and saw men in white. He pressed his face to the glass and looked toward the front and the back of the hotel. Men in white were approaching each entrance. In the parking lot, another two men in white stood ready to move.

Remember when Isaac said David had done something heroic that kept the rebellion alive? This was that moment. David had not yet been fired, even as Isaac became Gibion's number one enemy. This was an oversight. Gibion was a man of focus, and his narrow desire to kill Isaac caused him to drive all other thoughts from his mind. David simply had been forgotten. But it was a big mistake. David's continued employment allowed him to track the movements of the Gib-bots, to determine their target (Isaac), and to move in with a rescue attempt.

David was working in one of the control centers (there were twelve at that time). As he sat in front of a computer, he learned of Isaac's imminent danger. He saw the location of the cyborgs and guessed that Isaac would soon be killed or captured. Before standing to act, he opened a file and started scrolling through names. Delete. He removed the file with his own name. Delete. He removed the file with his brother's name. Delete. Delete. Other files were deleted. Then he stood up from his desk. He walked down the hall quickly.

The hallways of the control center were drab and gray. Each hallway was lined with four-foot tall cement pedestals in the shape of Roman columns that held dusty, plastic plants. Framed photos of government buildings, laboratories, and, landscapes lined the walls. David walked past door after door and finally came to his destination.

In front of a heavily armored door, two guards stood with guns. One was tall and overweight. He was dressed in a uniform that was clearly not tailored to his oddly shaped body. He held an AK-47 rifle in his hand. The other guard was short and built like the Incredible Hulk. His height was so similar to his width that the words "bowling ball" came to

David's head as he approached. The bowling ball also carried a rifle.

"Gentlemen," David said flashing his confident, movie star grin as he said it, "You are both in more trouble than you could know." They stared at him with confusion. "I was sent down here to ask you to explain yourselves." David paused after saying this to let the confusion and fear sink in. When the guards shuffled and stammered, David went on to accuse them of letting someone enter the room. He stated that the security violation had been seen on camera and that the entire facility security team was freaking out. No one was allowed in there. *Why* had they let someone in? *Who* had they let in? And *what* was he doing in there?

They assured David that they had not let anyone in. David laughed and told them that if they lied about it, they would be in even more trouble. The cameras, David explained, had shown them let someone in a few minutes ago, and they could either admit it and explain what was going on, or they would be arrested. David grew serious and explained that Reginald Gibion did not yet have a proper prison system, and in the current time of war, the penalty for any serious crime would be death. At this point, the guards were almost crying with defensive protests. David paused and smiled with pity, "Listen, gentlemen, I don't want to get anyone in trouble. You seem like good men, and if I were not told by the security commander himself, I would be inclined to believe you." David looked left and then right. He whispered, "They are rebooting the security system right now. The cameras will be down for another few minutes. If you are really telling the truth, show me. If there is no one in there, we might be able to calm this whole situation down."

The guards leaped at this offer. They quickly typed the code and held their thumbs to the two parallel scanners. The door clicked as the lock slid open. The short guard slowly opened the door. David stepped forward, stuck his head in the door. As he did, he pulled a baseball-shaped package from his pocket and threw it in. The two guards looked at him, confused.

"Looks clear to me. Must all be a mistake. I will inform the security team of your innocence. Now, if I were you, gentlemen, I would run." David, grinning widely. He turned and ran down the hall in a full sprint. The guards gave each other a look of confusion and then ran after him. As the three of them neared the end of the hall, there was an explosion that deafened everyone in the entire building. The door to the control room crumbled in flame and fire and smoke billowed out into the hallway.

As they ran away from the location of the explosion, three men in suits walked quickly toward them on their way to investigate the blast. As David passed them in the hall, they stopped and shouted, "Stop!" David did not stop. The security guards did. They stopped and spoke, they pointed and gestured, and soon all five were chasing David.

David got to the west exit well before they did and waved his badge over the turnstile sensor. Nothing happened. He tried again. Nothing. He turned and looked and saw that the group of five had doubled in size as more had joined the pack. They were about a hundred yards away. David stood back and assessed the door. The walls were concrete. The turnstile was metal. There was no way out.

David pulled two more baseball sized packages from his jacket pocket. One he placed on the turnstile. The other he threw at the oncoming crowd. He then walked over to a cement plant stand some distance down the hall and slid his body between it and the wall. He crouched down and sat on the floor, then he reached up and leaned the pedestal gently down over him. He tucked his head and his arms behind it.

Another explosion rocked the halls. This one had no steel reinforced door to soften the blow.

David was pelted with shrapnel and deafened. The dust and smoke gagged him, and he strained to see in the cloud. Groping and crawling, he made his way back to where the turnstile had been. Now there was a gaping hole through which sunlit smoke swirled. Twisted metal and broken concrete smoldered in front of the hole. David crawled over the rubble. His ears were still ringing, and blood was pouring from a wound on his arm. He could not hear the alarm, but he knew that it must be sounding because he could see the red lights flashing both inside and outside the building. He looked back at the spot where the chasing men had been. On the few occasions when, out of necessity, David would tell this story, his speech would slow, and he would grimace with grief as he came to this part. David had spent his life trying to save people. He had just ended the life of as many as ten guards. He turned and ran.

The security team was distracted and confused, and no one questioned him as he walked past the gate to the parking lot and found his car. No one stopped him as he drove away from the center and toward Ann Arbor. As he pulled into the city, he found a parking structure and abandoned his car there. He walked quickly into a small Italian restaurant that was next door to the structure. The whole restaurant became quiet and gaped as he walked in. He tried to smile, but his face hurt, so he walked directly to the bathroom. After looking in the mirror, he realized why everyone had been staring. His arm was a bloody mess. His face had concrete caked on half of it. His hair was almost white from the soot. His ears were bleeding. And his eyes were bloodshot. The entire left-hand side of his suit was completely torn to shreds.

He removed his jacket, rolled up what was left of his shirt

sleeves and started washing. He put his head under the sink and felt the water wash pebbles out. He then tenderly started to wash his arm. This was very painful and slow. He had to pull pebbles out from under his skin which led to more bleeding. He tried to staunch the bleeding with paper towels and soon the sink was a mess of dirt and blood. He removed the paper towel roll from the dispenser and used it to wrap his entire arm mummy-style as tightly as he could. He washed his face, cleaned his ears, and then removed his tie, unbuttoned his bloody and torn shirt, and threw it in the trash. He stood in his white undershirt staring at his cleaner and yet still very rough looking image in the mirror. He combed his hair with his fingers, straightened his shoulders, and flashed a smile in the mirror.

He walked out of the bathroom, smiled at the stunned diners who had been joined by several waiters and someone that looked like the manager, and walked back out the front door. As he exited, he pulled a $100 bill from his wallet and left it on the greeter's table. He would have said something clever about the mess in the bathroom, but his head was hurting too badly to talk.

AT THE SAME moment that David had successfully detonated a bomb in that control center room, Isaac had watched as the Gib-bots instantly become rigid in their places. He stared out his window and watched the three Gib-bots that were within his view freeze. He opened his hotel room door and saw a Gib-bot that had been standing by the stairs frozen. When he finally got the nerve to walk past that cyborg and the three still unmoving in the parking lot, he got into his car and drove away.

Over the course of the next few weeks, David and Isaac

reconnected and started to gather a small band of ex-Gibion employees and old friends and built their own "Third Party." Thanks to David's last-minute deletions from inside the Gibion secure server, the life profiles for David, Isaac, and ten or so other allies were gone. They were invisible to the systems of *Enduring Freedom* that Gibion was now using. This gave them a huge advantage over almost every other enemy of Gibion including most in the U.S. government. They were able to move without being tracked, talk without being heard, and start to build a counter to Gibion's – and the U.S. government's – power structure.

My parents and Jacob learned of the *Third Party* and considered joining. Jacob and David knew and respected each other. But Isaac creeped out everyone and, in the end, my parents and Jacob remained neutral. Sort of. They had even more secrets than the Third Party did. The most critical of this information was stored in hard copy form in a yellow envelope in my parent's bedroom safe.

CHAPTER FOURTEEN

As Jacob completed his story, it seemed like his physical strength had returned. David's work on his shoulder wound was doing its job. And with the returning strength came fire. Jacob's storytelling was growing more and more filled with his old rage. Toward the end, he started to punctuate sentences with muted exclamations. But when he finally finished, I felt like a man who had just had his first meal in a week. I felt satisfied. Finally, I had some answers.

We sat in silence, and I could tell that Jacob was thinking about other things. He started bouncing his knees as he sat. I looked at him, and he was burning holes in the back of David's head with his eyes. Occasionally, he would let out a sigh of disgust and shake his head. Finally, he started speaking, and his voice grew into a yell within just a few words.

"You are unbelievable. You and your brother helped Gibion get started. How many lives have been killed as the result of that? And now you single-handedly and without warning open up a third front, without resources or preparation, and happen to drag my family and me into it with you! You start a war you cannot fight. You start a war that you cannot win. The only way this will end is in death. You are going to die. I am going to die." He lowered his voice to a whisper and looked at Veronica and me. "They are going to die."

He continued, "You never stop." He stood up and groaned with pain but did not sit back down. He cursed and yelled, "I am *so* angry. I am *so* angry." I could see tears in his eyes as he spoke. "It was painless for you to do. This is the sort of thing you do. You have had a death wish since you left Gibion but how will it be for the rest of us? You follow your heart. The rest of us have lives. The rest of us have families. You are alone and have nothing to lose." Tears of either rage or pain streamed down his cheeks.

This whole time David sat with his back to Jacob giving no sign that he could even hear his words. He continued typing. But as Jacob said those final words, David stopped typing and turned swiftly around in his chair. His lip curled, and I thought he was going to smile, but it became a sneer. "You know nothing of loss, and you know nothing of what I still can lose." His words were soft and calm on the surface, but somehow they communicated rage that even Jacob's yelling had not. He stood. Jacob stood. I was sure that they were going to fight.

But the tension disappeared when we heard the noise. Veronica let out a yelp, and Elmo growled. I wheeled around to look. The noise was unmistakable: a garage door opening. I turned and saw it slowly open. In the bright light of the midday sun, I could only see a silhouette of the man standing in the doorway. But I recognized the voice.

"David, my David," the withered voice of Isaac spoke. "You have gone and joined the war. You have worked with these traitors," he waved his hands at Veronica, Jacob, Elmo and me. "You have quite upset and disturbed my careful plans. You are my brother, and I love you. But I came here to kill you." His hands were in his pockets but out from behind him stepped a fat man in a police uniform with a face the color and texture of melted cheese. He held a rifle that he was swiveling back and forth between David and Jacob.

"Why did you do all this? What are you doing?" Isaac was speaking to himself more than to David as he circled the garage looking at the contents on every shelf, desk, and wall. His hands were behind his back, and he moved slowly. He would occasionally mutter "why?"

During this time, David had risen to his feet and was watching Isaac circle the room. The entire time he smiled broadly. Finally, he interrupted Isaac's muttering. "Isaac, it is so good to see you!" He paused as though expecting Isaac to return the greeting, but getting nothing but a cold stare, he continued. "The last time I saw your face you were shooting at me. I hope you have not been worrying about it because you didn't do any permanent damage at all. You just hit the tire, and there was a perfectly good spare in the back. Would you believe that I was able to change that tire in only fifteen minutes? Really! Ask Veronica. Ask Thomas. Ask Elmo. It was fifteen minutes – it really was not a big deal.

"By the way, I totally understand your anger, and I think I might have behaved similarly if I was in your shoes."

Isaac stared at David blankly. David continued in his cheerful tone. "You know, I bet you are wondering why I did what I did? I too would be wondering that if I were you. And I am not sure I can answer the question properly. You know… it was the treatment of this poor child." He pointed at me. "That was not very nice of us, Isaac. For the record, he really didn't know anything." He hesitated theatrically. "I just couldn't watch the poor child lying there with all those injuries, being kept in handcuffs on the bed."

"Cuff," Isaac corrected.

"Hand *cuff*." David conceded. Then he paused and said, "You know Isaac, I have been thinking about that. I think that one is just as good as two when it comes to keeping a child from escaping." He waited for a response from Isaac, but Isaac said nothing. "You do know that he never actually escaped right? I freed him. The cuff had nothing to do with it." Isaac continued to stare.

An awkward silence followed. David and Isaac stared at each other, David with a big grin, Isaac with a dead stone scowl.

"Isaac," the cheese-faced policeman said, breaking the silence with a Boston accent; "we may not have much time. What do you want to do?"

Isaac stiffened and turned to look at the policeman. "Officer Hoover," he scoffed dismissively, "that is precisely what I am deciding upon. I am well aware of the time."

I was looking at Isaac, so I did not see what happened next. Veronica says that Elmo pounced at Hoover, without warning in one big jump. By the time I turned and looked, Elmo was on top of him. Hoover was yelling, and David and Jacob were running at him. Jacob ripped the rifle from Hoover's hand, and suddenly the whole situation was reversed. Jacob signaled for Officer Hoover to stand next to Isaac, and he limped over to that side of the room, nursing the place on his leg where there was no pant leg left. He was panting heavily and grimacing. Isaac's eyes were wild with shock at the turn of events. He looked like a caged animal. David smiled and winked at the dog. I heard him whisper, "Good old Elmo!"

Everyone stood silent for a few moments, and then David said, "Jacob, I fear we have waited here too long. If Isaac has found us, others will soon. I have done all I can here."

"Isaac," David smiled broadly and spoke in an exaggeratedly friendly tone, "and Officer Hoover," he turned and looked at the officer who stood frozen-faced, "I want to thank you sincerely for coming and bringing us this helpful weapon. I just thought that we would be in a better situation if we had another rifle." As David spoke, Jacob walked to the side of the garage, signaled for Veronica and me to follow, and walked out the door. David looked out the window and raised his eyebrows, "Isaac, you brought us a car as well! How did you know we needed a new car? Ours had blood all over it. And every cyborg on the planet was looking for it." He furrowed his brow and bit his lip in a look of sincere gratitude. "Thank you, Isaac. You are a good brother." The reflection on Isaac's glasses hid his eyes, but his face had now resumed its normal scowl and no longer showed any sign of consternation or surprise.

The car was cool. Isaac's car was a 1989 Land Rover with a third row. After our long trip with a giant dog in David's cramped car, this looked like paradise. David climbed in the driver's seat, Elmo jumped in the way-back, and Veronica and I piled in the middle row. Jacob stood outside with his gun pointed at Isaac and Hoover who stood with their backs to the side of the garage. David started to back out of the driveway, and when the door came parallel with Jacob, he jumped in the passenger's seat but hung out the open window, keeping his weapon aimed at the two men.

David pulled out of the driveway. As he did, I scanned the road and, to the north of the drive, I noticed a car parked in the distance. The car caught my eye; it had tinted windows and was parked in front of an abandoned building. I should have said something to David, but I did not. David turned to in the direction of the car, and as he did, a man stepped out of the car and lifted a giant gun to his waist. Everything seemed to be going in slow motion. Veronica spotted him and yelled, "Back up!" David threw the car into reverse. And then the shooting started.

The shooter was not dressed in white. He was dressed in a brown military uniform. The rear view window splashed glass as a bullet pierced it and then punched a hole in the roof just inches from Jacob's head. David looked at the hole, looked at us, and smiled with his eyebrows raised. Veronica and I climbed onto the floor and yelled to Elmo to do the same. As we huddled there, we saw Jacob climb over the seats into the way back with his rifle. We heard the deafening blast of his weapon as he fired out the back. David, to get out of the line of fire, pulled back into the driveway next to the garage we had just left.

"Got him!" Jacob said, and suddenly the chaos was over. Silence. "David, I think we are good to go." He said turning around and starting to climb back to the passenger seat in front. It was as he was climbing that the door next to me opened, and I saw the face that looked like melted cheese. Veronica's door opened, and we both looked up to see the gaunt bespeckled face of Issac. Officer Hoover was holding a small pistol and was pointing it at David's head.

Veronica and I were told to climb in the way back. With Elmo. On our laps. Again.

Isaac and Hoover climbed in. "Drive... Now!" Isaac said with as much passion as I think was possible with his withered voice. David pulled back out of the driveway.

As we sped back toward the village, the sun was setting, and the reds and purples lit up the horizon. Dark clouds overhead contrasted with the show of color and suggested that rain was on the way. The cool air reminded us that summer was not quite here. The tall grass that lined the road was filled with bright wildflowers, and when the wind blew, fluffy seeds scattered through the air like snowflakes. The world is a wonder. My life a few weeks ago was spent indoors playing video games. But real life is so much more. Filled with danger. Filled with grit. Filled with evil. But also filled with adventure. Filled with excitement. Filled with hope. I had lost everything, but through this loss, I had gained a new world. We had to fight this evil. We had to find my parents. We had to win. But at that moment, I knew that if I did not die, I would come to the other side changed and somehow better. The world was now on fire, and that fire brought color to what was once gray.

Isaac had given directions with a few brief whispered words and Jacob, who had taken over for David so that he could stitch Hoover's dog chewed leg, drove. We were traveling back in the direction of Ann Arbor but never directly. As we approached the city, Isaac had told Jacob to exit the expressway and to take old two-lane highways and side streets the rest of the way. But for the most part, Jacob drove without direction, and Isaac appeared to be satisfied with the course he took.

"Freedom was something celebrated in those days," the raspy voice of Isaac spoke. In the style of his brother, he spoke without prompting as though mid-conversation. "No one believes me about that anymore, but it is true. It was even taught in schools. Now they teach about freedom, but no one believes in *true* freedom. The idea of complete government control was something that made most people sick. But that is something everyone accepts completely now."

Jacob continued to weave through neighborhoods, and in the distance I could see Ann Arbor's skyline growing larger. After a few long moments of uncomfortable silence, David spoke. "Freedom is an excellent thing, but it doesn't make that which is bad suddenly become good," he said, smiling and twisting his neck to look at Isaac before turning back around. "For example, I might be free to shoot a child with a tranquilizer gun and then chain him to a bed in an effort to force information from him that he does not have, but that does not make it the right thing." Again he turned and caught my eye and gave a slight wink. I smiled back.

Isaac said nothing. He stared straight ahead, and there was no indication that he had even heard David. Officer Hoover also sat silently except for the occasionally heavy sigh.

From the wayback and with a giant dog on our laps, Veronica and I watched Jacob silently navigating the path. We were now in a small wooded area near a landfill. As we watched, I noticed that his head was lolling. I could see the side of his face, and he looked pale in the fading light. I was suddenly reminded of the fact that he was a wounded man who probably should be in the hospital. I wondered if he was doing okay. Then I wondered if it was safe letting him drive. I figured I should say something. "Do you think...," I began to say. As those words left my mouth, Jacob's head dipped, and he let go of the steering wheel. I don't remember what happened after that.

The next thing I remember I was lying in tall grass looking at the sky. The metallic smell of blood was in my nose and mouth. My face was sticky and tightened with that dry crusty life liquid. The ache I felt I knew would soon become pain. I could hear nothing but ringing. I could see nothing but smoke and sun.

Heat. Sun. Sun? The sun was going down last I remembered, but now as I opened my eyes it was high in the sky again. How long had I been lying here?

I could feel my toes. I could feel my fingers. Numb but there. The grass under my back felt like needles. The ringing in my ears started to sound like screaming. Screaming? As I focused my eyes, I slowly realized that the screaming was not just in my ears. The screaming was reality. And by reality, I mean outside of me. Someone, other than me, was screaming.

Sit up! I told my body, but my limbs refused. I had to move. I knew that. But I could not.

"Get up, son." The warm breath of a man with a Boston accent and a cheesy complexioned face whispered in my ear.

Hands grabbed my collar. Then the pain that I knew was there but had not yet felt arrived. My voice joined the screaming.

"Shut up, son." I felt my body being dragged through the tall grass, face up toward the sun. The light that seemed so bright darkened and then narrowed to a spot in the center of my vision. That spot grew increasingly small, then a dot, then no light at all, and then blackness.

I woke again and heard birds singing. The temperature that had been cool the night before had changed. It was hot. I was glad to be out of the sun. Hoover moved me into the trees, and I was surrounded by shades of green mixed with the colors of flowers. I breathed in the smell of dirt and plants. In the distance, I could hear road noise. Closer, I could hear the bubbling of a stream.

Veronica was sitting next to me. Her face was filthy. Her eyes caught mine. She frowned and said grimly, "David says I broke my arm." She held up her left arm for me to see. It was wrapped tightly in cloths with a stick tied to the outside of the wrapping. "But at least *we* are alive," she emphasized the 'we' and then hesitated. I panicked.

"What do you mean? Where is Jacob? Where is Elmo?"

"Isaac was thrown over there," she said nodding to her right, "when the car crashed. He is dead. It is super gross. I woke up right next to him." She became silent again.

"What about Jacob?" I felt like screaming again.

"He is alive but not doing so well. David carried him down to the stream and is working on trying to clean his wounds and get him sewn up." She hesitated again. "Elmo is fine. He went with David."

"What happened?"

"Jacob lost consciousness while driving, and we crashed. Isaac was thrown from the car and probably died right away. David and the cop dragged us all out of the destroyed car and into the tall grass. As they were doing that, drones started flying overhead, and we had to take cover. They pulled Jacob and me under the trees but didn't have time to get you out of the grass. He figured that the safest thing was to leave you until the coast was clear. The drones kept coming back over and over. David says that they must not have identified us or they would have sent troops already. But something about that car wreck caused them to really want to check things out. They have not been back in a while. That is a good thing."

As she spoke, David walked out of the trees followed by Officer Hoover. He limped, and his pant leg was torn up to the thigh. His sleeve was gone. No smile was on his face. A few years ago, my cousin died of cancer, and I could hardly move my face muscles without crying. I remember clamping my jaw and being careful not to blink so that the uncontrollable weeping would not return. David's eyes were wide open. His jaw was set.

"Children," he said calmly but with a fire that he had never shown before, "This is not your uncle's fault. The gunshot wound was far greater than I knew. Your uncle may not live. My brother is dead. We are now in the middle of this war. Today, we have buried our first casualty. Tonight, they will bury hundreds."

CHAPTER FIFTEEN

WE WALKED AWAY from the road and through the field. The unseasonably warm morning was cooling as dark clouds hid the sun and threatened rain. David and Officer Hoover had constructed a gurney for Jacob out of two branches, Hoover's jacket, and David's sport coat. And we made our way through the wooded countryside. Elmo was the happiest of the bunch enjoying his outdoor life. He had caught and eaten a rabbit earlier in the morning which was super gross but appeared to nourish him. None of us had eaten since last night. Elmo, to his credit, had offered us some of the rabbit, but no one was hungry enough to take him up on that.

As we walked, I tried to get David to answer some questions. I asked about my parents. Neither David nor Officer

Hoover knew exactly where they were. David said that Sam (the man who died on my living room floor) had been monitoring government and Gibion communications that night and had learned that both entities were well aware of the valuable intelligence my parents had collected. Both wanted it. And both had sent forces to my house. Sam had been in the army with my father, and the two had once been best friends. Although Sam's work with Gibion and then Isaac had driven them apart, Sam still felt strong affection and loyalty. When he realized that my parents were in danger, he wanted to go to their house to warn them, but Isaac objected. Isaac thought that it was a death mission. Sam went anyway. That was the extent of the story that David knew. Why, where, or how my parents had been taken was unknown. Veronica asked what happened to her parents. Neither David nor Officer Hoover knew that either, but they said that it was possible her parents, with their very close ties to my parents, were suspected of also having the same information.

I asked about the war. Who were we at war with? The government? Gibion? Both, according to David. But Gibion had much more power.

I asked about the "Third Party." Who was it loyal to it? Now that Isaac was gone, who was in control? The Third Party consisted mostly of people who had been criminals before the war that either just wanted to disrupt things or hoped to somehow clear their records and start new lives. Many were former employees of Gibion that had been kicked out for bad behavior. Officer Hoover said that he had no idea what they would all do now that Isaac was dead. He thought they might be interested in joining us, but David was not so optimistic. "I contacted almost every single one of them from the garage. Not a single one wanted to join us. That might change now that Isaac is gone," he said this and choked on the words, and I was reminded that he was mourning the loss of his brother, "but I doubt it."

We trudged through a forested area for what seemed like hours. Jacob was unconscious the whole way. After about three hours of walking, we came over a hill and found ourselves looking down at the back side of a travel center next to the expressway. With three fast-food restaurants, a gas station, and clean bathrooms, the lot was full of travelers making their way into the building. I had been in similar places with my family during road trips, but I had never approached one on foot before from the back. It looked strange to see a familiar place from an unfamiliar angle.

"I will go in," David. We all looked at him. He looked like a cartoon of someone that had had a bomb go off in their hands. His shirt was torn and covered with blood. His beard was ripped off on the right side of his face (probably from the accident). His pant leg was frayed and almost completely gone. He was at once comical and frightening.

"Uh," Veronica said after a few moments of everyone awkwardly looking at him, "You are a mess. I will go. What do you want me to do?"

"No," David said shaking his head. "I am not sending you. Every step we take from here on is an act of war, and if either Gibion or the government identifies us, we probably will not even know we are being killed before we hit the ground. I will go. I am not sending a little girl with a broken arm."

"Little?"

"Ok. I am not sending a young woman with a broken arm. Not to fight my war."

"Listen, I know you have not looked in a mirror lately, but you look like you have been playing catch with hand grenades. You cannot go anywhere in public until you get majorly cleaned up. And I think you are going to have to shave your beard – half beards are not really in style this season. "

David looked at Hoover and me, and we both nodded in agreement.

"Maybe you have a point." David turned to Officer Hoover, "You go."

"No way. I am not sure I look much better than you." He waved his hand at his torn sleeve and bloody knee. But the truth is that he did not look that bad. I think he could have totally done it. David clearly thought the same and turned his head with a look of disgust but did not argue.

"Well, Veronica, Thomas cannot go – he is a wanted man, and his picture is being circulated on every electronic device in the country. Jacob cannot go – he is mostly dead. And apparently, Officer Hoover thinks his torn sleeve disqualifies him. So, if I cannot do it, that leaves you."

"Gee, thanks for the confidence."

"What about your arm?"

Veronica said that the pain meds were working, the arm felt fine and that she would manage. So David gave her instructions. "We need you to call these numbers." He pulled out a folded piece of paper from his pocket and started writing a list of phone numbers. "When they pick up, say two names: Digory and Uncle Andrew. If they say, Uncle Andrew, hang up. If they say Digory, give them this number." David wrote down a final phone number.

"Once you have done that, come back here as quickly as you can."

"Got it," Veronica said. She then bowed her head, and I could tell she was praying. David bowed his head with her. After a moment, she straightened herself and moved down the hill. The tall grass was up to her waist. Elmo whined as she left. I sat down next to him and watched her go. She stepped over a culvert and into the back of the parking lot.

None of the travelers noticed as she turned the corner of the building and walked in the door.

We then sat there for what seemed like hours. Jacob had finally woken but was still mostly out of it. He looked barely alive. His skin was the whitest skin I have ever seen. His white undershirt was soaked with blood, his injuries showing clearly through the cloth. His shoulder (from his scrap with the Gib-bot), his leg (presumably from the car accident), and his forearm (also from the car accident) all had destroyed his clothing with blood. Other bruises were visible most notably a big gash on his forehead.

As the day wore on, I increasingly felt my injuries from the accident. I had a full body ache. Also, I had a huge bruise on my rib cage that was sensitive to the touch. I guess that is where I landed when I was thrown from the vehicle. And my head was throbbing, and I could feel the drumming of my pulse in my temples.

The only ones in our crew that didn't look particularly hurt were Officer Hoover and Elmo. Elmo sat by me. Officer Hoover stood a little off near the woods talking with David. I was not sure what they were talking about, but Officer Hoover kept shaking his head and saying no. David was speaking calmly and intently. As David spoke, I could see him trying to clean himself up. With his fingers, he brushed his hair to little effect. He was also ripping his shirt sleeves in an effort to make it look less like he had been blown up by a Looney Tunes bomb. It was not working, and he gave up. The conversation continued for a while, and then Officer Hoover walked away from David and stood on his own looking down at the travel center. David walked back to us but did not speak.

Time passed slowly. We all sat there and watched people come in and out of the travel center. Large truckers would waddle in, cars would pull up, families would pile out of the car, and kids would run into the bathrooms. Occasionally, people would lead dogs out of their cars to allow them to relieve themselves on the strip of grass next to the building. Elmo would look intently upon his fellow dogs. He would perk up his ears and even lurch forward as though he was going to run down and greet them, but he restrained himself and stayed on the hill with us. Officer Hoover said nothing the whole time. David rarely spoke but would occasionally exclaim, "Veronica, you are taking much too long?" or "Veronica, what in the world are you doing in there?"

After a while, I walked away from the travel center back into the woods and looked around. I found another small stream (or maybe the same one) and washed my face. The water was very cold and, with the air which had turned cool again, made me shiver. Elmo had followed me, and he drank deeply from the water. I looked around at the trees. I remember hiking in the park behind my house and feeling great about being away from my parents and alone in nature. Now nature reminded me that I wanted nothing more than to be with my parents. My eyes got hot, and I felt tears coming. Elmo bumped his nose into my ribs, and I hugged him and held on. His fur smelled like wet dog, but he was warm and familiar. I could not hold back the tears anymore. I cried.

I was there hugging my dog and crying when I heard David and Hoover talking with excitement back on the hill. I turned around and saw them looking down at the travel center. I quickly washed the tears from my face in the river, stood up and started walking back. As I approached, I could see Veronica coming up the hill. She had at least ten plastic bags hanging from her right arm and a giant smile on her face. As she got most of the way up, David and Hoover met her and relieved her of the bags. The three of them walked back up together.

"What took you so long?" Hoover asked in a gruff voice.

"I had to make a million phone calls," Veronica said indignantly. Then she smiled and added, "And I went shopping. Get away from the bags! I want to present my presents." She moved to edge us all away from the bags.

"Veronica," David said smiling, "since you brought presents, I will forgive your tardiness. What was the response to the phone calls?"

"Every single one was Uncle Andrew with one exception – one Diggory."

"Well, one is better than none. May I suggest that before we have Christmas in April, we move a bit further out of sight of the travel center?" He turned to Veronica, "Are you sure no one suspected you?"

"Pretty sure. At least no one seemed to notice me," she said as she helped to collect the bags and move them down the hill away from the parking lot. We stopped near the trees, and Veronica began to present what she bought.

"For David, I got... quite a bit." She pulled out an orange hoodie with a generic "MICHIGAN" (clearly the state, not the school) written across the chest. "I know – not your style. But they didn't have a 'Jos A Bank' at the travel center, so you will have to live with this." She threw it to him. "And this." She threw him a pair of jogging pants with "MICHIGAN" written down the leg."

David looked at the clothes with disgust for a moment before giving a half smile and nodding gratefully. She then pulled out a package of razors, baby wipes, bandages, and a bottle of hand sanitizer. "I guess you might need these too." She hesitated and then said, "You really do look terrible. You will look much better with all this, trust me."

She then presented the rest of her purchases. She gave a sweatshirt to me and one to Hoover. She had a full outfit for Jacob as well. She then pulled out a treasure trove of food. A massive number of granola bars, snack mix packages, beef jerky, mixed nuts, a few candy bars and eight large bottles of water. Then she held up two large bags of dog treats for Elmo to see.

I will admit this was the happiest moment I had had in a long time. We had gone without food so long that I had forgotten I was hungry. Being able to clean up with wipes, sanitize my hands, bandage my cuts, and then dig into the food, was a joy that is hard to describe. Hoover seemed pleased as he snapped into a Slim Jim. Elmo ate treat after treat as Veronica fed him. You could tell that Veronica had spent time in the bathrooms there. Her hair looked like she had washed it, her face was clean, and I noticed that she was wearing a new pink "MICHIGAN" jacket.

As we rested and ate, David walked over to Jacob and used the wipes and the sanitizer to start cleaning him. He tore off his shirt. I could now see the extent of his injuries. His shoulder was black with bruises and the hole from the Gib-bot was swollen and red around David's stitches. David finished the wet wipe bath and then massaged his shoulder with sanitizer. Jacob winced as the alcohol burned in the wound but did not fully awake. We looked away as David also removed what remained of his pants and cleaned his lower half. When he gave the sign that he was done, we turned around and saw Jacob fully clothed in travel center generic "MICHIGAN" clothing. Still pale and sickly, but a little cleaner and less scary looking. David then sat him up against a small tree and started to drip water into his mouth slowly. He asked Veronica and me to continue the process and walked a few steps away.

David went to work on himself. After I told him about the stream, he walked down there and came back looking much cleaner, freshly shaved, and wearing his ridiculous "MICHIGAN" outfit. Veronica started laughing when she saw him. That got me laughing. Elmo started barking. Hoover shook his head. David smiled and raised both eyebrows in mock surprise.

"Veronica, despite the questionable style choices, you did good work in there. I should have thought of all this, and you did. I am glad. Thank you."

"You are very welcome. And for the record, my style choices were very limited. It is a travel center after all."

When we were done, we had full bellies, clean hands, and faces, David had shaved, and we were all dressed like weird generic "MICHIGAN" cheerleaders.

"The next thing we need is transportation," David continued talking to himself. His eyes were on the parking lot. Then he raised his voice and said, "Hoover, you and I are going to go get a car. Kiddos, you stay here with your uncle. If we can get transportation, we will pull around to the back of the travel center. Collect all our supplies together here and get ready. If we are not back in twenty minutes, something must have gone terribly wrong. If that happens, I advise dragging your uncle somewhere he can be found and trying to escape back into the woods. I have no more of a plan than that."

CHAPTER SIXTEEN

DAVID'S WORDS TERRIFIED ME. The idea of losing him was too much for me right now. But we did not have to worry long. David and Hoover walked down the hill, and we watched them enter the parking lot. A white commercial van pulled in as they walked up, and the driver jumped out and made the major mistake of leaving it running with the doors unlocked. Without even changing their pace, David and Hoover had jumped in the van and were backing out. They pulled behind the building and ran up the hill to help carry Jacob down. We saw the poor driver of the van running out after us as we pulled out onto the expressway.

"You guys stole that poor guy's van," Veronica said.

"Commandeering," David said. "We are soldiers at war in perhaps the most important fight our nation has ever been in. Military actors are allowed to commandeer property in times of emergency to advance the cause."

"Hmm. It looked like stealing," Veronica said and grew quiet.

The next exit up, David pulled the van into a gas station, stepped out of our vehicle, and crouched behind another car in the gas station parking lot. A few seconds later he came back with a new license plate, screwed it onto our van, and we were on the road again.

"Thomas, please get your envelope out. We are going to do some planning as we drive," David said. As time passed, he was starting to act like his old self again – strangely cheerful and overly proper. I pulled the folded envelope from my sweatshirt pocket and looked at it. It had been such a long time since I had taken it from my parents' bedroom safe. This envelope, Elmo, and I were the only ones who had been there when this adventure began. It was now rain-damaged and dirty, and Elmo and I bore our scars from the adventure.

"Now, we know that the Ann Arbor center was bombed by the government because we saw the jets and the resulting frozen Gib-bot. We know the Pinkney location is destroyed because we blew it up." He turned and smiled at Veronica and me with raised eyebrows. "That leaves nine more locations we need to hit. And I think we had better hurry. The government forces will be attacking Gibion very soon. Desperation is setting in. They have no nuclear capabilities, and he does. They must be trying to move quickly because they think that he is getting ready to strike. They are probably right. Gibion was planning some tactical nuclear strikes to establish his position by the end of this year. The government probably figured that out and is trying one last desperate ploy to stop him. They bombed Ann Arbor, the most obvious and dumbest location that Gibion could have chosen. But I doubt they know the locations of the other centers. If they did, they would have at least attempted to destroy them by now. They may have some guesses, but I think that they are probably just hoping that Ann Arbor would slow Gibion down. I doubt that."

Hoover spoke, "So, what is your plan?"

David grinned. "Officer Hoover, are you joining us? I was not sure you were on our side!"

"Not sure there are a lot of sides left to choose from. But, for the record, I have not decided yet. Fighting seems like suicide to me, and I think I may just lay low."

David nodded but said nothing.

Silence followed. Broken by Hoover, "So, what is your plan?"

"Let's go in order of location. The children, dog, and I got #4 the other night. The USA got Ann Arbor, # 2, with the bombing. What number is closest to where we are?

As David spoke, Jacob stirred and seemed to be waking. He even muttered a few things before dropping back into sleep. After a few moments passed, David reached over and turned on the radio, and we drove without conversation. It was so strange hearing regular radio. DJs making dumb jokes, commercials, and regular music that I used to listen to back when life was normal. He rolled through the stations for a while and stopped on a classic rock channel. The familiar music of the Beatles, the Who, and Elvis once again reminded me of my parents and my time in a normal home. I closed my eyes, and sleep almost immediately overtook me. Within a few moments, the sound of the radio was gone, and I was dreaming again. When I awoke, I was staring at the ceiling of the van, and I was leaning against a sleeping

Veronica. My sweatshirt had become twisted and tight around my torso, and I straightened it. I stretched my achy limbs, put my feet on the carpeted floor, and opened my eyes again. We were still driving, and I watched for a while as cars passed us. Elmo was sitting next to me, and he whimpered – ready for a bathroom.

"Good morning, sunshine," the voice was familiar. Jacob?

I turned around and, to my surprise, Jacob was sitting up. He was awake and smiling... well, not exactly smiling but something less than his regular scowl.

My sleep cobwebs cleared immediately. Jacob was doing surprisingly well and seemed almost his regular self. He asked many questions about what he had missed and even laughed when we told him the story of Veronica and the travel center shopping trip. But after we spoke for a while, his questioning turned to David and Hoover.

He asked about their plans. How did they ever hope to successfully destroy the nine remaining facilities that were almost certainly on high alert now that two of the facilities had already been bombed? Gibion, Jacob reminded us, had been accumulating military might for years, and Jacob estimated that his ground troops may now be equal to that of the government. "For those keeping score at home," he said darkly, "Gibion's army is probably the biggest army in the world." How could we, an army of one very injured man, a fat policeman, a doctor, two kids, and a giant dog, take down the world's most powerful military? Jacob wanted to know. And I thought he made a lot of good points.

"Jacob, those are all excellent points. And I commend you for thinking of them. I, too, shared some of those concerns, but the manner in which you have thought things through just moments after being unconscious is quite impressive. You know, you banged your head very badly. I was worried you were brain-damaged. But I am glad to hear that your brain appears to be in good working order. Better than good, in fact, excellent working order I should say.

"Officer Hoover here has an even more pessimistic view than you, by the way. He is sure we are doomed and is thinking about dropping out of our little operation. I, of course, am happy to grant exit to anyone not comfortable moving forward. I would not share the glory with anyone who is not fully on board with what we are doing. But let me remind you what we are doing.

"You all know Gibion. The man is brilliant, charming, and a motivator of men. No one can doubt his skill. He could have done anything in life. But he chose super-villain. And I really think that speaks to his character. Jacob, I am not alone in my opinion that allowing a man such as that to become the unchallenged dictator of the world is a bit disquieting.

"And that is our problem. He is on the verge of taking down the U.S. government. And the U.S. government deserves it. But if there was one organization worse than our own government it is Gibion's. Absolute power in that man's hands is something we all need to realize would be quite catastrophic, to say the least.

"And so, Jacob, I think that you, and I. And Hoover. And Tommy. And Veronica. And Elmo. We have the chance to do something that few do. We have the chance to save the world from evil. And that is a wonderful thing. Growing old in a nursing home does not sound that attractive to me. Dying saving the world from a super-villain? That sounds pretty good. Jacob, we are all going to die. The question is when. The question is how. But we are going to die.

"The ancient man feared dying a death without glory. Today's man just fears death. But count me classical. Count me among those who would rather die in a blaze of glory than live and know I could have done more.

"And so, I say that we take a moment to pray. To resolve

in our own minds what we are going to do. And then all who are with me can go with me. All who wish to run away, I will not hinder."

With this, David pulled off at an exit and turned right. He pulled into a gas station and turned the car off. He bowed his head down and placed his forehead on the steering wheel and was silent. Hoover looked at him like he was crazy. He turned his head around and looked at Veronica and me. We all turned to look at Jacob – his head was bowed too. There was a strange silence in the car that felt like it lasted hours but was probably only minutes. Then David raised his head, Jacob raised his head, and they looked at each other.

Hoover opened his door. Before stepping out, he said, "I am out. I think this is a fool's mission. Not enough people. Not enough money. Not enough weapons. We will just die. I have no interest. I am not sure what I will do, but I just cannot do it. It is suicide."

He stepped out of the car and walked toward the gas station door. Before reaching it, he stopped and turned around added, "Good luck." David looked at him but did not respond. Jacob cursed under his breath and muttered something about cowardice. Then he looked at David and said, "Of course I am in, you drunken idiot. And I did not need your inspiring speech."

The two remaining adults in the car turned and looked at Veronica and me.

"I am in," said Veronica with little hesitation.

A few more seconds of silence followed.

"Me too," I finally said. I was not going to more of a coward than Veronica.

CHAPTER SEVENTEEN

"WE HAVE THOMAS'S ENVELOPE," David said, "and that gives us more of an advantage than we could have dreamed of a few weeks ago. Jacob, we do not need a full frontal attack as we did before. We can be more tactical and strategic. We have schematics for every facility. Sewer systems, keypad codes, and passwords, we have everything – assuming the information is still good. Further, the envelope lists insiders at every facility who might be sympathetic to the cause... if needed.

"I am not saying it will be easy, Jacob. I would never say that. But I am saying that the information in that packet provides us enough information where we can put together a plan that makes something once impossible, possible.

"Thomas's wonderful parents were able to identify security flaws of some sort at each of remaining locations. If we act with stealth, speed, and courage, we can do it. We can save this country... and the world."

There was silence for the next few minutes.

"You do realize that we will need to be successful every time right? Eight of nine is not enough. We destroy all nine or we die pointless deaths."

"Very true, Jacob – that is why I did not say this was an easy venture."

"So where do we start?"

"I don't think we have any choice but to do it geographically. We need to move fast, and our only means of transportation is this van. That means there will be hours of driving between locations even with the most strategic routes. And I am guessing, after the first one or two, we will not be able to use the most strategic routes. They will start blocking roads and monitoring the air. I think that is the biggest challenge that we will have." He turned around and faced us for a moment and winked as he said, "Be thinking of solutions to *that* Thomas and Veronica."

"Ok," Jacob said holding the envelope in his hands and shuffling through the papers, "There are a few that are almost equal distance to where we are, but I suggest we start with #6, near Findlay."

"Findlay, here we come."

From looking at the map we found in the glove compartment, the drive to Findlay was about ninety minutes. The time passed quickly as Jacob poured through the page describing #6.

"The main entrance is on the west side. And it looks like that is the most heavily guarded. There are two smaller entrances to the north and the south that are also well protected, but it appears the security systems are not quite as extensive. If we somehow could get into one of those doors, the way to bring down the control center is pretty easy. The data banks are on the east side of the building. Just need to head down that hall and throw the explosive in that direction, and it should do it." He paused and lifted his head. "How many explosives do we have left? Nine or more I hope?"

"We have six left," David said confidently without turning around.

"Wait," Veronica said, "How is it possible that these places are so easily attacked? A single bomb is bringing these places down?"

"The control centers were not built like military fortresses," Jacob said. "Gibion had to build them in such a way that they would be thought of as harmless. If the government thought that they were anything more than high-tech offices, they would have paid much more attention. But Gibion was able to build them without any outside interference. The problem was exactly as you stated; they are weak and exposed. But Gibion thought that he could deal with that problem by making them invisible. No one knows where they are. Their location is completely absent from all maps, all satellite images, and from any mention on the internet or in government databases. In other words, they are very vulnerable if you can find them." He slowly looked at each person in the car individually, "And we can find them. We will do one at a time. Start with #6 and then go until we destroy them all. Or die trying." He said these words without any emotion. He continued, "So, everyone, please think of ways to blow things up without bombs. We only have six of those explosives left."

The conversation continued, and it was decided that David, being the only healthy adult left, would be the one to actually approach the centers. He would walk confidently up to the gate, inform them that Gibion sent him, and give the necessary passwords listed in the envelope. Upon being let in, he would throw the explosive toward the correct door and run. Simple plan. Could go wrong. Probably would go wrong. But that was the plan.

The rumble of the road continued as David drove. He turned on the radio, and Elvis Costello sang *Veronica* as the rest of us listened. After a while, David spoke as though out of a dream. "Music is magical," he said, "When we talk about freedom we cannot forget music. The one thing our government has not stopped is music. I thank God for this. Beautiful and untamed. Why haven't they banned this? Who can be satisfied with the managed and efficient world they are trying to create when we hear this coming through the air? No one. They made a mistake when they did not silence the radios."

When I was four, my grandmother lost me at the mall. Or I lost her. It was probably my fault, but hey, I was four. I was looking at the fountain or something like that. Anyway, something hit me for the first time when that happened – the world is a big place. Trying to find one person in the endless sea of humans in the almost endless number of places was an insurmountable task. And that was a mall. Not really that big in the grand scheme of things. I now find myself lost in the whole world. Where was the world I once knew? But in the face of this new world, I was grateful for one thing: purpose. We were saving the world. And although we were hopelessly outnumbered and outgunned, the fact that we knew our purpose and direction and reason for existence gave meaning to the hopelessness. It struck me that, in my short life, the best moments have not been moments of comfort. They have been moments of purpose. And I felt purpose now. I loved my parents. I wanted to see them again. I loved my home and old life, and some part of me wanted to return to that some day. But saving the world was something worth dying for. I was ready.

Time passed quickly, and before I realized we were getting close, Jacob told David to exit the expressway. We pulled onto a dirt side road. It was early evening, and the sky was becoming darker and redder in the lengthening days of late spring. David turned off the headlights, and we sat. Jacob spoke bluntly with his old angry tone.

"That is #6 is right across that field. We could drive up to the gate in a display of confidence. But if we did that and anything went wrong, we would all be dead. Another option would be for you to hike across the field and approach on foot. That might also raise questions – especially if someone saw you before you got there. But you have the codes and passwords (assuming they still work) and with your confidence, you might be able to deal with that. And the upside would be that there could be no search of your vehicle. No trying to hide two kids, a cripple, and a giant dog. You just walk up to the gate like you have always been there, give the passwords with confidence, and walk in."

"Jacob, that sounds like an excellent plan. I see one potential flaw. It has to do with Veronica's fashion choices.... "

We all looked at David and immediately realized what he was talking about. He looked like a cross between a Russian mobster and a tourist. He was wearing a full sweatsuit with "MICHIGAN" written across his chest and down his leg. There was no way he would just blend in. He looked the opposite of authoritative. He would probably get laughed at.

"We need to get you some clothes," Jacob said after a moment. David turned the car on, did a U-turn, and we drove back toward the expressway. There was an old gas station near the exit, and we pulled into the driveway kicking up gravel and grinding to a halt in front of the single old-fashioned gas pump. David got out and then leaned his head back in. "We might be less suspicious if the kids came in. I will look like a regular dad rather than a strange man in a sweat suit." Veronica and I climbed out of the back seat leaving Elmo and Jacob behind.

As we walked into the gas station, I hungrily scanned the shelf of candy. I reached out and ran my fingers past the rack of M&Ms, Skittles, Snickers bars, and Paydays. Behind the candy was a wall of coolers filled with Gatorade, Pepsi, and bottled water. The wall in the back had old Budweiser posters with horses and bikinied women. We walked to the counter. We were greeted by a man with a stained white tee-shirt and a smile that looked like he had just swallowed phlegm. His nametag said "Hunter."

"Hunter, I am in need of directions," David said cheerfully. "I need to know where I might be able to procure some proper attire. Nothing special. Reasonable quality would do."

Hunter stared, swallowed, stammered, and then grew quiet.

"He needs to buy some nicer clothes," Veronica clarified.

With that, Hunter proceeded to give directions to the Walmart. We were supposed to go toward town and then turn at the creek. When we "got to the old Snyder house," we should turn right and then it would be not too far from there. David listened patiently and opened his mouth as though he were going to respond when the shelf of M&Ms, Skittles, and Paydays crashed over behind us burying our feet in candy. The deafening noise caused me to duck and twist around to look. We saw Jacob and some man wrestling on top of the tipped over shelf. The man was wearing dark khaki pants and a crisp dark khaki shirt that looked almost like a uniform but was unmarked by any flag or logo. The fight was wild and desperate. The man had Jacob by the hair and Jacob was pummeling his arm and rib cage.

David walked calmly to the counter and grabbed a rack holding metal cigarette lighters, lifted it above his head and brought it down on the back of the man in khaki. The man crumpled to the floor and lay still.

"Jacob, I know you have a reputation for a temper. I do hope that this fight was worth the battle. We have a much larger fight in front of us. And poor Hunter's store here is now a mess."

"You don't recognize his outfit?" Jacob said panting through his teeth.

David stopped, looked, smiled, and raised his eyebrows. "Hunter, thank you for those directions, but I do not think we will need that trip Walmart after all."

Jacob pulled the shirt and pants off of the man and tossed them to David leaving the man in an undershirt and boxers. We speed walked back to the van. Jacob limped behind us.

As we reached the door, we heard, "You folks better stop right there." It was the voice Hunter's. We turned around and saw a 12 gauge shotgun pointed at us.

David turned and smiled at Hunter. He signaled with his hand for us to climb into the car, and Veronica and I got in. Jacob reluctantly did the same.

"Hunter," David said, "how do you feel about our government?"

It turns out Hunter did not like the government. It turns out that Hunter was a member of some anti-government militia that had long suspected half the things that the government was actually doing. He didn't know anything about the Gibions, but David didn't muddy the waters with that. By the end of the conversation, Hunter was trying to help us. He loaded us up with snacks and drinks. He couldn't bring himself to give us his shotgun, but he sent us on our way with his blessings. Within a few moments, we were back on that dirt road looking at the field next to #6. David was wearing all khaki. He had got some baby oil from Hunter's station, and his hair was oiled and perfectly combed. He seemed much happier in his new clothes.

Jacob reviewed the plan. "You will have to hurry to reach the south gate at exactly 8 pm. According to the report, that is when they change shifts, so you will be getting a new guard. The procedure to enter is this. You will say, 'The weather this time of year is unpredictable.' They will tell you to wait and then ask you your name. You will answer, 'Frederick Nietzsche.' They will ask your mother's name. You will answer, 'Betsy Ross.' They will scan your pupils with their reader (nothing will come up thanks to your deletion) and then you will have to type in the number code. Can you remember all that? "

"I think I can, Jacob, thank you."

"When you hear the sound, the gate will open, and you will walk in. According to this, there is no further security protocols or passwords."

"No search of person?"

"If you follow those exact phrases, they will think you are in the highest ranks of the Gibion leadership. They cannot search you. You could search them if you wanted but not the other way around. You then walk in, and you will need to get the device down that hallway and put it in front of the double door near the end. Then run."

David was silent. He knew that he had to do what he was being told. But he didn't like the idea. Everyone in the car knew that if one code had been changed, if one protocol was different, David would be dead.

"It will work," I said trying to sound confident, but I felt like a silly little boy.

"Thomas, I agree. It will work."

David got out of the car and started to hike through the field on our right. He ran, surprisingly fast, along the line of trees. The growing darkness hid him soon after he left the car. We may have caught a few glimpses of him moving stealthily through the trees, but he was mostly invisible.

Time passed slowly as we waited. Was he now walking up to the gate? Was he saying the phrases? Would the phrases work? Was the guard giving him a hard time? Knowing David, he was probably giving the guard a hard time. Maybe David would insist on searching him. But he would want to move quickly. Maybe he was in the door now. Maybe he was moving down the hallway. We had no way of knowing. We just looked out over the dark field. And suddenly it was not dark. Suddenly a massive explosion across the field told us that David had been successful. "Start the car, Veronica," Jacob said. Veronica jumped into the driver's seat and brought the van rumbling to life. Seconds later, David came running with a giant grin on his face. Veronica jumped into the back seat as David climbed into the van and quickly turned it around. We were wheeling toward the expressway again. I looked back and saw a plume of smoke. Cars were stopping along the side of the road to look. As we drove by the gas station, we saw Hunter standing outside looking at the smoke. He saw us, lifted his fist high, and whooped as we passed.

CHAPTER EIGHTEEN

THE CAR WAS OVERFLOWING with giddy joy. Out of eleven Gibion control centers, three were now gone. We had a long way to go, but suddenly things seemed promising. The amazing coincidence of getting the Gibion uniform. The fortunate fact that Hunter was a crazy militia man, happy to let us go so long as we shared his mission. The envelope's flawless instructions. And David's problem-free operation. Everything went perfectly. If our future efforts went even half this well, we would be victorious and done in just a few days! Even Jacob seemed happy.

The windows were rolled down, and Elmo had his head sticking out breathing in the wind with his mouth open wide and his tongue out. David was smiling as he drove. Veronica was talking constantly, asking David to go over the details of his story again, laughing at Elmo, and asking Jacob how he was feeling. Strangely, it was the wrestling match with the Gibionite that had really brought Jacob back to life. He needed a shot of adrenaline and a battle to fight. His wounds were healing nicely. His pain was subsiding, and he seemed almost healthy.

Night had fallen, and the streets were lit only by head-lights. The sound of the wheels and wind from the open windows filled the car, and soon even Veronica's talking ceased, and we sat happily in the car as we drove. Jacob had mapped out our path to the next center, #8, and we antici-pated about a two-hour drive.

The time passed slowly. As we got closer, it began to rain, and we rolled up the windows. Jacob started reviewing the notes for # 8. He outlined the three entrances, and he and David debated which approach was the best. In the end, they decided that it would be best for us to go straight to the front door. Both David and Jacob started to discuss the possible heightened security. They hoped that we could get there before the Gibions could react (updating security codes and procedures), but it felt like we could not get there fast enough. Our ecstatic mood wore off as we drew closer, and it was replaced with heaviness and worry. I could see Veronica praying quietly, and Jacob reread the document over and over.

But once again I found my mind drifting. As I watched Jacob plan, I was struck by how much he looked like my father. And this caused an overwhelming sadness to come over me. I realized how much I missed my parents and how much I wished that I knew where they were. I looked at Veronica, and I knew she was going through the same emotions. We might die here. This may be the end of our short lives. And we might never see our parents again. If they were alive, how heartbroken they would be when they learned we were dead.

"Jacob, take a look at this," David said calmly. Jacob did not look up immediately. David did not repeat himself, but as Veronica and I looked up, we both made the sorts of shocked noises that got Jacob's attention – and he looked up. On the horizon in front of us, there was a massive fireball and a tall pillar of smoke. The outlines of Blackhawk helicopters hovered above the fire, and David pulled off into a Taco Bell parking lot for us to look. "It appears," David said, "that our government has taken care of #8 for us."

We stared with mouths open. Speechless. David broke the silence. "Who would like some tacos?" He pulled into the drive-through.

After we all ate, used the bathrooms, and let Elmo roam on the grass by the edge of the highway for a few minutes, we piled back in the car.

"So, how does this change our equation?" Jacob asked.

"I think that it changes nothing," David responded.

"So, we should just keep going?"

"Yes, I think that the government does not know all the locations. No one does but us. They are desperate and attacking what they know. I think that things are speeding up very quickly now. We may be too late."

"God let that not be true."

"We will see. Let's move."

David put the car in gear and pulled out of the parking lot. He turned right and started back on the expressway. As we rumbled down the entrance ramp, Jacob began to read through the envelope and the map. "#7 looks like our next best shot. Go north until you get to I-475 then go west. It is about two hours away."

We turned on the radio and started to listen. There was a short report on the news. According to the broadcaster, a warehouse fire had broken out, and firefighters were using helicopters to douse the flames. It was amazing how easily and quickly the government was able to craft this false narrative. I remembered back when David had first told me about the war, and I had not even known there was a war. I wondered how a war could be going on without the public knowing it. Now I knew.

David changed the station and found a Tigers-Red Sox baseball game. Miguel Cabrera was at bat, and there were two outs. David Price was pitching. But my attention was pulled from the familiar ballpark sounds. Up ahead, the traffic was stopped dead. Our car came to a stop.

"Traffic jam? Seriously?" Veronica said, exasperated.

Jacob swore and leaned over and pressed the car horn for about 30 seconds. He swore again and slammed his fist on the dashboard. "We can't have any delays. Our only hope is speed. Gibion is probably reeling right now, and every facility is probably being locked down, passwords are being changed, and additional security forces are being put in place as we speak. What is going on with the traffic?"

Veronica was the first one to notice the radio. The sounds of the stadium crowd and announcer had stopped, and a radio host was talking with a strange urgency.

"Turn it up!" she said, pointing to the radio.

David complied, and we all listened.

"...unbelievable... again, if you are just turning on the radio it appears that something horrible has happened...(the host whimpered)... Ladies and gentlemen, reports are just coming in, but it appears a major attack has happened in Washington, D.C. Oh, my God...(more sounds of crying)... It appears... a nuclear bomb..."

We listened in stunned silence. As we sat, people started getting out of their cars and walking around talking on cell phones. Some were hugging. Many were crying. The news had spread. The worst imaginable thing had happened.

"Oh my…," Veronica gasped with her hands covering her face.

"The monster did it. He really did it. He said he would do it, and he really did," Jacob muttered through his teeth.

"His back was against the wall. This is an act of fear as much as anything," David added.

"Nuclear bomb?" I asked without even being able to process what I was saying. "Nuclear bomb?" I repeated.

"The amazing thing," Jacob said flatly, "is that these very poor people do not even know there is a war going on." He opened the van door and stepped out. Leaning back in the door, he added, "They will know soon."

What would we do now? Veronica and I peppered David with questions as Jacob limped toward the crowd of people that were congregating in the middle of the road in front of us.

"Who did this?" Veronica asked.

"The devil," David replied.

"It was Gibion," I said. I could see what had happened as though I had witnessed it. Gibion was being attacked. Four of his eleven centers had been destroyed. He had one trump card. He was the one-eyed man in the land of the blind. He had the bomb. No one else did, thanks to his ADK-9. Destroying Washington without warning was a horrible thing, a murderous thing, a subhuman thing… and also the smartest and strongest move that he could have made. Washington is (I probably should say was) the home of his enemy, the U.S. government. President Adam James lived there. The Congress was there. That one unexpected strike may have killed most of our government officials. And it was impossible to strike back in kind. Gibion's centers were spread throughout the country and often near cities. Not only did the government not have nuclear capability, they couldn't even do anything more than precision bombings. And if they were not sure where the centers were, they could not even do that.

David raised his eyebrows and looked at me, "Thomas, you have started to guess the mind of the Devil."

"Why would he?" Veronica said.

I had guessed the answer, but I remained silent waiting for David to answer. David did not answer.

"Where are my parents?" I said out loud but to myself.

"Not in Washington, I think," David responded reading the reason for my question correctly. "Gibion would not put them in Washington only to blow them up. If they are alive, they were not killed in the blast."

"My parents, too?" Veronica added.

"Yours, too," David said without emotion.

Jacob ducked his head back in the car, "Turn up the radio. There will be an announcement from the president in five minutes."

We turned up the radio. It was the same voice, still stammering and crying, still talking about Washington. It was a nuclear bomb. It had been confirmed. Lots of stories of devastation. Lots of stories of death. It was a horror show. But it was real. We sat silently.

Then finally, the announcer got quiet. Then he stammered, *"Uh... I think the president is going to talk now... uh...."*

Then the familiar voice of President James spoke,

"My fellow Americans, today, less than one hour ago, a bomb was detonated somewhere near the center of Washington DC. It appears that this was a nuclear bomb. The devastation is overwhelming. The death toll is... horrible. On top of that, there are many, many gravely injured.

"I have ordered emergency workers in the region to provide assistance. I ask the public to keep their distance. The city will have dangerous levels of radiation, and you might put yourself in danger.

"But... I... the situation is out of control. For quite some time, we have been fighting an insurgency group named the Gibionites, named after their founder, Reginald Gibion. We have been fighting them in secret. And they... they... they are winning. They have technology... they have weapons.

"Ladies and gentlemen, our nation is in trouble... pray for Washington. Pray for our nation. Pray....

"People of America, I am so sorry. I cannot believe that it has come to this. But after consultation with what remains of my cabinet, with what remains of Congress, we believe... stepping down would be the best thing for our nation. We are surrendering. We are setting aside our weapons. Effective midnight on Saturday, the United States of America surrenders to the Gibionites. We have no other choice. More resistance would lead to more death.

"So that there will be a smooth transition of power, the generals will continue to report to me for the remainder of this week, but by Saturday, they will be serving at the will of Reginald Gibion."

The radio went silent. The radio host did not return. Just dead air.

"So, what do we do?" Veronica asked.

"We keep going. It is Monday. We have six days. We do not stop. We speed up. We kill the..." Jacob concluded his rant with a long list of words that my parents told me not to use. He panted when he was done. He slammed his hand against the dashboard.

"Jacob, I like your spirit," David spoke with his old vigor and cheerfulness. "I agree. We should keep going. We should go, and we should die."

Jacob did not respond.

"Wait, die?" Veronica asked.

"Jacob knows very well that we cannot destroy seven more of the centers. The government has now surrendered. That means that we will be the only enemies. All of Gibion's focus will be on us. We would be lucky to get one more. But Jacob is right. That is better than quitting.

"As I told you, the classical man feared dying an inglorious death. The modern man just fears death. Jacob is a classical man. Better to die in a blaze of glory than to live in slavery to Gibion."

"He will kill us anyway," Jacob added.

"Jacob," David asked with his voice rising as though he were discussing philosophy, "what should we do with the children?"

David turned around as he drove and looked at Veronica, then me, then Elmo. He smiled with tight lips - a sympathetic smile.

Jacob sighed deeply. "We drop them off at the next exit. They will survive on their own much longer than they would with us."

"No!" I shouted. "I am not just going to walk away from you. My parents are gone, maybe dead; you two are the only family I have."

"Me, too," Veronica added.

"Where you go, we go," I stated.

David shrugged, "Thomas, I truly appreciate your words. With my brother dead, you and Veronica… and Elmo…," He said with a smirk that made me think he still thought the name was funny, "you are the only family I have."

"But guess what?" Jacob interrupted with a combination of love and anger, "Family doesn't take their kids into war. They protect them. You are not coming!"

As we spoke, David started turning the wheel of the car to the right. He was turning directly toward the cornfield on the side of the expressway. The car struggled to get over the culvert, and David plowed through the old wire fence dividing the road from the field. The noise of dry corn stalk stubble from last fall's harvest scraping the bottom of the car prevented any conversation until we reached the side road that was running parallel to the expressway.

As soon as we could hear, an argument started. Veronica and I argued to stay with David and Jacob, Jacob spoke loudly against the idea. David remained mostly silent. Elmo started barking. But in the end, Jacob would not change his mind. David agreed to drop us off at the next McDonald's with some cash for a hotel and food. And Veronica, Elmo, and I found ourselves standing outside an exit somewhere off US-23, in front of a McDonald's with $300 cash in our pockets.

David and Jacob drove off. We watched them leave.

"Those guys are leaving to die," Veronica said.

CHAPTER NINETEEN

WE STOOD in front of the McDonald's. It was part of a trucker's oasis. In addition to the McDonald's, it had a Wendy's, pay showers, a million DVDs, a whole wall of dolls (probably for truckers to take home to their daughters after long trips), a row of CB radios, and a truck wash which was on the other side of the parking lot. It smelled like potatoes for some reason. The fluorescent lights flickered. Outside was a large parking lot with trucks parked on the side and cars coming and going in front. Everyone seemed to be on the move. Everyone seemed scared. Conversations were limited, but when people did talk, they spoke of Washington.

The enormous lady behind the counter looked at us as we

walked in. We had left Elmo outside. People entering looked at him warily. But it was not just that he was a huge dog – everyone was on edge anyway. I was worried as we entered the gas station that my face might be recognized (a few weeks ago the government plastered my face on every mobile device), but no one was thinking about that. Everyone was thinking about the words of the president. Everyone was thinking about what would come next.

Veronica and I did not know what exactly to do. We talked about maybe calling a taxi, finding a cheap hotel, and camping out to watch the news and see what happens. But before we could do much we heard a familiar voice with a Boston accent.

"Hello, kiddos."

We turned around and saw a fat man wearing a ridiculous "Michigan" sweat suit. His face looked like melted cheese.

"Hoover?" Veronica said, raising her voice in amazement.

"Yeah... I guess we must have been heading the same direction. What happened to David and Jacob?"

"They left us."

"They're going on without you? Even after what happened?"

"Yeah, they are still going. But it is 'too dangerous' for us," she said, punctuating her words with air quotes.

"It's too dangerous for everyone in my opinion. I am not sure how all this is going to turn out, but I don't think it is going to turn out good. We're all in trouble. Gibion's insane. I knew him years ago and never thought he was capable of doing this. He just blew up Washington." As he said that, Hoover grabbed his thin wispy hair in his fist and grimaced as though he were about to cry. Then he looked up at us. "I want to help. We need to stop him. This is further than I thought he would go. How do I help?"

"Well," Veronica said with a smile, "do you have a car? Because we have a map."

"I can get a car."

I just couldn't take this. "What are you guys talking about? How are we going to do anything other than be killed? What can we do? We have a giant dog. We have a girl with a broken arm. We have clueless me. And we have a fat cop... No offense Hoover." I had to add that as I realized how bad that sounded.

"None taken," Hoover said shrugging.

"That is our army. That is all we've got. David is smooth and confident. He knows how to act and what to say. Maybe he is insane, but it works. No one ever questions him. But there is no way that will happen with us. Us going up to the gate of any of these places would be suicide. We would be dead."

"Do you know what changed my mind?" Hoover asked with a flat voice.

"What do you mean?" Veronica asked.

"The last time you saw me, I was the one checking out of this whole project. And, Tommy, I agree with you that we do not have a chance. I agree that we are not as good as David and Jacob. I agree we will probably all be killed.

"But as you all drove away and I stood at that gas station alone, I realized that I had just walked away from any chance of being a decent person. My whole life I have been a screw-up. I was the fat kid growing up. I flunked out of college. Then I became the corrupt cop. Then I got kicked out of Gibion's army. What haven't I messed up? Someday I am going to wake up old and in a nursing home with tubes sticking out of my nose and arm and realize that I did nothing worthwhile in life. I decided at that moment that I am not going to die with tubes in my nose... Kids, I am not asking you to come. It is an offer. If you guys want just to stay put and hide in some hotel somewhere, feel free. But I am going. Just give me the envelope."

I hesitated before speaking. Hoover was old. He could talk about dying because he was way closer to death anyway. I was fourteen. Veronica was thirteen. But then I realized that Hoover was realizing what I had realized earlier. Purpose makes life worthwhile. And what was this but a moment of great purpose in the history of humanity? A president had surrendered the nation to a terrorist organization. A new nation was going to form. What would it look like? I remember reading the biography of George Washington for a history class. I remember wondering what it would be like to live in such a momentous time. A time that history books would record every event that happened. And I realized that I was in a moment like that. I realized that if Jacob and David... and Veronica, Hoover, Elmo, and I... were successful, we would be the ones in the history books. And I realized I wanted that. I did not want the history books to include a sentence saying, "And then Thomas went and hid in a motel until the dust settled."

"I'll do it," I said.

"Me too," Veronica added without hesitating.

We looked at Elmo standing outside the door staring at each person as they walked in. He was in too. We knew that.

"Ok," said Hoover, "now we have to get a car. You guys wait in here." He looked around the parking lot and then left the store to the right of the doors, past Elmo and out of sight.

As we waited, we watched the activity outside the doors. There were long lines of cars at each of the gas pumps. People were agitated and worried. But one thing I noticed was that all the movies that show people devolving into madness and violence in times of great national trouble got things wrong – so far anyway. People waited, and people paid for the gas they got. Despite the fact that no one knew exactly who was running our nation. Despite the fact that our capital was now a pile of ashes. Despite these facts. Everyone was respecting each other's property.

Except for Hoover.

"Get in!" He yelled from a police car that had just rolled in front of the doors. He got out and pushed Elmo into the back seat. Veronica and I came running and jumped in. I called 'shotgun' and sat in the front seat. Veronica did not protest and hopped in the backseat with Elmo. Hoover floored the accelerator, and we sped out of the gas station and back onto the expressway.

"How did you get this car?" Veronica asked.

Hoover smiled. "Cops sometimes park cars on the sides of highways to slow down speeders. I know because... well, I'm a cop. It belonged to no one, and my guess is that no one will notice for a while given the recent events."

"Cool," Veronica said wide-eyed, "can we turn the lights on?"

As we drove down the highway, we planned. I pulled out a map we found under the seat and set it next to the yellow envelope. "Where should we start?" I whispered to myself. It would not be helpful or good if we did the same locations as David and Jacob. In fact, it would be a disaster if we showed up at the same time. We had to coordinate somehow which ones we were going to attack without actually being able to talk to them. David had thrown our cell phones out. We had no way of communicating with them.

"Well," I answered, thinking as I spoke, "we know, roughly, the plan that Jacob mapped out. He said that they were going to attack as quickly as possible which meant always attacking the next closest facility."

"Right!" Veronica said leaning into the front seat to look over my shoulder unable to control her excitement. "The government just did #8. So Jacob said they would be doing

#7 next. Look," she pointed to the map, "It is right there. They might already be there."

"Well, how about we do the opposite? How about we start at the furthest facility and work our way back. That way we meet David and Jacob in the middle?"

"I like that plan," Veronica smiled.

"Sounds like a good enough plan for me," Hoover grunted, "but first we need some more explosives. David and Jacob took the six that we had left. Just navigate me toward our next target, and I will think about it on the way."

Veronica answered for me, "The furthest facility is #10. It is way up near Traverse City. Get on I-75 and take that almost the whole way."

Hoover nodded and followed that course. It was a long drive. The map said that it should be about 5 hours, but because of the many people on the roads and frequent traffic jams, it took five hours to get into Michigan again. Even if the roads cleared right now, Hoover said it would be another 4 hours best case. We had all been up all night. We had left the gas station around 11 pm, and in the early morning hours finally, Hoover decided we had to stop. He had an idea to get some explosives but did not want to bring us with him. We would stop, and Veronica and I would try to get a three or four hours sleep, while Hoover went hunting for bombs. We stopped at a motel. Hoover got a room (using my money), ordered a pizza for us, and then left with the car. Veronica and I made our way into a room that smelled like a combination of fish, soy sauce, and cigarettes (despite the fact that the door had a large 'no smoking' sign on it). But it was clean enough, and we were exhausted. Elmo slept on the floor. Veronica took a quick shower and collapsed in one of the beds. She immediately started snoring. I collapsed on the other, and Elmo jumped up at my feet. I was tired, but when I put my head on my pillow, I suddenly could not sleep.

My mind was racing. Tomorrow would be #10. We were probably going to die. This was probably my last day on earth. I was fourteen years old. I had not done anything. All my life, I had imagined what I would do when I grew up. What sort of job would I have? Would I have a family? Would I have kids? Where would I live? The answer to all of those questions would be 'not applicable.' I would die as a teenager and probably be forgotten altogether. And my parents, if they were still alive, would never find out what happened to me. And it would be over. I fought back tears. But I did not cry.

When we woke in the morning, I was sore all over from the ride. My nose had become accustomed to the smell of the room and no longer noticed it. I took Elmo out and realized that we had slept too long. It was bright outside, and the maid was making her way down the long line of doors facing the parking lot. Where was Hoover? Veronica joined me on the balcony, and we looked down at the lot.

We packed up our few things and walked down to the lobby. We were just beginning to panic when the police car came flying into the lot. "Get in!" yelled Hoover, and we obeyed quickly. I noticed that the car had bullet holes riddled in the sides, and they had not been there the night before.

"What happened?" Veronica asked.

Hoover ignored the question and was looking in his rearview mirror as he drove. After a while, he seemed satisfied that no one was following, and he calmed.

"Old Hoover still has a few tricks up his sleeve," he said speaking of himself in the third person. "This is a fireworks paradise around here. I remembered busting an illegal fireworks operation a few years back, and I figured I might be able to find some M-80s if I went back to the house of the guy I busted. Sure enough...," his speech broke off with a satisfied sigh.

"What is an M-80, and who did you think was chasing us, and why are there bullet holes in the car?"

"M-80s are quarter sticks of dynamite that are used as big firecrackers. I've got four huge boxes of them in the trunk."

"Who did you think was chasing us?" Veronica repeated.

"Oh well... Apparently the warehouse had some sort of alarm on it, and apparently, they don't take kindly to people stealing their M-80s in the middle of the night. Those people are crazy. I got four boxes loaded, and then the gunfire started. Just barely got in the car, and got away. Pretty sure we lost them now, though," he said as he looked in the rearview mirror again.

Spring was now over. Sunlight baked the car as we drove, and the air conditioner struggled to keep up. But it was not the heat that was making me sweat. The closer we got, the more panic started to overtake my heart. I wanted to run away. I looked at Veronica, and she looked as scared as I was. But when I asked her, she said that she was not scared. What a liar.

Hoover gave us instructions on how to convert the M-80s into explosives. It involved a lot of very delicate unwrapping of M-80s and then some tight packing of the powder into a metal tube that Hoover had found in the warehouse he robbed. He thought maybe the crazy people that owned it were making explosives of their own. Hoover gave instructions on how to make the fuse, and by the end of our drive, we had a crude explosive sitting in the front seat of the car between Hoover and me.

After a few more hours of driving, the map showed that we had come to our exit. We pulled off and drove on a two-lane highway for another hour. Then we pulled off onto a dirt road and weaved our way toward the 'X' that I had drawn on the map last night when Veronica and I had started our navigation. I calculated that we were still about three miles away when Hoover pulled the car off to the side. I heard the gravel and loose stones under the tires as we slowed. He turned into the field on our right and drove into the middle of a small stand of pine trees. The branches scraped on the windows and hood and the car stopped.

"This is as far as we should go," Hoover said. "We need to walk the rest of the way – staying under cover the whole way." He hesitated and looked around. Hoover was nervous. Sweat poured down his cheek. His cheesy face looked shinier and paler than normal.

"Don't you mean *you* are going to stay under cover?" Veronica asked. We had been assuming that Hoover would go alone as David had gone alone. His using the term 'we' was weird.

"Yeah… I can do it alone," he said, but he raised the end of the statement as though it were a question.

"Wait," Veronica said, "You are not backing out are you?"

"I am just not sure I am the right guy to do it. I might still be in their databases. David said I was deleted, but David is a drunk, and even his brother didn't trust him. If their face scanners recognize me, I might walk up to that gate and get shot on sight. I honestly do not think that it will work."

I got angry at this point. "Hoover, what are you talking about? I *know* I am in their databases. I was on everyone's tablet not that long ago, remember? I am a wanted man. If you do not walk up to that gate, no one is going to walk up to that gate. Why did we even come here?"

"I'll go," Veronica said.

"No," I said.

"Why not? Because I am a girl?"

"No… well sort of. I am just not sure how many thirteen-year-old girls with broken arms the Gibionites have in their ranks. They might doubt you are a high ranking Gibionite official."

Hoover was silent. His sweat dripped, and his eyes were wide.

"Hoover, you are the one that gave that inspiring speech. What happened?" Hoover was silent. "Why are you all the sudden so scared?"

"I am sorry. I don't know what is wrong with me."

"Listen, I am just a kid. I have no idea what to do in situations like this. My dad once told me that being brave is not an emotion, it's an action. He said that when he was fighting in Iraq, everyone was scared, but the brave were separated from the cowardly based on whether they fought anyway. I think that this might be a moment like that. I think you just need to go in. I think it is okay that you are scared. I am super scared. I could not even sleep last night. I know Veronica is scared."

"No, I am not."

"Yes, you are Veronica, I can tell. But, Hoover, you can do it anyway. You can go in. Dad said that sometimes the soldiers that were the most scared did the most good. You have to stand when you feel like running."

Hoover looked at me for a moment, nodded, and opened the door and stepped out. "Keep the car running," he said.

It was somewhat comical to watch that fat cop run in and out of the trees. I hoped that the Gibions were not watching the field because he was the opposite of stealth. He would duck behind a tree, and we could see both sides of his fat belly on each side of the tree. He would then run to the next tree and "hide" behind that.

The plan was for him to go up to the gate and to say all the right code words, just like David had, and to basically follow the same plan. The problem was that he did not have a Gibion uniform as David did. He was still wearing a very shabby looking "Michigan" outfit. It was torn at the elbows and stained with blood.

We watched him run out of sight and then waited. The next hour felt like forever. But about an hour later we saw an explosion in the distance. About fifteen minutes after that we saw Hoover running toward us as fast as the fat man could go. His face was red, but he was smiling broadly. When he got to the cop car, he jumped in, threw it in gear and pulled out of our cover of trees. He spun the car around and got back on the road.

"They were totally not ready," he said grinning. "Their gates were open; they were moving trucks in and out. I think that their guard was down for some reason... I climbed on the back of a truck coming through the gates and crouched low. No passwords. No questions. No nothing. As soon as I got in the gate, I jumped off the truck, walked up to the east door and tossed the explosive down the hall near the control center (just like we said), and I ran like crazy. It was amazing."

"They thought the battle was over," Veronica said in a thoughtful voice. "The government surrendered. Gibion feels like his enemies are all defeated."

"He will know he has enemies now. If his guard was down, it will be back up now," I said as Hoover pulled back onto the expressway.

"Start making another bomb," Hoover grunted.

CHAPTER TWENTY

WE TURNED on the radio and listened. The voices were an endless discussion of the aftermath of Washington and the President's announcement. Gibion had made no appearance or statement. At that moment everything was in a state of uncertainty. Hoover thought that Gibion was building a government and would appear when he felt things were secure and stable. We ignored most of the discussion; the three of us almost certainly had more information than anyone on the radio.

But one thing did interest us. There were a few veiled

discussions about four explosions in southeast Michigan – one in the Tecumseh area, one in the Toledo area, one in Bellville, and one near Walled Lake. I looked at the envelope; the four locations were close to #11, #9, #5, and #7. We got frustratingly few details from the radio discussion (they seemed somewhat uninterested in such a minor explosions in mostly rural areas), but we hoped that it proved David and Jacob had been successful. Those four would have been the logical next steps. But given that we went to the furthest location and they went to the closest, they should have already had time for several more attacks. But four seemed almost too good to hope for. We listened intently for any indication of any other attacks. #3 might be the next logical location, but nothing about any other explosion in any other area came up.

We decided to head for #1. It was closest to us and far enough away from anything David and Jacob would attack. It was about a two-hour journey from where we were.

We pulled into a gas station to fuel up. Veronica took Elmo to the grass by the road, and I went in to load up on as much food as possible. I opened the door. I looked around. The shelves were pretty bare. Since the nuclear bomb hit Washington, shelves were becoming emptier. When it snows hard, people always go out and buy milk and bread; I guess I should not have been surprised that a nuclear bomb and a government overthrow would cause people to buy a bit more stuff. But some food remained. There were Hostess treats. There was a basket of mostly spoiled old fruit by the door. And there were still several bags of chips. I grabbed those and the last remaining bottle of Gatorade and three bottles of water. I also grabbed a bag of overpriced dog food. I hauled all this up to the counter and paid.

I was only inside for a few moments, but when I came out, everything had changed. I saw Veronica hiding with

Elmo behind a hedge in front of the gas station. I saw two men dressed all in white next to the police car. One of them held Hoover's arm behind his back and was marching him to a black van that was across the street. He pushed Hoover into the back while the other Gib-bot climbed mechanically in the driver's seat and started the engine.

I cannot explain my actions at this point. I never liked Hoover much. He was weird, ugly, and was a coward about half the time. But he had been brave enough to change his mind about helping the fight. He had been brave enough to suck it up and to go destroy #10 (after a little coaxing). But none of that went through my mind at the moment. It was more a reaction of anger and fear. I dropped my gas station groceries and charged. As I ran, I stopped and grabbed a snow shovel that was leaning against the gas station wall. I approached the van and turned the shovel around and put it through the open window. I had meant to hit the Gib-bot, but it slid off his shoulder and into the steering column. He was just pulling out and the wheel locked on the shovel handle, and the van smashed into the Ford F250 pickup parked in front of the van.

"Hey, what did you do to my truck?" The voice was from a man across the street – a very large man. He was tall – basketball player tall – he had a shaved head and tattoos all over his shoulders that were exposed under his small white tank top. He was built like a bodybuilder. Anger was on his face, and he was walking our way. The Gib-bot got out of the driver seat. Looked at me blankly. Looked at the man blankly. Then without hesitation, stepped toward the back of the van and opened the door. The other Gib-bot, with Hoover over his shoulder, hopped out. The two of them started speed walking away from the scene down the grassy island between the sidewalk and the road. They moved across the street toward a parking lot behind the gas station.

"Hey! You are *not* just going to walk away, buddy!" the man started to follow them yelling. I went back and grabbed my shovel and ran after the three men. He broke into a trot and started to catch up to the two Gib-bots and Hoover. Running full speed, I caught up with the angry man and checked my speed to match his. He looked at me, looked at the shovel, and tilted his head slightly in confusion before turning his attention back to the Gib-bots.

"What are you doing with that guy?" The man asked looking at Hoover. He was still angry, but now confusion entered his voice. He was just getting a good close-up look at the Gib-bots and was probably realizing how not normal they looked. His voice modulated as he spoke, but he continued to talk.

"Put that guy down. You smashed my car... I am not letting you just run away."

But the Gib-bots just kept walking away as though they did not even know the man was there. But then the huge man suddenly lunged at the Gib-bot who was not carrying Hoover. The Gib-bot stepped quickly out of the way causing the man to miss and crash to the ground, and the other Gib-bot set down Hoover and grabbed the fallen man by the back of his neck driving him into the ground.

Did I mention this guy was a mountain of a man? I think that if he were anyone smaller, he would have been finished. But with one Gib-bot on his back and the other holding his face to the ground, the man did a push-up and lifted them both up. He then got up to his knees. He then stood up. With Gib-bots gripping him, he proceeded to start spinning and twisting. One of the Gib-bots fell backward to the ground. The other remained latched on the man's back. He reached his arm around the man's neck and held on. I could see the man's face getting redder and redder as the Gib-bot tightened his choke hold.

Then I saw a red blur out of the corner of my eye. It landed on the back of the Gib-bot and went rolling to the ground with him. As they rolled away from the giant, I could now see Elmo latched on the Gib-bot's neck. I saw a combination of blood and metal underneath Elmo's jaw. The Gib-bot twisted and pulled at Elmo's face, but his jaw did not let loose. He stood up, and Elmo hung from him like a necktie. He then started smacking and twisting at the dog trying to break him free.

Meanwhile, the other Gib-bot had gotten up and was coming back to the fight. The giant man had also stood again and was standing next to Elmo and the Gib-bot looking for a way to join in the fray. As he saw the second Gib-bot coming, he turned towards him and squared up to him with fists raised. The Gib-bot walked up to him but then stopped. He started to scan the growing crowd of people surrounding the melee. He seemed to be looking for something. After a moment he turned and started to walk away. The other Gib-bot, with his neck bleeding and metal hanging out, followed him in lockstep. He approached the intersection in front of the gas station with the crowd following close behind them.

A gray Honda Accord was sitting waiting for the light to change. The Gib-bots walked up to it, opened the door, and pulled out the small bald man in a white polo shirt behind the wheel. They put the car in gear and sped off.

The crowd stood silent. Watching them drive off. I turned around and looked the carnage. The massive man was now sitting down rubbing his neck. Huge red bruises showed the outline of where the Gib-bot had gripped him. I turned and looked at Elmo. Elmo was lying still on the ground. As I ran to him, I saw Veronica had emerged from the crowd, and we both fell in front of him. I was relieved to see Elmo breathing and trying to get up. Veronica called to the crowd for water, and soon someone came with a bowl. After a few minutes, he was standing and tentatively walking around with a slight limp.

But then the police showed up and started making their way through the crowd. "We better get out of here," I said, remembering that the police were not my friends. Then I wondered if that was still true given that our government had just surrendered....which side were the police on now? Veronica and I, with Elmo limping behind us, ducked through the crowd back toward our car.

"Where is Hoover?" Veronica said, and I realized that we had left him unconscious on the ground. I turned and ran back, but by the time I made my way through the crowd, the police were kneeling next to him and radioing for medical help.

Both of us backed away and moved toward the car. "I'm driving," said Veronica. She jumped in the driver's seat and turned the key. I opened the back door so Elmo could jump in and then sat in the passenger's seat.

"What are we going to do about Hoover?" Veronica said through her teeth as the police car rumbled to life.

"We better go," I said. "I think they are going to take him to the hospital. Hopefully, he is ok but not sure it will do any good for us to wait for him. If those cops see us, we could be done. And there are still at least two, probably more, control centers left on the list."

Veronica slid the transmission from park to drive, and the car rolled into motion. I scanned both sides of the street and twisted around to see behind us. Two more police cars rolled onto the scene.

"We cannot leave without Hoover," Veronica said hesitating.

"Look, Elmo and I almost just got killed saving him. We saved him. He is alive. We have to go, or those police will be questioning us soon – and we are sitting in a stolen police car! We will be put in jail. We have to go."

Veronica didn't respond, but as soon as the two police cars passed, she hit the accelerator and headed west, back toward the expressway.

"Why would the Gib-bots go after Hoover like that?" Veronica asked as she changed lanes. The truck behind us slowed. I think he would have honked if we were not driving a police car. Fortunately, he could not see Veronica driving - not too many people would believe she was a cop. "I mean why didn't they go after you or me…" She turned around and looked at Elmo, "or him? It makes no sense!"

"I think it makes sense. I think that Gibion doesn't care about you or me that much anymore. He probably thinks we are mostly harmless kids. Right now, I think that Gibion is much more interested in David, Jacob, and Hoover. He knows they are behind the recent control center attacks. I am not sure how he was able to track down Hoover, but I am sure he is desperately trying to track down David and Jacob too."

"So what do we do?"

"I… have no idea. Keep going after the control centers, but I don't know how. We are both kids. So far, the strategy has been for an adult to walk up to the door, act like they belong there, and say the codes found in the envelope. I don't think that is an option for us. No one is going to believe we belong there."

We discussed this briefly, but lacking other ideas, we decided to stay on course for #1. As we drove, the car was silent. With the silence, came dread. It was never going to work. There had been more than a few times during this trip when I was sure we were going to die, and now I was more convinced than ever. If we attempted this, we *would* die. As I was lost in these fearful thoughts, Veronica broke the silence.

"My dad used to say that underdogs are more likely to win wars than the favorites," she said thoughtfully, "because underdogs are forced to use tactics that the favorite does not think of. We need to start thinking of new tactics. The 'walk up to the door like you belong there' tactic will not work anymore. They are not that dumb. And I am sure that, by now, the codes are all changed anyway. Heck, they probably have helicopters with guns flying over each center by now. We are going to have to think of new ways to do this."

"Uh…. Ok; but saying 'we should be creative' is a lot different than actually being creative. Do you have any ideas?"

Veronica didn't say anything for a moment. I began to think that she was not going to answer. The rumble of the car, the sound of the tires, and the wind through the open back window replaced the sound of our voices. Then Veronica sighed deeply, looked at Elmo and then at me, "What if we go after Gibion directly – the person, not the control centers?"

I had to give her credit for thinking creatively, but the statement was ridiculous on many levels. First, how would we find him? Second, what would we do if we did? I imagined our whole government had probably been desperately seeking to find him for years. And they had the power of the NSA, CIA, and FBI. They obviously failed. So, are two kids and a dog going to find and kill the guy that the most powerful government in the history of the world could not kill?

"Hmm, that is an idea," I said trying to be nice.

"Shut up, Tommy. I know you think it is dumb, but I *do* have ideas."

"Ok, I am listening."

"You said that you think all Gibion's attention is on David and Jacob right now right? Maybe that is why he has not even bothered to appear to the nation to tell everyone what is going on. He is panicked. He has lost up to nine of the eleven centers in the last few weeks. If something happens to the last of them before the official government transition, the deal could fall apart. He might not be able to maintain his power. That is why he bombed Washington when he did. That is why he is searching for David and Jacob. He feels vulnerable even at this moment that should be his triumph."

"Okay. So?"

"Okay. This is what I am thinking. We show up and turn ourselves in at the gates. We explain who we are and what we have been doing, and we say that we want to stop David and Jacob because we are afraid of more nuclear bombs. We demand to speak to Gibion directly. The envelope will prove that we are who we say we are."

"That is your plan?"

"Yeah, I think it will work."

"Or they will just shoot us."

"Gibion is panicked about David and Jacob. He is focused on stopping the attacks. If we can go in and make them believe that we can help stop them, I think he will do anything. He'll be happy to meet with us."

"Ok, well I doubt it will be so easy, but let's suppose for a moment that is true. We get in front of him and then what? They are not just going to let us walk up to him with guns, neither one of us knows karate... I haven't seen this guy, but I am guessing any attempt to hurt him would fail miserably."

"Remember Frodo?"

"You are talking about Frodo the Hobbit?"

"He had no idea how he was going to get through Mordor. They just went to the gates and figured it out."

"That was a book. This is real life. And we do not have a magical ring. And, you are a nerd."

Veronica stuck out her tongue in response before

returning her attention to the road as she passed a truck. Silence and the sound of wind followed. The sky was gray and bleak. The grass on the sides of the highway was brown and dead. Discarded plastic cups, bottles and litter spotted the median. The whole scene felt like Mordor.

"And which one of us is Frodo and which is Sam anyway?"

"Oh, shut up! It was an analogy!" she shouted with an exasperated laugh, "You know what I meant. When things are bad, you have to do the right thing and figure out the next step when you get there. We are in that situation, Tommy." Her face got serious, and her voice became low and soft. "Everything that has happened this past week is big. This is a moment for the history books. There may be some Broadway musical someday where they rap and sing about everything that we are doing.

"I don't know what is going to happen, but I know that we cannot just keep trying to destroy these control centers. And I know that if we could get close to Gibion, maybe we could figure something out. I know that the longer we wait, the harder it will be to do anything. If you are too afraid, give me the envelope, and I will do it."

"I am not afraid, ok?"

"Then let's do it! Let's figure it out when we get there. Maybe we can push him off a balcony or something. And maybe we will lose. Like David said, it is better to die doing something good than to live knowing you let bad things happen. I think not doing this would be bad and doing it is the only good we can do."

"Okay," I said. I knew she was right. I just didn't like it. I didn't want to do it. But she was right. "Ok. I am in. You are right. But, for the record, we are going to die."

"Okay, I will enter that in the record. And then maybe they can add that to the musical."

CHAPTER TWENTY-ONE

We DECIDED that we would just continue our course to #1. We would first hide the envelope somewhere so that we could easily access it later (but bring copies of two pages as proof for Gibion). Then we would walk up to the gates, talk to the guards, tell them that we wanted to help Gibion catch David, show the copies to convince them that we were not just crazy, and hopefully get to Gibion.

That was the plan. It was not much of a plan. But that was the plan.

As we approached #1, we realized that its location was of a different sort from the others that we had attacked – it was in the middle of a village. The sign by the side of the highway as we entered the village read, "Manchester – Home of the

Famous Chicken Broil." The speed limit dropped from 55 mph to 35 to 30, and we rolled into the old downtown. We turned right at the blinking traffic light, crossed over a bridge, and passed an old red mill, a pharmacy, a florist, two antique shops, a pizza place, and a gas station. Then there were two residential blocks with old houses. We then came to a small park full of flower gardens. We turned right and drove between two churches across the street from one another. We turned right again on the road behind the churches and on our left was a 15-foot cobblestone wall that was covered with ivy and obscured by small trees and weeds that grew between it and the road.

"It's on the other side of that wall," I said.

"Where is the gate?"

I scanned the page from the envelope. "I think there is a driveway up here," I said pointing, "We go down there."

"Ok, but we better do something with that envelope first. Remember? We need something to offer Gibion when we get to him, and we cannot have him just steal the whole thing from us. And we never made copies."

"Yeah." I looked around in the car for a place to hide the envelope, but I knew they would search our car. "Turn around. We need to find a place that is not in this car." Veronica turned the wheel and slowly started a U-turn. She suddenly slammed on the brakes as a red car speeding in the other direction passed us. She then finished her turn and headed back toward the churches.

"Stop," I said. "Pull behind that church." St. Mary's Catholic Church stood on the corner, and I got out of the car. The church was old; its walls were made of uncut field-stone. I walked around to the front of the church and passed a statue of Mary holding a baby Jesus. The front stairs had fake green grass on them, and I started walking up. I got to the large wooden doors and pulled. The door was not locked.

As I stepped in, I smelled the lingering aroma of incense. I looked around. The sanctuary was narrow and long. The walls were white with ornate gold wallpaper strips decorating them in intervals. I looked for a place to hide the envelope.

As I turned to the right, I saw a staircase leading to the basement. I climbed down the stairs and at the bottom I found a small office. Inside was a desk, a long window bench, a cabinet... and a copy machine! I hurried to the copy machine and made copies of the first two pages. I then looked around for a place to hide the envelope. I lifted the cushion on the bench, and the seat moved – it had a compartment under it. As I lifted it, the smell of old dry paper filled my nose, and I could tell that this bench had not been opened in years. I pulled out the envelope and slipped it inside a large book of sheet music. It fit nicely inside, and I piled other books on top of it. I closed the bench, stood up, and walked back out of the church.

Within a few minutes, we were heading back to #1. We turned left into a small gravel driveway with heavy branches and shrubbery on both sides. As we turned in, I saw the red car that had sped past us when we were on our way to the church; it was parked just past the driveway. We slowly wound our way down the driveway and finally came to a gate. We got out of the car, leaving Elmo, and saw two guards sitting down in chairs on both sides of the entrance. They seemed surprised to see us and stood up looking at us. Scrambling for their rifles, they pointed them at us yelling, "On the ground! On the ground!"

We quickly got on the ground as the guards continued to yell and threaten us. They came over and searched both of us roughly. Then the big guard pulled out a plastic twist-tie. I yelped as he pulled my arms behind my back and secured my wrists together with the plastic. They did the same to Veronica, and she cried out when they pulled her broken arm behind her back. They dragged us to our feet again and pushed us back against the car.

The whole time they said almost nothing to us, only occasionally speaking to one another about how to proceed. Oddly, they seemed afraid of us. They kept looking around. They were talking to their radios with stress-filled voices. "High alert!" one of them kept saying into his walkie-talkie. I think that they had heard about the other attacks and our showing up made them think that something big was about to happen.

"We want to see Gibion! We can help him!" Veronica yelled. They looked at her and then looked at each other. One of them gave a nervous laugh and shook his head. Neither directly responded. They pulled us away from the car and led us through the gate. The picked me up by the arms, and pain ripped through them. I screamed and heard Veronica also screaming. Her broken arm was being twisted, and her pain was unbearable. When they realized her condition, they loosened the tie and allowed a bit more space for her to straighten the broken arm. I looked back and saw Elmo still in the car with his head sticking out the half-opened window, barking like a mad dog but unable to get out.

They dragged us through the cobblestone gates that certainly were there long before the control center was. We were pulled past many nervous-looking soldiers who almost flinched as we yelled and kicked. The gate closed behind us, and our handlers pulled us toward a metal-sided brown building. We came inside, and a tall man stood watching us as we fell to the ground. He scowled. The guards picked us up off the ground and dragged us toward the wall. My arms were hurting, and I wrestled to free myself from their grip. The guard behind me tripped and pulled me down with him.

For a moment there was commotion, and although I had not intended to struggle, I was now pulling away from the guard. As this commotion continued, the tall man did not move but appeared to grow visibly agitated.

"Don't you dare!" he finally screamed, and everyone stopped moving. We immediately grew silent. "Don't you dare resist like you are the victims here..." His eyes were narrowed, his nostrils flared, and he bared his teeth in rage. "You are the ones that have killed so many of our men. You are responsible. I wish I could choose what would happen to you. If I did, you would die a slow and painful death." He walked towards us, and we crawled back in fear. The other men stepped in front of him. They argued in whispers for a few moments. I was realizing that everyone was both furious and afraid of us. The stories of the successful bombings were well known and images of me, Veronica, David, Hoover, and Jacob were posted all over the wall behind the angry man. There was even a photo of Elmo.

Despite the fact that Gibion had just been declared ruler of the most powerful nation on earth, his followers feared Veronica and me. It was so strange.

Both Veronica and I kept saying that we wanted to talk to Gibion, but the men all ignored us. Phone calls were made. Lots of talking that we could not quite hear. Finally, the tall angry man came up to us and squatted so that his eyes were level with ours. He had long hair, a thin mustache, and bulging muscles. With a deep voice and an unidentifiable accent, he spoke, "What are you doing here? Trying to blow us up?" We did not have time to respond when he continued, "Well if you think we are going to take you inside the control center, you are mistaken. You are probably going to die. Just so you know. But we are going to move you first. Way away from here. Not sure what sort of ideas you have, but you are going to be taken where you cannot do any damage."

"We want to see Gibion," Veronica said.

"I bet you do."

"We have the information he is looking for. We can help him find David and Jacob."

"I have no idea who you are talking about, but you are not going to see Gibion. No one sees Gibion. He is the president now you know."

"You will get in big trouble if he learns you killed us without giving him this information."

The man paused and stared blankly.

"Ask him," I added. "Just ask Gibion."

He turned and looked at the other men and smiled broadly. Then he looked back at us and straightened his face with another blank stare. "Just call up Gibion, huh? You do realize who he is right now right? Why would he want to talk to two dumb kids?"

"You know that Gibion has put everyone on high alert," Veronica blurted out. "You know that control centers have been blowing up left and right. You know your men are panicked. We know why. If you kill us and Gibion finds out we could have helped...," Veronica shook her head and clenched her teeth as she said, "He will be so mad at you."

The big man turned and looked at his men again. No smile this time. He stood up and ran his fingers through his long hair.

He walked over to the phone on the wall and picked it up and started talking. Both Veronica and I strained our ears to hear what he said, but we could not. He was gesticulating as though he were angry. The call took forever. My hands started to hurt as the tie cords that bound them behind my back dug into my wrists. I looked at Veronica, and she had tears of pain running down her cheeks. How long could this take?

Finally, the big man hung up the phone. He stood and

looked at us. He then walked over to a thin guard who had been standing at the door, whispered in his ear, and walked out of the room. The thin guard stood thoughtfully for a moment and then signaled to the other men in the room to grab us, and we were carried out of the room.

I was heaved over the shoulder of a guard, and I looked over and saw that Veronica was in the same situation. We walked back out of the door and back toward our car. As we left the gate, we saw a large pickup truck sitting next to our car. I felt myself being lifted over the tailgate into the bed of the truck. They dropped me, and my back hit the metal, and the wind was knocked out of me. Veronica was yelling as I was gasping for air. I then heard barking mixed with cursing. That was followed by a yelp. Then I heard the grunting and groaning of men lifting something heavy, and a moment later a giant pile of red dog crashed into the back of the truck with Veronica and me. I twisted and saw an unconscious Elmo lying beside me.

Veronica stopped yelling, looked at Elmo, and then looked at my scared face. "He is alive, Tommy, I can hear him breathing." As she said these words the thunder of the truck's diesel engine coming to life silenced all talking. Vibration and shaking indicated that the truck was put in gear. As the truck lurched forward, I slid back and hit the tailgate; Veronica slid into me and then Elmo slid into Veronica.

Dust and wind swept over us. For what seemed like an eternity we slid around the back of the truck feeling the bumps of the road, the turns in the highway, and the speeding up, occasional stopping, and accelerating. I felt each of these maneuvers with my body as I slid around in the back with Veronica and Elmo crashing into the tailgate, wheel wells, and cab. I was able to shield my head a little with my arms, but before too long, I could not take it anymore. My arms were going to fall off. Just as I was ready to give up and just start letting my head smash, the truck stopped.

We heard the doors creak open. Feet walking on gravel. Veronica groaned, "Elmo needs to lose some weight... and you... both of you were killing me."

"I had both of you slamming me into the metal wall. I think that is worse," I responded. We were interrupted by the sound of two men talking.

"Put them inside. And then let Hugo Carmody know that we are here."

"Should we lock them up?"

"No, just leave them tied up and keep an eye on them. We won't be staying long."

The tailgate creaked open, and we twisted our necks to see three men standing there, all dressed in brown Gibionite uniforms like the one that David had once borrowed. They pulled Veronica out first and carried her to the building by her shoulders and feet. Then they came back and got me. I groaned as they grabbed my now very sore arms and legs. They shuffled across the dirt driveway, opened the door to the building and dropped me on the floor next to Veronica. A moment later, Elmo was dropped in as well. I looked at him and saw that his legs were now bound with plastic pull ties.

As we lay on our sides, bound and in pain, I looked around. The inside of the building was dark at first; the only light was coming through the curtained windows. As our eyes adjusted, I could see that it looked like an office build-ing. There were many tan cubicle walls, desks with mostly empty docking stations and high-backed adjustable desk chairs on wheels.

"Well, this didn't turn out like I expected," Veronica said. "They don't seem too interested in David and Jacob."

"I don't know. We are still alive. I think something we said may have made an impression."

Elmo stirred, and I was happy to see him open his eyes. "Hi, Elmo! Good boy. Are you alright, boy?" Veronica said in that high pitched voice everyone always uses with dogs for some reason. Elmo licked his lips and tried to twist to get up, but his paws were twist-tied together, and the ties held. So after twisting for a while, he stayed there.

Seeing that Elmo was alright brightened my spirit, and as Veronica and I spoke, we reviewed what we thought would happen. Veronica was convinced that these guys were not taking us to see Gibion, and if we were lucky, we would be put in some jail somewhere (she did not say what would happen if we were *not* lucky).

I was more optimistic. Maybe it was just hopeful thinking, but I kept reminding myself that Reginald Gibion would *want* to see us. We had what he wanted. We had the envelope. We could help him find David and Jacob. Those were important things to him. It seemed to me that they were taking our claims seriously, and something changed when the big guy was on the phone.

We lay on that floor for the next day. Twice during that time, Gibion's guards would enter, give us food and temporarily loose our bonds so that we could eat. When we were done, they would tie us up again. The night was difficult sleeping on our sides with our hands behind our backs. Poor Veronica had a tougher time with her broken arm, and although she never complained or even admitted being in pain, I would hear her whimper during the night. In addition to the physical pain and discomfort, the mental anguish during this time was incredible. There was a strange combination of fear, anticipation, and boredom. We tried playing games and talked about everything we could think of, but much of the time was spent in silence, lying together, worrying about what would happen next. Then finally, early in the afternoon, our boredom ended.

The door opened, and a man stepped into the room. He had the size, dress, and shape of a goon in the Italian Mafia. His thinning hair was greased back. He wore an expensive suit. He had gold rings on his fingers. His wide shoulders matched his wide, fat face. He had no beard, but the dark stubble on his chin left a shadow that reminded me of Fred Flintstone.

"Good afternoon children. I am the new president, Reginald Gibion, you requested a meeting with me?"

CHAPTER TWENTY-TWO

REGINALD GIBION STEPPED into the room, looked at us, looked at the dog, and stood with his arms slightly away from his sides. Elmo showed his teeth and growled.

"I was told you were here to help," he said, and his voice was smooth. It reminded me of David's voice only deeper and less affected. "We have a noble cause, and your help is appreciated. Unfortunately, time is tight, and your nation depends upon your immediate cooperation. I was told you could lead me to David and Jacob?"

The sudden presence of Gibion himself came as a shock to both of us, and we were tongue-tied. A long awkward silence followed while Gibion stared at us.

"Where is David?" he said. He paced as he spoke. "It is essential that you tell me right now. I know that you have heard bad things about my men and about me, but we are looking out for our nation and for the equality and well-being of everyone in this land. I care about you. I care about everyone. Things are going to be good. I promise you. Our government was broken. We can fix it. We will make it better." He leaned toward us and looked deeply into my eyes. I had to turn away. "But we cannot do it with David doing what he is doing. I am not sure what David has told you, and I am not even sure why David is doing what he is doing. But I know that his actions are going to hurt a lot of people. I don't know you, Thomas. And I do not know you, Veronica. But I do know that you don't want to hurt anyone. Help me stop David, and I promise that not only will I not hurt him, but by doing so, you can guarantee that no one else gets hurt either. This war will be over, and there will finally be peace." His voice was compelling. As he spoke, his words seemed to ring true and reasonable.

Now, if you remember our plan, this is the moment both Veronica and I were hoping for. Our whole plan had been getting to Gibion, and we had accomplished that. But neither one of us had done any planning beyond that. I think our plan was to kill him somehow, but killing is not really something kids do, and now that we were looking at him and listening to his compelling speech, the idea faded.

But what were we going to do? We really should have planned better. And we did not actually know where David and Jacob were anyway. We both remained silent.

Gibion walked over to us and crouched down. "I care about our nation's youth, and my whole mission is to make the world a better place for young men and women like you. So I would never want to hurt you. But I also do not like the idea of watching my new nation be attacked by a traitor. And I do not have much time. You told Hugo that you could help find David – now is your opportunity. Where is David?"

Silence.

Reginald smiled a genuine smile. But his words were a not-so-subtle threat. He stared at us. He took a half step over to Elmo and reached out and patted his side. Elmo growled.

"Veronica," Gibion said staring at Veronica. "Thomas," he said turning to me. "Your parents miss you. I am sure you miss them. When was the last time you saw them?"

My head spun, and suddenly the fact that this man was the man who knew where our parents were and could reunite us came rushing into my mind. My parents? The world always felt safe when I was with my parents. The world was insane now. I longed to hear my dad's voice. I longed to feel my mother's touch. I longed for normal. I longed for life before all this.

"You do realize that I am the president now?" Gibion spoke slowly, "I know exactly where your parents are. The government took them, but now I have liberated them. But I need to find David and Jacob. I need that. And it would be so good for the nation if I did. So I need you to answer the question."

He spoke clearly and with purpose. He stared at us with a half smile that seemed both beneficent and threatening at the same time.

"We can help," I said. I was not sure why I said it, but I thought it was the right answer at the moment. I felt like we needed to buy time. And there was a big part of me that just hoped he would let us see our parents. "I have the envelope."

Veronica gasped as I spoke. I looked at her, and her mouth was open in disbelief. "Shut up, Tommy!" she shrieked.

"No, do not shut up Tommy," said Reginald Gibion, "What exactly is the envelope?"

"Pull the paper I have in my front pocket out." He reached down and carefully removed the folded two copies I had made from the envelope. He looked at them for a moment. Then he crumpled them up and threw them across the room.

"So this is how!" he said grabbing his hair in his fists and frowning with his teeth showing. "How many copies are there of this?"

"We have the only copy. Hidden. No others. David is going off memory."

I am not sure why I was talking at that moment. On some level, I was just following our plan. But, and this is embarrassing to say, some part of me was no longer thinking about my country. I was no longer thinking about honor or glory. I was thinking about my parents. These past months had made me grow from a kid to a soldier, but now I wanted to be a kid once more. I was a kid missing his mom and his dad. I don't think that I would have betrayed our little band, but I was never given the opportunity. Because as I opened my mouth to speak, the door opened and Hugo, the tall muscle-bound guard, walked in.

"Mr. President," he said interrupting. Gibion turned around with a look of anger and fury on his face. I thought he would hit the man, but the man did not flinch as Gibion approached him. He said calmly, "A message that you will want to see."

"Your life depends on how much I want to see it," Gibion said, checking his anger for a moment. "Read it to me."

The man looked at us and hesitated. "I am not sure they should hear it."

"They are my friends, and what I hear they can hear."

Hugo proceeded to read the letter. I can tell you exactly what he said because, as I write this, I now have that letter in my possession. It is handwritten and in cursive. Not easy to read at points, but the man with the bulging biceps read it like a pro.

"*DEAR REGINALD,*

"*I do hope you are doing well. Congratulations on your newfound presidency! Color me impressed! I always told Isaac that you had potential, and you proved me right. Unfortunately, I cannot tell that to Isaac because he is dead, and you are responsible for his death. Anyway, Jacob has reminded me that I don't have time to reminisce anymore ~ I need to 'cut to the chase,' as they say. The reason I am writing is that I want to let you know that your presidency, although new, is in great danger. There are two principal causes for its danger: first, as you, with your quick wit and superior powers of deduction, have probably ascertained, we know the locations of your remaining control centers. Second, we are now in possession of the weaponry (guns, rockets, tanks, and etc.) that would allow us to destroy them quite easily and quickly. Now, I realize that you only need these centers for a few more days as your transition to Washington takes place. But, unfortunately for you, you do not have a few more days. In fact, I would guess that you do not even have one more day.*

"*That is unless you, Jacob Burke, and I meet and discuss the new government. Yes, Mr. President, we are willing to negotiate. The idea of a new government actually sounds quite good to both of us. As you know, both of us were vocal critics of the old regime and worked in our own ways to overthrow it. You have now done that (and bravo!), but we think that it is important that we help you set up the new government so that the result will be according to everyone's liking.*

"*For this reason, we request a meeting with you in person. I propose 5 pm today at the Mongolian Grill on the corner of Main St. and Washington St. in downtown Ann Arbor to discuss what this might look like.*

"*I am not one to threaten, Reginald. I trust you with every fiber. But if I were writing this to someone I did not trust, I would warn them that a failure to appear, any efforts to deceive, or any sort of action that would undermine a parley between old friends would*

*bring down fire from heaven on your remaining control centers. All
your plans would be destroyed. You would be just like Adam James
– not president anymore. But you are an old friend and a very
smart man, so I will not threaten at all and look forward to
meeting with you over a nice meal of grilled meat and vegetables,
Mongolian style.*

"Your friend and admirer, David Rogers

"PS: Fair warning that I have no idea if Mongolian Grill is
actually in the style of the Mongolians. I do not know any Mongolians and have never been there myself. Maybe we can ask the wait
staff when we are there.

"PPS: Bring Thomas and Veronica with you, if you would be so
kind. They love Mongolian Grill, and I would not want them to
miss the meal. Also, bring Elmo – and, if you want a giggle, ask
Thomas how he got his name."

THE BULGING MAN read every word, including the post-
scripts, with a low voice, articulating each syllable clearly.
When he was done, Gibion stood up straight and stroked his
jaw thoughtfully.

"What time is it, Hugo?"

Hugo looked at his watch. "11:30 am."

"I need to think about this whole situation, but be
prepared with the helicopter. If the meeting is going to
happen, we will need to leave soon."

Hugo turned to exit. "And Hugo," Gibion said as the big
man left, "I needed to hear that very much. Thank you."

"Of course, sir."

Gibion turned and looked at us. Then he crouched beside
me and whispered in my ear, "Thank you for your willing-
ness to serve, Thomas. It will not be forgotten. Your parents
are safe, and if you continue to be helpful to me, I promise

that you will see them again." With that, he stood and left the room.

Veronica looked at me with wide eyes. "This is a little crazy, don't you think?" I said nothing. She went on, "Do you think that David would really join forces with Gibion?"

I didn't need to think about that. "No, I don't. Not for a second. And I can guarantee that Jacob would not. I have no idea what they are doing but partnering with Gibion is not it."

"I think you are right." She hesitated. "But David was friends with Gibion once..."

"Well, he is not anymore. No way."

"Ok...," she said with a sarcastic lilt to her voice. Then she said something that hurt, "Just now, were you thinking about giving him the envelope?"

"No!"

"Yeah, you were."

"No, I was trying to buy time."

Veronica pursed her lips doubtfully, and let it go. We waited in silence.

Hugo returned. He stepped through the door, looked at us, and smiled. One of his hands was behind his back. He stepped toward us and pulled out a knife. Veronica shrieked. He laughed and crouched down. "Shut up," he said still chuckling, "fortunately for you, the president says that I can't kill you. You are going to see your traitor friends." He used the knife to cut our bonds. He stood back up and started walking out of the room.

"You forgot Elmo!" Veronica said as Hugo walked away. He turned and raised an eyebrow, looking at the still hogtied dog. He looked like he was thinking. Then he started walking to Elmo.

"Yes, that would probably be easier than carrying him," he crouched in front of the dog, started to cut the bonds and then stopped. "If he attacks me, I will kill him. Can you guarantee that he will not attack?"

"He won't attack," Veronica said.

A few moments later, Elmo was up and walking. Initially, he growled at Hugo, but Hugo left without incident.

A few minutes later, Hugo stepped back in and motioned for us to follow. And we found ourselves climbing into a Blackhawk helicopter. A pilot sat in the front, and Gibion sat next to him with headphones on. Hugo was in the back with Veronica, Elmo, and me. We buckled into the bench in the back. The wide bay door on my right was still open, and as we lifted off, Hugo stood, holding the side of the door and looking out over the edge.

The noise, wind, and vibration were deafening. I leaned over, still buckled in, and looked out the door. I saw the countryside from above. Old farmhouses with old barns. Rows of planted crops. Fields full of cattle. The pungent smell of a pig farm. Soon we passed over the village – the dam, the mill, and the small downtown. People looked up at us as we passed. Everyone seemed afraid and almost crouching as they saw our helicopter.

Since the nuclear bomb had been invented, only two cities had ever been bombed, and only the very elderly are still alive to remember either of those. For most people, nuclear warfare was something that was only rarely discussed and thought unlikely – and unthinkable. But now our capital city was gone. Thousands of lives were gone. And our president had publicly surrendered. But people were still living their lives.

I remember hearing the story of London during the Second World War. Great Britain's experts had predicted that if the Nazis bombed the city, there would be widespread panic. People would flee to the countryside, and factories would cease production. And as a result, the war would be lost. Hitler, making the same assumption, ordered the bombing of London. As bombs began to fall, everyone expected the worst. But there was no mass panic. Very few fled. Production continued. And the people remained firm in their morale and resolve.

I would have expected that a nuclear bomb and a governmental overthrow would shut down our whole society. I would have expected widespread anarchy. None of that happened. The country continued almost as though nothing happened at all. Except for the looks on people's faces – there you could see fear and confusion.

Now we were once again above cows and cornfields. We passed over a lake, a trailer park, and a horse farm. Slowly, we began to see subdivisions, schools, and strip malls as we came to the outskirts of Ann Arbor. The skyline of the city rose into view, and the chopper moved toward it. As we passed over a massive parking lot and an expressway, the skyline that was distant just a moment ago was upon us. We passed over the football stadium and hovered right over the center of the city. We slowly descended toward the top of a parking structure. Looking down, I saw at least one hundred soldiers, dressed in the Gibion uniform, waiting for us with guns. A black heavily-armored Hummer was also parked there awaiting our arrival.

When the chopper came to rest, Hugo jumped out and then turned around and helped Gibion out. I walked to the edge of the helicopter, and Hugo grabbed my arm as I jumped to the ground. He did the same for Veronica. Elmo jumped out after us. We were overwhelmed by the combination of helicopter noise, the heat of the early summer, and the brightness of the cloudless sky. We were ushered to the Hummer and put in the back seat. Hugo climbed in the driver's seat, and Gibion sat in the passenger seat.

"Can I assume the arrangements have been made?"

Gibion said as the door closed and noise of the chopper was muted enough to talk.

"Yes. They will have no weapons. We have sharpshooters on every building. And the streets are blocked off."

Gibion nodded and grew silent as the Hummer made its way out of the structure. After circling down the eight floors, we turned right toward Main Street and almost immediately stopped. Gibion and Hugo got out and nodded for Veronica and me to follow. The streets were empty, and security forces stood visibly at the end of block preventing people and traffic from coming our way. I looked up the street and saw on the corner the Mongolian Grill. In front of the restaurant, sitting in the outdoor dining area and smoking a cigarette, I saw David. Next to David was Jacob. A bottle of wine was on the table, and I could see that David was enthusiastically telling a story to Jacob. Jacob was ignoring him and staring at us. Actually at Gibion. He looked angry.

CHAPTER TWENTY-THREE

DAVID SMILED, stood, and opened his arms to embrace Gibion as he approached. Gibion stepped back and extended his hand far from his body to offer a stiff handshake which David cheerfully accepted giving a warm two-handed handshake. He then turned and laughed as he saw us and gave both Veronica and me warm side hugs, patted Elmo on the head (along with some 'good doggy' talk) and encouraged us to sit at the table. The whole time Jacob sat staring a death stare at Gibion, not even acknowledging that the rest of us were present.

Soon the five of us sat at the table outside the Mongolian Grill with David talking the whole time like we were all old friends. The waiter (who was clearly frightened) came and took our order. We did not, as is the custom at the restaurant, go in to pick ingredients or watch as the food was grilled but instead just listed what we wanted and the waiter went in to arrange things.

As soon as the waiter left, Jacob interrupted David's story about the first meeting he had had with Gibion (in the 'good old days'). "Listen you...," and he added several curses, "you just murdered a million people. You are a monster, and if David were not here, you would be dead right now. I would jump over this table and rip your heart out with my bare hands." The two guards that had been standing away from the table moved closer. David started laughing as though Jacob were making a joke and then tried to continue his story. Gibion squared his shoulders and sat upright and returned Jacob's scowl.

"I murdered no one," he said, again interrupting David, "you murdered many. President James murdered many. But I murdered no one. Warfare is not murder. Every king, every president, and every general has killed during war, and we do not call them murderers. Only when the cause is not just is the leader to be called a murderer. And my cause is just. I speak on behalf of the people. I speak on behalf of fairness and equality. The government that claimed to be the United States was illegitimate and illegal. Everything I have done and everything I am going to do will fix what is broken in this nation. When I fix what is broken, I will turn things back over to the people. I am here to promote fairness and equality. That is it.

"The USA has been nothing but harmful. Under my leadership, we can reshape the world. We can ensure equality and peace that the world has never seen before. Poverty will be gone. War will be over. You and you and you...," he said with his finger moving around the table and stopping for a moment in front of each of us, "will be remembered as the people that worked against the progress of history. All generations will remember Reginald Gibion!" He slapped his chest theatrically then repeated, "They *will* remember me." Hugo nodded with approval and gave a slight grin. "I toppled the most corrupt and murderous government in the history of the world. I will be the George Washington, the Jefferson, and the Franklin wrapped up in one. All generations will remember me."

David smiled sympathetically and said nothing. Jacob's face looked like he had just smelled a fart, his legs stiffened, and his hands pressed on the table looking like he was poised for a jump. I saw the guards move even closer now, directly behind Gibion, with their eyes on Jacob.

"Well," David said, "that was certainly a statement made up of words. And it sounded as though those words were intended to justify the bombing of a multitude of innocent people. And well done with that. It was a very good effort. But we are not here to argue about the justification, or lack thereof, of that bombing. We are here to talk about the future." Gibion glared at him but said nothing, and after a sip of water, David continued. "Reginald, as you know, Jacob and I have been able not only to locate your control centers but to destroy them. In the recent weeks, of your eleven control centers, we have destroyed nine. And, if my calculations are correct, that would leave two remaining.

"Yesterday, Jacob and I put the mechanisms in place to destroy the last two. We are well aware that you will need them only for a few more days, and therefore we had planned on just destroying them quickly to put an end to your little effort. That *is* well within our power. But, then I posed a question to Jacob. Do you know what I said?" David paused and looked at Gibion as though he expected an answer. Receiving none, he continued, "I said, 'Jacob, why destroy Gibion? Why not work with him?' Did I not say that Jacob?" David turned to Jacob, and Jacob said nothing. He continued, "I said that we are in one of those very rare situations where a new nation is being built. A constitution is being written. And why cause more turmoil and confusion when a peaceful new government is possible?"

Gibion sneered, "What are you talking about? First off, I think you are lying. Second, this madman here can hardly keep from attacking me. I do not need you. I do not fear you, and I think whatever game you are now playing is ridiculous."

"I think you *do* fear us," David said dropping his voice and his smile for a moment. "I think you fear us very much. You are so close to victory, and you know that we could paralyze you right as you are about to cross the finish line." David smiled again and changed back to his friendly tone as he said, "But we do not need to be friends. Many of the founding fathers were not particularly fond of each other. Adams disliked Franklin. Hamilton hated Jefferson. Jefferson disliked Adams. And we all know how Aaron Burr felt about Hamilton. But, with the exception of Hamilton, they all survived, and the nation became, until this week, the most powerful nation in the history of the earth. Now, we have the opportunity to be the new founding fathers. We have the opportunity to build the next great nation. The greatest nation!" David spoke in a measured way as he said all this, and all the cheerful calm had given way to a slow passion that was very inspiring.

I was even inspired by the idea of it. For a moment. Then I remembered the dead. The million dead in Washington. Mothers, fathers, daughters, and sons. Gone. Millions of others would probably suffer and maybe die from the radiation and fallout. This man sitting in front of us was a murderer on the level of Hitler or Stalin. I looked at Veronica, and she raised her eyebrows. How could David do this? How could Jacob do this? What was going on? My head was spinning.

The two waiters returned with our food and drinks. But no one ate. Gibion sat silently staring at David with narrowed eyes. Finally, he said, "You have nothing. You cannot destroy anything. You are out of options. And this is a desperate last attempt. And now you are going to die." He pulled out a handgun and pointed it at Jacob. Jacob did not flinch but continued to stare coldly at him.

"Have it your way. The moment you drew that gun, you lost another control center. One left. Pull the trigger, and you will have zero." Gibion looked startled, and turned and looked at the guards, and then back at Hugo. Hugo was talking into the white bud hanging from his left ear. I could not hear him, but I heard his voice rise, and a panicked expression fell on his face.

"Mr. President...," he said faltering.

Putting the gun back in its holster, Gibion stood up and put his hands on his head. His eyes were wide, and he paced without talking. After a few moments, he spoke.

"Give me some time."

"Reginald, there is no time."

"Ok. How is this going to work? I mean... what exactly do you want me to do?"

"We want some guarantees with some of your skin in the game. Jacob here has developed a series of checks and balances to ensure that both of us are protected from one another. I told him he was crazy to not just trust you, but you know Jacob, always suspicious.

"The basic structure we are proposing is this: As our new government takes over the reins from the U.S. this week, Jacob and I will select exactly half of the high-ranking military leaders – your team and our team will work together, or there will be a bloody civil war. The three of us stay together physically during the entire transition. Once we have our people in place, we work together to draft a constitution.

The details of that can be worked out later, but we thought that you could have the executive power while we maintain legislative authority. Essentially, we make the laws you enforce them and fight the wars."

Gibion interrupted in a shout, "What? The whole reason I did this was to be able to craft the laws that will be put in place! I am trying to build a new society, one in which there will no longer be envy and inequality and injustice. You know my background. I have economic plans that I have devised that, once implemented, will improve our economy and better the world. I have already ended the threat of nuclear war. My next accomplishment will be ending the threat of poverty. I cannot do that if I am not creating the laws." He spoke these last few sentences with passion and earnestness ending his sentence with a sad but wise tone as though he were reading poetry.

"You ended the threat of nuclear war, huh?" Jacob said sarcastically. "You just dropped the first nuclear bomb on a city since World War II! I look forward to seeing what you do with poverty!"

Gibion ignored Jacob and looked at David.

"I understand," David replied. "How about this – table that for now. We will work out an agreement on the legal code when we have more time. For now, we will just make sure that we share power. The fact of the matter is that at this time you and we are in a stalemate. No one can win without the other."

Gibion paused for a long time. Once my schoolmate caught a squirrel in a box, and we peeked through the holes, and I remember how pitiful and scared it looked. Gibion had the same look in his eyes. He stammered in his speech and kept glancing back at Hugo. He signaled for Hugo to come over and asked him more details about the destroyed control center. It was #3, just south of Flint, the most fortified of all the centers. That meant that only #1, Manchester, where Veronica and I got captured remained.

"Ok." He said finally.

The plans were made for David and Jacob to bring in a combination of Third Party loyalists, ex-military, and family members to help run our side of the military leadership. Gibion would also maintain his portion with his current loyalists.

The conversation seemed to be complete. The waiters had come out several more times, but only Veronica and I had eaten anything. David gave the other three meals (that had been untouched for the entire conversation) to Elmo. But right as I thought everything was settled, the real debate started.

"One more little thing," David said as we were about to get up. "We will need the formula for ADK-9." Everyone sat back down. Gibion was silent, so David repeated, "We need ADK-9." Gibion shook his head, and much shouting followed. Several threats. But in the end, David refused to budge and threatened to blow up #1.

The wind blew, the sun that was high in the sky when our meeting started, was now sinking, and the air was cooling. Gibion stood frozen and dead-eyed. Shell-shocked. A short time ago, he had become the ruler of the world's most powerful country. Now he was about to give his primary source of power to two enemies. He started unbuttoning his shirt in the middle. He unbuttoned one button. Then a second. Then a third. Then he reached inside the open shirt, and his bare chest showed. A red raised lump on his skin that looked like an enormous burn became visible. He took a knife from the table and...

To be honest, I have no idea what he did. I looked away. I asked Veronica what happened, and she also was looking away. But the next thing I knew, he was holding flash drive that was slimy. By the time I opened my eyes his shirt was buttoned again, but a crimson stain marked the middle.

He signaled to Hugo who brought a leather bag. From the bag, he pulled a computer. Gibion opened the computer and inserted the flash drive. We watched as he clicked and dragged files. A moment later he pulled the flash drive from the computer, wiped it clean on his shirt, and handed it to David.

David took it, smiled, and nodded appreciatively. He handed it to Jacob who pulled a tablet from his jacket and inserted the flash drive. After a moment, Jacob nodded and pulled the flash drive.

The exchange had been made. The most important technology since the Manhattan Project had just been shared with my uncle!

David stood and smiled. Jacob stood. Veronica and I stood. Elmo stretched lazily. We walked as a group back to Gibion's car. The plan was for us all to stay together until power was transferred. But all this planning and everything we thought was happening no longer mattered.

Screaming around the corner came a baby blue, rusty Ford Bronco. Standing up through the sunroof was a man with a machine gun firing away and yelling. Gibion's troops scattered. Hugo grabbed Gibion by the arm, and the two dove behind a pillar. But David and Jacob stood. When Veronica and I started to run, they grabbed us and whispered to stay still. The Bronco burst through the mini-roadblock that the Gibions had set up with cars and men and pulled right up to us.

I could now recognize the man with the machine gun up top.

"Hoover?" I gasped.

He nodded and fired off several shots. David and Jacob jumped in the car, and Veronica, Elmo, and I all followed.

Soon the Bronco was driving away at dangerous speeds. A man I did not know was driving. Hoover climbed in and smiled. He looked around the car. "The team is back together!"

The car rocked back and forth as we navigated over sidewalks and around stopped cars in a desperate attempt to get out of the city. The rocking of the car caused Jacob to wince. I was reminded of all the pain he had suffered in the past few weeks. Gunshots, beatings, car crashes and explosions coupled with almost no rest or sleep. All that must have been taking its toll. David noticed his wincing too. "Jacob, here," he said pouring some pills from his jacket pocket into his hand and holding them out. "These will help with the pain." Jacob shook his head, cursed, and did not turn around.

"You look hurt," Veronica said. "Why don't you take them?"

"Yes, I hurt. But unless I am dying, I think taking pills is dumb. Pain is a signal your body gives you to help. It helps you move the right way to prevent further injury and promote healing. We feel pain for a reason. Humans have relied on pain to survive since creation, but now modern thinkers have it all figured out... silence the signal!"

"Jacob, well said. I do hope that the very helpful signal of pain will not throw off your aim," David reached under his seat and pulled out a gun, handed it to Jacob, "we have some shooting to do."

CHAPTER TWENTY-FOUR

I LEARNED the driver's name was Rick. And Rick was amazing. He wove in and out of the city. It was like a real-life version of *Need for Speed.* He was getting us out of town. He turned right and then left and then down an alley and through a parking lot. We pulled onto Huron Street trying to get out to the expressway. But despite his excellent driving, Rick did not live long. And our escape did not last long either.

I was the first one to hear the sound. It was unmistakable. The sound of Gibion's Blackhawk helicopter. Everyone started looking at the sky, and soon we saw it closing in on us.

"Pull into that lot!" Jacob yelled. The car swerved into the gravel parking lot on our right and stopped. Jacob screamed,

"Everyone out! Everyone out!" He kept repeating this until the car was empty, and then he and David led a wild race to the trees on the other side of the lot.

The rat-tat-tat of machine guns came from the chopper, and Rick crumpled, never to rise again. Hoover screamed and grabbed his leg. Jacob grabbed Veronica and me and pulled us down just behind the tree line. "Crawl!" he yelled, and we all started crawling away. Except for David. David stood. He stared at the helicopter.

"Get down David, you lunatic!" Jacob yelled, punctuating his command with curses.

David stood unmoving. The gunfire from the helicopter ceased, and the man with the machine gun sitting in the helicopter door looked at David as he stood as an unmoving target.

"What are you doing?" Veronica shrieked.

David turned his head and said, "Veronica, Thomas, Jacob, I am going to have a chat with Reginald Gibion. You have the formula. The hope is in your hands. Run. Goodbye, Elmo."

"You are insane!" Jacob yelled.

"Death is not the end. And there are more important things in life than living," David said, grinning at us, and then marched out into the parking lot with his right hand palm forward to the helicopter.

Jacob pulled us away. I didn't understand. What was David doing? How would he survive? Why was this happening?

We made our way back into the trees. Soon we came to a red wooden fence fifty or so yards into the trees and on the other side was a backyard. We could see the helicopter still hovering above the gravel parking lot. Jacob looked back and then signaled to us to climb over. He crouched and linked his hands together and nodded. Veronica stepped on his hands, and he heaved her over the fence. Then I followed her. From the other side of the fence, I saw Hoover climb over (groaning and crying in pain as he did). Then I heard Jacob mutter a complaint, and suddenly Elmo's head appeared over the fence. Then his paws. Then his shoulders. Then his butt. Then his tail. Then he fell over, and I could hear Jacob panting from the effort. A moment later, Jacob was scrambling over the fence.

The five of us sat in the backyard of a small brick ranch house. A large vegetable garden lay between us and the home. Jacob, leading the way, ran toward it. He jumped over the garden and got to the sliding glass door. He pulled, and it opened. Hoover, Veronica, Elmo, and I followed him in. We found ourselves standing on a linoleum floor in what looked like a dining room connected to a kitchen. I could hear the TV blaring in the next room. Then, out from what must have been the living room, came a scrawny man with pimples wearing an Avengers t-shirt. He looked around the corner and started screaming. Then four Chihuahuas came running out from the hallway barking wildly. Despite the man's screaming and the dogs' barking, all of our eyes were staring out the back of the glass window at the helicopter hovering over the parking lot on the other side of the tree line.

"What is David doing?" Veronica screamed.

"He is giving us time," Jacob said.

"Time to do what? He is going to die!" Veronica sounded as though she were going to cry. But Jacob did not answer. He turned and walked toward the man who was now yelling at us to get out of his house. I thought Jacob was going to punch him by the way he walked at him, but before he reached him everyone's attention was turned to Elmo.

Elmo had been nipped one too many times by the little dogs and now was barking ferociously while showing his teeth. The four dogs instantly silenced as did everyone in the room. Even Jacob checked his step and turned around – but only for a moment. The moment that Elmo stopped barking, Jacob spoke in a low steady voice to the pimply young man. "What is your name?"

"Sean."

"Sean, we need to use your computer."

Sean pointed Jacob around the corner to a coffee table. It was in a small living room that was darkened by lowered blinds. The room was a mess. Shoes were scattered by the front door, beer bottles and Coke cans almost completely filled the table, and the couch had a bird's nest of blankets on it.

"Nice decorating," Jacob said as he looked around.

"Wasn't expecting guests to pour in through my back door."

"Fair enough."

"What are you doing?"

"Saving the world."

Jacob pressed the 'on' button, the sleeping computer blinked to life, and the loading screen came on.

"I hold in my hand the secret to ending nuclear war forever. It is dangerous in the hands of one man but the most wonderful thing when in the hands of all men. If your internet is working, I plan to get this to every major government in the world within the next few minutes." Jacob turned and looked over his shoulder, "Hoover, that chopper move yet?"

"No," came Hoover's groaning voice. Looking back in the kitchen, I saw him sitting on the floor. Blood was pooling around him. Veronica moved to help him. She asked Sean about medical supplies, but Sean had nothing. We had to settle for some paper towels and duct tape. Veronica tied the paper towels tightly around his leg and started wrapping the duct tape around to stop the bleeding. The whole time we watched the helicopter above the lot.

It was strange that it was lingering so long. Suddenly, we heard 'rat-tat-tat' of the machine gun. Veronica looked at me with sadness in her eyes. We realized David was gone. I felt like I had been punched in the gut. My head spun, and I wanted to scream and cry at the same time. I went to the window and looked out. I reached for the handle to open it. I had to go out and see him. I had to see if he was lying there dead. What sort of a man does not even try to save a life? Who was I to stay here safe? I pulled on the door. Veronica put her hand on my hand and pushed the door closed. "He died so that we could continue the mission," she said, and tears were in her eyes. "I want to go too, but we cannot help him now. All we can do is try to finish what he died to make possible. We need to help Jacob. We need to stop Gibion. Or we need to die as David did."

I crumpled to the floor and cried. Veronica fell next to me and cried. Elmo came over to us and started licking our faces, and I reached out and grabbed his fur and pulled him in to hug him. I wanted to stay there and cry forever. But Veronica was right. David gave us marching orders. And before we could grieve long, we heard those orders coming from the next room.

"We've got trouble!" The internet was down. Jacob had been saying that he was surprised that neither Gibion nor the government had shut down the internet (both had the ability), but if Sean's house was any indication someone finally did.

Jacob walked back into the kitchen and looked at Hoover. His cheddar face had turned to mozzarella, and he was grimacing. Jacob looked angry. "You probably cannot move can you?" Hoover said nothing, but Jacob said, "We are going to have to leave you with Sean." He looked at Sean. "Sean, do you want to save the world?"

Sean said nothing.

"You can help by helping Hoover. He needs to get better without talking to any doctors. He needs to rest here. You need to clean his wound, stop his bleeding, and let him rest. If the people in that helicopter find him, they will kill him. And then they will torture you. Then they will catch us. Then a tyrant will rule the world. Keep that fat police officer hidden and safe, and you might make it into the history books." Sean nodded, and Jacob signaled to Veronica and me to follow him.

We stumbled out the front door and into a quiet neighborhood on the west side of Ann Arbor. Jacob was moving east in a direct line without regard for streets or sidewalks. Occasionally a chain link fence would block our path and Jacob would place one hand on top of the fence and jump it without slowing down. Although he was walking, his long strides and efficient movements made it so that Veronica and I had to run to keep up. Elmo had no trouble keeping pace except at fences where Veronica and I would have to help heave him over. Jacob did not slow and did not appear to care if we kept up or not.

We came to a neighborhood park, and by running, we were able to catch up with Jacob. As I came alongside him, I asked, "How did you and David know that we were with Gibion?"

"I think you saw us. We were in that red car sitting by Gibion's driveway when you pulled into #1. We were getting ready to attack it when we almost hit Veronica doing a U-Turn in the middle of the road. When we realized it was you, we tried turning around to follow but didn't see where you went. We drove back to the control center driveway and waited down the road for you to come back. When you came up the hill, we were going to cut you off, but the crappy car David stole after we ditched the van stalled, and we just sat there and watched you turn in. By the time we got the car running, that pickup truck with the three of you in the back was rumbling down the driveway."

"How did you blow up that control center while we were at the Mongolian Grill?"

"Remember that 'Digory' phone response that Veronica got at the travel center?"

"Oh yeah… I almost forgot about that," Veronica said from behind us.

"That was Rick. Rick was a contractor at a U.S. government missile site north of Lansing. Rick is also the reason we were able to reconnect with Hoover. He intercepted a government flag that Hoover was in a hospital and got there before Gibion or the Feds could."

"Rick was a hero," I said, suddenly sorry that I had only known him for a few moments.

"Yes, he was. But if we fail, his death was in vain." Jacob picked up his pace, and Veronica and I had to jog to catch up to him again.

"What are we doing now? Where are we going?"

"We have to get this information out to the world. That is going to be very hard without the internet."

"So what is the plan?" Veronica added. "Find internet somewhere? Starbucks?"

"Not unless you want coffee. I am pretty sure the internet is down everywhere."

"How can you be sure?"

Jacob pointed at the baseball diamond where there was a crowd of kids chasing each other around. "How often do you see a busy playground when the internet is up and running? Xboxes and PlayStations across the neighborhood must be down."

Veronica nodded, "You are probably right." She then yelled at the kids, "Hey!" The kids looked at us. "Is your internet down?" They shouted back that it was indeed down.

Jacob kept walking. We left the park and were once again walking through random yards.

"So, the internet is down. Now what?" I asked.

"Time to go old-fashioned. Old fashioned might work better anyway."

"What is old fashioned?"

"Paper. Newspapers. Printing. Hard copies. Physical copies. The formula is not that long. We are going to print it up. Mail it out. Hand it out. Throw it from rooftops. The whole city will get a copy. We are going to be old-fashioned newsboys. We are going to be old-timey preachers, handing out gospel tracts."

We were starting to enter downtown. The small ranch houses had become two-story old homes. We passed an old corner store, a shuttered brick factory covered with graffiti, and under a rusty train bridge. We wove through a gravel parking lot full of cars and found ourselves, once again, on Main Street, downtown Ann Arbor, just a few blocks from the location of the negotiation.

Jacob did not slow. "We need to get to *Thrifty Printing* on Detroit Street. I know the owner. He will help us."

We turned north on Ann Street, left on Fourth Street, and came to Detroit Street. We passed Zingerman's Deli and were back in a neighborhood of apartments and old homes. As we approached the corner of Division Street, Jacob stopped in front of a tall painted brick building. A faded painted sign hung above the door with an arrow pointing up. *"Thrifty Printing,"* it read. Jacob opened the door, and we climbed up the steep staircase that smelled like cigarette smoke and mold. At the top of the stairs was a door with the name painted on it in stenciled letters. Jacob knocked. There was no answer. Jacob slammed the door with his fist so hard that I thought he would break it. *"Open!"* he shouted.

"Uh…. Who is it?"

"It is me – Jacob."

"What do you want?"

"I need something printed."

"At this hour?"

"What time is it?" Jacob said softly to me. I looked out the window next to the landing and could make out the clock on the Kerrytown bell tower.

"It is about 8:30 pm."

"It is not that late Laban! Open the door."

Laban opened the door tentatively. Jacob pushed it open almost knocking Laban down and waved us through. Once inside, he closed it and locked it behind us.

"Hey, what is going on? No dogs in here!"

"Shut up Laban. We need to get something printed fast."

"Jacob, I am really busy."

"No, you are not. Not anymore. This is all you are doing." Jacob took out his thumb drive with the formula on it and plugged it into Laban's laptop. After complaining a bit, Laban agreed to get his printer started. Within a few minutes, the formula was being printed in packets of paper. It was fifty pages of diagrams and chemical formulas. Each packet, once printed, was stapled and set aside.

"Print 1000 of those packets," Jacob said. As he spoke, he looked out the window. I looked over his shoulder, and I could see three men in dressed in white with white hair standing outside on the street. Jacob swore.

CHAPTER TWENTY-FIVE

"OK, TOMMY, LISTEN TO ME," Jacob said turning and looking me in the eye. "I am going out there to deal with those guys. You and Veronica stay here with Laban and get as many copies as you can before those guys," he nodded to the Gibbots outside the window, "start up the stairs. Then you drop every copy that you have in this bag," he held up a backpack that Laban had found for us, "and climb out that window and run."

His angry face softened. His eyes watered. "Tommy," his voice cracked, and I thought I might see the unthinkable sight of my angry uncle crying, "I am going to die out there. You will probably die too. We are both at the end of our lives now. But this life is not something to cling to. There is a greater purpose. You, Veronica, and I have done what we can do. We will die fighting. Our death will be a glorious one."

He sniffed, wiped his nose with the back of his hand, and straightened his shoulders and back. His voice lowered and hardened again. He then said out loud to everyone, "But no one is going down without a fight! Let's get this information out. Let's stop Gibion." He then whispered to himself, "And with God's help, we will."

He bowed his head silently with his eyes closed for a moment. He stood. He walked out the door. I heard his heavy steps descending the stairs. Then through the window, I watched him run out the door to the south and the three men in white chased him out of sight.

The printer spit out packet after packet. We looked out the window, straining our eyes in the direction that Jacob had run. Time seemed to go by very slowly. The sound of the printer. Laban standing silently watching the printer. Elmo panting and pacing around the small office.

"They are coming back!" Veronica yelled spotting the Gib-bots before I did. But soon I saw them, too. There were only two of them now, but they were coming our way. We ran to the printer and grabbed the stack of packets. It looked like maybe one hundred or so had been made. We dropped them in the backpack, tried to zip it, could not zip it, pulled a few out, zipped it, put it on my back, and climbed out onto the mossy roof. I stopped and climbed back in. I reached over and grabbed the flash drive out of Laban's computer and put it in my pocket. Then I ducked back out the window.

The air was crisp and filled with the smell of leaves. I lay down on the roof and edged my feet into the air. Veronica looked at me and smiled. I didn't have time to be afraid of heights anymore. I dangled from the gutter before dropping ten feet to the ground and fell onto my back. Veronica and

Elmo followed. From upstairs, we heard Laban talking to someone. His voice was raised and sounded frantic. We ran trying to stay out of the line of sight of those windows.

We cut through three backyards and into a small group of trees. Coming out on the other side of the trees, we were now on Depot street. The three of us continued to run east. "What are we doing?" Veronica said panting beside me.

"Uh... We are trying to get away from the weird guys in white."

"No, I mean what is our next step? I thought the idea was to start giving these away." She gestured to my backpack.

"Who are we going to give them to?"

"I don't know, but I am guessing someone is better than no one."

Ahead, I saw a bus coming. I could hear the breaks squeal as it approached a stop about 200 feet in front of us. I waved to the driver, and we ran to get on. The driver was not sure about Elmo at first but allowed us on when we insisted. As the bus pulled away, we saw the Gib-bots running toward us. But they grew smaller as the bus drove and soon were out of sight.

"Now what?" Veronica said, sighing as we turned around and faced the front of the bus. Elmo panted, sitting in the aisle.

"Let's think," I said. "We need to get these in the hands of the people."

Veronica gave a thoughtful look. "Do you remember the story of Paul Revere?"

"The 'the-British-are-coming' guy?"

"Yeah."

"Did you know that he was not the only one that went out to spread the word that night?"

I shrugged.

"Nope. There was another guy who also went out

spreading the word. But apparently, Paul Revere was better connected. He knew the right people to give the information to. He was familiar with the movers and shakers in the area who were sympathetic to the cause and went to them. That allowed those people, the movers, and shakers, to spread the word too."

"Okay…"

"Are you seriously not getting what I am saying?"

I stared blankly.

"We need to start handing these out to movers and shakers who are sympathetic to fighting back against Gibion."

"I don't know anyone in Ann Arbor except for Laban, and he does not strike me as a mover or a shaker."

"Yeah. Who should we talk to? Who knows the most people?"

I thought for a moment. I thought about the people I knew who knew the most people. "Politicians, and pastors?"

Veronica smiled. "Where is the nearest big church?" she shouted to the bus driver.

"Next stop is near St. Thomas," the bus driver said.

We got off at the next stop and hurried toward St. Thomas. The church was beautiful and huge. It was constructed with cut cobblestone. The bell tower was tall and magnificent. The stairs to the front door were concrete.

We walked up the stairs and opened the door. The smell of incense and candles filled the air. The sanctuary was huge. Wooden pews with red cushions filled the space. Large stained glass windows surrounded us but were darkened as the sun had now set. We looked around and saw no one.

"Hello?" Veronica yelled.

At first, we had not noticed the woman wearing the clothing of a nun who had been kneeling, in the front pew, in prayer. But when Veronica yelled, she stood and started coming our way. She looked angry. She placed her finger to her lips and speed-walked in our direction.

"Young lady," she said in a deep voice with an accent that sounded German and almost growled, "This is a sacred place, not a playground. I will thank you for keeping your voice down and showing some respect."

Before entering the church, we had planned on coming in and blurting out the need, giving whoever we met a few packets, asking them who else they thought we should give them to, and going away. But this nun's grouchy attitude had thrown both of us off. I found myself apologizing, and Veronica got quiet.

"And what is that thing doing in here?" she said pointing to Elmo.

Even Elmo started acting shy.

"Please, ma'am," Veronica said, and her voice cracked as though she was going to cry. The nun looked at Veronica, and she gave a slight smile.

"My dear," the nun said, and her voice had softened, "I am Mother Catherine. I work at the school next door and was here praying. But what is it I can help you with?"

Veronica and I told her the whole story. It was not well told. We did not know where to start. Veronica started. I interrupted. Veronica interrupted me. We went back and forth. The whole time Mother Catherine listened without talking. Occasionally she would nod quietly, but for most of our story, she stared at us with narrowed eyes.

When our story was done, the nun raised her eyebrows. "Thank you for that. If I understand the situation correctly, we need to get this information to as many important and influential people as possible? We need to get this," she pointed to the backpack, "out to the world?"

We nodded.

"This is really a small thing." She then started to mumble

loud enough for us to hear but clearly was just speaking to herself. She listed names as though we knew who she was talking about. "David Schneider is a fundraiser for the school, and he would be very helpful... Jenny Gleason knows everyone... Paul Davis would be perfect... Governor Thompson has an aide who lives down the street and might be able to get a copy to him." Finally she paused, looked at us, and said, "Let's get started, shall we?"

We followed her to an office behind the sanctuary, and she found a map of the city and an address book from her drawer. She pulled out a pen and tried to write on the map. The pen was dry, and she scribbled in a circle trying to get it started. No ink came out. She threw the pen in the trash and got another pen from the drawer. She scribbled again. This pen worked. She started to read the address book and then write on the map. Within a few minutes, she had sketched out a plan. We would canvass the city, dropping off copies with important and influential people that she thought would be sympathetic to our cause. She stood up, put on a gray sweater over her habit, and said, "Let's go."

We followed her down a hallway and back outside. Soon we were half walking, half running down the street. She led us through the neighborhoods. Old two-story houses lined the street. We ran up to doors marked on the map, knocked, and after offering a brief explanation to the person that answered, kept going. If no one answered, we left a packet. For these, Mother Catherine would hand-write a short message on the front page. Then we would keep running.

We had 53 packets (Veronica counted as we distributed). We went late into the night passing them out. It was sort of awkward knocking on doors in the middle of the night, but the residents would always respond with kindness when they saw Mother Catherine. We were even given food and drink to keep us going on our way. As we handed out the last packet, Mother Catherine looked at her watch. It was 3:02 am. She smiled at us with satisfaction on her face.

"If what you told me is true," she said with a half smile, "the world will never see nuclear war again." And with that, the enormity of the idea hit me. For my entire life and my father's entire life and a good chunk of my grandfather's life, nuclear war had loomed as a menace over the world. It was a doomsday weapon that, on some level, everyone believed would someday destroy the world. And now it would not. Now it was gone. Nuclear bombs were worthless. Or at least they would be. As soon as cities were protected by ADK-9 – which, if Mother Catherine was correct, would happen soon.

"What now?" Mother Catherine said.

"I have no idea," I said.

"Sleep," Veronica said with a note of desperation in her voice.

"Very well. Back to the church. I will inform the priest that you will be sleeping in the pews."

CHAPTER TWENTY-SIX

I WOKE up stiff and sore. I groaned. I heard Veronica groan from the pew across the aisle. I rolled and came crashing down on Elmo who was lying on the floor below me. He crawled out from under me and stood in the aisle and stretched. Veronica looked up at me. "Whoa," I said, "that is some serious bedhead." Her hair was standing almost straight up in the back and was matted to her forehead in the front.

"Shut up. Yours looks worse."

Mother Catherine came hurrying in just as I was about to tell Veronica that it was not possible to look worse. "Children, get ready. I fear we rested too long and too soon.

"On television, they are announcing the transition of power right now. Effective at midnight tonight this man,

Gibion, will take complete control of the entire U.S. military. Our efforts tonight may have ended future nuclear wars, but that man in control could still be a tyrant in the old-fashioned way. We may not be able to stop him, but we should try. Grab your things, use the bathroom, and meet me outside by the car – we leave in 5 minutes."

We hurried, and soon we were on the road. Mother Catherine's car was pretty bad. It was a red 1984 Datsun station wagon. The seat belts did not work, and I am pretty sure its top speed was 55. It is hard to express how frustrating it is when the future of the world depends on how fast you go, and you are getting honked at for going too slow.

We were on our way to what remained of Washington where the handoff of power was going to happen – at midnight tonight. The map said it was an eight-hour drive which would put us there around 8 pm, but at the pace we were traveling, we would be lucky to get there before the midnight handoff.

The reporter on the radio described the planned ceremony. It is not easy to hand over the keys to the most powerful military in the world. In order to make it happen peacefully, everyone in the military with the rank of general or higher would agree to step down and leave the country with their families. They had to be on airplanes by midnight to be assured safe passage. President James and his family also would be leaving as soon as the handoff was complete. All lower ranking military personnel would be given a choice to swear loyalty to Reginald Gibion or turn over their weapons and return to civilian life. For the past week, Gibion had been hiring as many mercenaries as possible to supplement his already formidable army.

What would happen tonight would be the *official* handoff. All access codes, military passwords, documents, and secrets would be handed over. The president would officially sign his resignation, and all nine Supreme Court justices would be present as the Constitution of the United States would be nullified in favor of a dictatorship. The announcer on the radio, repeating Gibion's statement, assured listeners that this would be a temporary state and that democracy would be restored as soon as order was established and all members of the "corrupt United States government" were removed.

Gibion would be there in person to accept his new role. He obviously feared last-minute trickery by the U.S. government because also present would be hundreds of Gib-bots along with a massive showing of his own security force. What was not stated by the announcer but was evident in his voice and in the faces of every person we saw was the looming threat hanging over the whole affair. The fear everyone shared was palpable: No one wanted any more bombs to drop.

Mother Catherine said that we needed to inform someone high up about the fact that the nuclear bomb was no longer a threat, that in theory, every city in the world could be made safe tonight.

It was almost eleven in the evening when we finally reached the outskirts of Washington. The wreckage of the city was shocking and dark. Emergency vehicles blocked major roadways into the city. About 30 miles from the city, we left the expressway and made our way through corn fields and rural highways. The event was at McKinley Mansion, an old country house that was for generations used by senators for weekend outings, social events, and meetings. It was outside of the city and far enough away from the blast radius. Mother Catherine had to stop to ask for directions a few times, but eventually we found ourselves approaching the mansion via an old country road. For such a momentous event, I was surprised by the small-ness of the crowd outside the gate. In fact, there were only two press vans parked in front. We stopped and talked with them.

The press, like everyone else, was afraid. With the collapse of the government, many feared that the new president would crack down on a free press. Some had chosen to walk away from the profession altogether, but many more just decided to report from the safe distance of newsrooms. The very few reporters that did show up made it clear that they were also doing it out of fear: They said that they were afraid of *not* covering it. Gibion might lash out if no one showed. They were prepared to say whatever Gibion wanted them to say and were sitting outside the mansion awaiting instructions. Gibion's team had already been in contact with them. One cameraman had been allowed inside to record the event. Everyone else was supposed to report from outside. We parked our car and got out.

The reporters paid little attention to us. In the growing darkness, we were able to slowly move away from them into the night. When we were a safe distance away and into the woods on the east side of the building, we started to plan. We could see the helicopters lined up in the field behind the house. Soldiers from both sides were eyeing each other as they stood near the front gate and in the landing area. At midnight, the helicopters would carry all the higher level military members and their families out of the country. Their pilots were already sitting in them, engines running, getting prepared for the journey.

We needed to get in the building without drawing the attention of Gibion's soldiers. We needed to alert someone higher up in the U.S. government that we had ADK-9 and that Gibion's nuclear threat was no longer credible. Hopefully, they could figure out how to delay things from there. The security was massive though. Behind the press line, there was a cement barrier that prevented anyone from ramming through. Behind that barrier stood hundreds of Gibionite soldiers and several large tanks were also parked there. Behind them a chain link fence had been constructed with barbed wire above it. Black hawk helicopters circled overhead. If the control centers suffered from not enough security, McKinley Mansion overcompensated. Getting through was not going to be easy.

But you do not need to break through if you can just walk through. Mother Catherine in her nun's habit was an intimidating woman. The plan was for her to walk up to the front gate as if she belonged there. She would walk slowly and confidently past any guards at the door, and if anyone tried to stop her, she would make them feel like they messed up for even talking to her. I was skeptical. Mother Catherine laughed and said that if she carries herself with confidence, no one questions a nun. She lowered her voice as though she were confessing something terrible and said that she occasionally used her uniform to get backstage at the opera to meet the singers. When in her habit, no one had ever stopped her from going where she wanted.

So, Mother Catherine would get inside and start spreading the news to the U.S. government leaders. That was the whole plan. Veronica, Elmo, and I didn't really have a role. We were to sit outside and wait. If Mother Catherine's effort failed, it would be up to us to figure out another plan.

At 11:37 pm, Mother Catherine left us and walked around the corner to the front gate. She confidently walked up to the guards, looked past them, raised her hand to wave confidently at someone inside, and stepped around the guards who did not stop her. She was inside as easily as that!

But then the very unfortunate thing happened. The man she had waved to walked up to her and started talking. Then there was commotion around them, and the man raised his voice in alarm. Mother Catherine tried to walk away from him, but the man called to the guards. Within seconds, the guards from the gate had tackled Mother Catherine, and she was being led back out of the gate in handcuffs. The guards and a group of people from inside were gathered around a military transport truck, and she was put in the back.

"Ok, we are up. I am going in," Veronica spoke quickly. "I am going to get inside, hide, and look for opportunities to talk to U.S. government people. You stay here. If I get stopped or if you do not hear from me by 11:55 pm, you figure out how to get in from the side and try to stop things." Veronica said this without waiting for me to say anything and then ran for the gate. I looked at my watch, 11:41 pm.

With all the commotion of the guards arresting Mother Catherine, Veronica was able to walk up to the cement barrier unnoticed. As the guards laughed and watched the nun get dragged into the transport truck, Veronica jumped the cement barrier and ducked behind the shrubbery next to the chain link fence. When the drama of Mother Catherine's arrest was complete, the guards walked back out to the cement barrier leaving Veronica behind them. She slipped out from behind the shrubs, crawled inside the chain link fence and dove into the bushes lining the driveway that led up to the front door. And she was in.

I took Elmo back around the side of the mansion. From there, I looked past the cement barrier. I looked past the tank that was parked between the barrier and the chain link fence. I looked past the handful of guards pacing around the tank between the barrier and the fence. I saw the old original McKinley Mansion stone wall that divided the yard from the field. I knew that if I was going to position myself to help Veronica, I needed to get past the barrier, guards, and fence. Then I would need to get over that stone wall. All within the next few minutes.

As I stood and thought, the hatch to the tank opened and

one of Gibion's soldiers raised his head up and smiled. "Hey," he shouted to the guards standing there. They looked and he waved for them to come over to him. He ducked back into the tank and pulled out a bottle of wine, some paper cups, and a hand-held radio. He climbed out of the tank and sat on the tire treads. The five soldiers that had been pacing the fence walked over to him. He turned up the radio and I could hear the host talking about the events inside the mansion. As the host spoke, the driver of the tank uncorked the bottle. "We will toast at the moment of victory!" he said with excitement in his voice and he poured the wine into the six paper cups that he had lined up on the tread.

As I took in the scene, I suddenly saw something. The height of the tank was almost the same height as the chain link fence. With a running start, I thought I might be able to clear the fence and land on the stone wall behind it. I looked at my watch, and it was 11:49. The second hand spun around slowly... the sound of helicopter engines in the field rumbled... Elmo panted beside me... 11:50.

I crouched as I ran from the far side of the tank hoping that the darkness and angle would shield me from their view. I came to the back of the tank and put my foot on the tread. I could hear the voices of the men on the other side. I climbed up the side of the tire tread and looked over the fence, past the wall, and I could now clearly see the mansion. In the dark, I could see lights on inside and people moving around. The yard was empty. Large French windows showed a full spectrum of the dining hall. I could see U.S. military soldiers lined up rigidly by the wall. They all looked nervous. I also could see Gibion's men. They did not look nervous. They swaggered as they walked, and I could see that many of them were smiling and laughing.

Then in the next room over, I saw President Adam James. He was standing in a crowd of soldiers that were making their way toward the dining hall right in front of the French window… 11:51pm. Then I saw several Gib-bots enter the room and everyone turn to look at them… 11:52pm.

Where was Veronica? Three minutes before I had to move. I looked over and could see that the guards were already drinking the wine. I eyed the gap between the fence and the stone wall and was pretty sure I could make the jump. Elmo whimpered. I really did not want to leave him down there. If I had to create a distraction, he would be helpful. But how do you get a giant dog to climb on top of a tank and jump a fence? I climbed back down. I whispered to Elmo what we were doing. Do dogs understand human language? Science says no, but Elmo always seems to understand. I led him next to the tank, pulled his paws against the tread then climbed under him and tried to lift. His front end slid forward, and I found myself with his back end on my shoulder and his front end on the grass. Elmo looked at me like I was crazy… 11:53pm.

I ran back to the line of trees to try to find something to help. Near the edge of the woods, there was a scrapheap of old discarded construction materials. In that, there was an old metal tub. It was heavy, but I lifted the front end and dragged it back over to the tank. The tub was about three feet tall and a few feet wide. I turned it over and told Elmo to jump. He did not respond. I climbed up the tank again, and with a whisper-yell, I called him.

If dogs could fly, cats would probably not climb trees. But I now have an idea of what that would look like. Elmo ran, jumped on the tub, and cleared the tire treads landing on the back of the tank. His paws scratched the top of it and he twisted as he landed but he was up. I looked at my watch… 11:55pm!

Still no Veronica. Time to move. The people in the window were moving around a table. I could see that the final handoff was about to happen. I took two steps and jumped. I cleared the chain link fence, landed for a moment on the stone wall, lost my grip, and tumbled into the yard of McKinley Mansion. A second later, Elmo followed (much more gracefully). I got up, gasping for air, and crawled behind a tree that was halfway in between the wall and the house and tried to hide. It was too thin, and I had a giant dog with me. It was just a matter of time before someone noticed me. I had to get in that house right now. I looked up, and a rotten branch hung low over my head. I reached up and grabbed it. It broke off with a crunch.

"Hey, you!" a Gibion guard yelled. I ran, branch in hand, toward the house. I heard gunshots. I felt a bee sting my calf but kept running. I was now 10-feet from the house. I could hear shouting and more gunfire. Five feet from the house. Elmo ran next to me. I brought the heavy branch down upon the French window pane. There was an explosion of glass. I stepped on the window sill and started to climb through. Elmo jumped in after me.

We jumped down into a large room. It looked like a medieval dining hall. Banners with embroidered family crests hung from the ceiling. Paintings of men on horses lined the walls. A fireplace was roaring on the west wall. But I barely noticed all that. What I did notice were the people. There were probably at least 100 people in the room – far more than my estimate from the outside. The crowd was clearly split between U.S. government and Gibion allies. Everyone had guns. Everyone was staring at me.

Climbing through the broken window, I had cut my hand pretty bad, and it was bleeding on the floor. There was also blood in my shoe for some reason. I could feel it filling up. That bee sting on my calf was hurting terribly now too. Elmo growled next to me. I turned slowly looking for the president. I saw him. He was standing by a table holding a pen.

"Don't do it!" I yelled. But my voice faltered. I realized I could not speak clearly. My head was cloudy for some reason. I tried to walk, but my leg with the bee sting did not work. I fell. As I lay on the ground, I saw people coming toward me. I saw Gibion walking my way too. Behind him, I saw the president still standing with a pen in hand. Behind him, I saw a plant. Behind the plant, I saw Veronica. She was climbing out and moving toward the president. As Gibion's big hands grabbed me, I saw Veronica whispering to the president. "Thomas, I am so disappointed in you. And you are much too late," Gibion whispered in my ear. Then things went black.

CHAPTER TWENTY-SEVEN

I OPENED my eyes when it got too noisy to sleep. The noise was rude. I wondered why my mom was allowing it. I wanted it to stop. I was so tired. The noise did not stop. "Quiet...," I tried to yell and then readjusted my arms under my head. But the noise grew louder. Then I recognized the noise.

Gunshots. Lots of gunshots. I opened my eyes. I was lying on the floor by the fire, and I was looking at a battlefield. U.S. government soldiers and Gibion's soldiers were shooting machine gun fire at each other using tables, chairs, and doorways for cover. I had no cover.

And it was chaos. The dead lay all around. The large open space of the dining hall was a no man's land between the two rooms on the north and the south. On the north side, I could see Gibion soldiers reaching out firing off rounds and then ducking back behind the wall and turned over tables for cover. On the south side were U.S. government soldiers doing the same. The thick stone walls provided excellent cover for both sides, and eventually, those behind the tables were killed or fell back behind the stone walls. The room was full of bodies, but the killing appeared to be over. No one was landing shots now despite the hail of bullets.

This stalemate was broken by the Gib-bots. Without warning, a man in white stepped out from the north and walked toward the southern room. He was followed by another, and another, and another. The U.S. government soldiers filled each of these cyborgs with bullets. The bullets tore their clothes and the surface of their bodies but did not significantly slow them down. They kept walking with deadly calm determination toward the southern room.

"Fall back! Fall back!" I heard soldiers scream as they realized retreat was required. The room continued to fill with Gib-bots marching. The U.S. military fired off more rounds as they retreated, tearing the flesh of the Gib-bots, but they did not stop marching forward. Until suddenly they did. In the middle of all the shooting and mayhem, the Gib-bots froze. They suddenly stopped marching. They became strange gory white manikins, dripping blood but standing perfectly still. Silence followed for a surreally long time. Faces looked out from both sides of the room.

I knew what it meant for Gibion's cyborgs to freeze suddenly. I had seen it before. I immediately realized that someone had destroyed the last control center. I think that Gibion knew as well. What we did not know, at the time, was the story of how it happened.

THIS WHOLE STORY has been told with so many falsehoods and confusions that I have tried to limit what I have said to what I saw personally to ensure that everything was correct. But here I feel required to violate my rule for the sake of explanation. This was related to me by Sean himself.

Remember Sean? The guy with the Avengers shirt and the Chihuahuas? The guy we left Hoover with? Well, it turns out that he was actually a pretty good guy. And he was studying to be a pilot. After we left his house, he sat and talked with Hoover as Hoover was bleeding and almost dying. He learned about what we were doing and decided that he wanted to help. Sean was one of the few that actually paid attention when Enduring Freedom was rolled out. He never liked it and never forgot about it. While Hoover fought back from the edge of death, they planned. And as they planned, they became convinced that they could do only one thing – attempt to destroy the final control center. Hoover secured a bomb from an abandoned Third Party warehouse on the west side. And a few hours before midnight, as Mother Catherine, Veronica, Elmo, and I drove (at 55 miles per hour) toward Washington, Sean and Hoover departed from the Ann Arbor Municipal Airport. Getting Hoover, who still struggled to move, onto the plane was not an easy task. But soon they were in the air heading to the final center 20 miles southwest of the airport.

THE MANCHESTER CONTROL CENTER came into view. Sean flew low. As Gibion's guards fired up at him, Hoover aimed for the southwest corner (the location of the database according to the envelope). Hoover had never played sports in high school. His cheesy complexion and hefty build certainly offered no indications that he was an athlete. His sickly inability to even get on the plane without a herculean effort by Sean made what followed even less predictable. Hoover leaned out the open door of the plane, reached back his hand, and threw a strike that, if a scout for the Detroit Tigers had been watching, would have generated interest. The bomb fell, hit, exploded, and at that very moment, miles away, every remaining Gib-bot froze.

I HEARD Gibion yell to his men to attack. The Gibion cyborgs would not be helpful anymore. Gibion's men came running out through the door, and as they weaved between the frozen Gib-bots, gunfire broke out from the southern doorway. The first few Gibionites fell, but thanks to the confusion and the fact that many of the U.S. government soldiers had already retreated, Gibion's men got through. I could not see what happened, but I heard lots of screaming and shooting.

Reginald Gibion then came strolling into the room from the northern door. A few minutes later, Hugo came back. He saluted Gibion, "Adam James is dead. So are most of his generals."

Those words were a load of TNT in my chest. The president of the United States of America was dead? His generals were dead? That meant we had lost. Gibion had secured every military code. For all the public knew he was also the globe's only remaining nuclear power. He could walk out that door, get into one of his helicopters, fly to the nearest military base, and he would be the most powerful ruler in the world.

But he was not quite ready to do all that because at that moment he noticed me craning my neck to look at him. Despite all his power and success, the sight of me made him mad.

"President James is dead. David is dead. Jacob is dead," he

said walking over to me with a smile on his face. "And now," he raised a pistol from his waist and pointed it at me, "you are dead, too. So it goes for all who oppose Reginald Gibion." I closed my eyes, ready to die.

This story started with a dog bite as I lay in bed. And it ends with a dog bite as well. Elmo always was a smart dog. He also is pretty defensive of me. When Gibion raised that gun, Elmo, who had been keeping guard over me, jumped. Once again, I saw a dog fly. A red blur. Being hit by a flying Elmo is not fun I am sure. Gibion fell hard. His gun flew. Hugo was clearly surprised and turned to help but fumbled with his gun. "Bam!" came a gunshot from behind him. Hugo crumpled to the floor. Veronica stood with a pistol smoking in her hand. She dropped it, shocked at what she had done.

I prepared for the worst. Gibion's men would come in, kill Elmo then probably kill Veronica and me. And Gibion, if he were still alive, would be installed as president after all. But something strange happened. A soldier wearing a brown Gibionite uniform came in alone. He looked at the scene with wide eyes. He looked at Veronica. He looked at me. He looked at Hugo's body. He looked at Elmo who had now backed off Gibion but was still growling at him. Then he looked at Gibion – bitten and bloody but still alive on the floor. "Shoot the dog!" Gibion yelled. But the man did not shoot Elmo. He did something strange. He pointed his gun at Gibion. His finger tightened on the trigger. A shot rang out. And Gibion was no more.

I never found out who that man was. There are many rumors and theories, but no one knows for sure. But I do know that David and Isaac could not have been the only ones who had signed on with Gibion in his early days only to regret it later. That man had probably been waiting for a moment like that and took advantage of it when it came.

After shooting Gibion, he dropped his gun, walked out of the room, and disappeared never to be heard from again.

The U.S. and the Gibionite armies were both now leaderless. The president and the generals were dead. Gibion and Hugo were dead. There was nothing for these armies to do but to go home. As soldiers came back into the room, one by one they surveyed the scene, put down their weapons, and slowly walked back out. As they left, I heard conversations about going home. No more gunfire. No more war.

And as we sat there in that room the house emptied. Outside, I heard helicopters taking off. The fire in the fireplace died down, and the room darkened. I asked Veronica to turn on the lights, and she said the lights were on. But things kept getting darker. Then all the light in the room narrowed in front of my eyes. I placed my head down. Darkness. I could hear Veronica saying my name, but her voice got further and further away. Silence.

———

I OPENED MY EYES. A white ceiling. A needle taped to my arm. A bag of fluid connected to the needle. Flowers next to me on a small table. A TV in the corner of the room. I tried to sit up, but my head hurt. Then I saw her, smiling at me with her long brown hair and her beautiful weatherworn face. It was the face of a childhood that had been lost. "Mom," I said. When she heard my voice her mouth opened and her eyes widened, and she smiled. She looked like she had been crying, but was now overcome with joy. Behind her stood my father. "Hey pal," he said.

Both my mother and father came to me and wrapped me in their arms. Their embrace, their smell, their movements all were at once so familiar and yet seemed like ancient memories. What followed was laughter, tears, and more laughter. I wanted to ask them what had happened to them. I wanted to tell them what happened to me. But before I could start asking and telling, I noticed a figure lying on the other bed in the room directly behind my father.

There lay a man with his arm full of needles and bags of fluids surrounding him. He flashed a large grin. "David?" I asked.

"Thomas, what a pleasure it is to share this hospital room with you," he said this, and I waited for some explanation as to how he was now in this hospital room with me. But only a long smile followed.

"I thought you were dead."

"No, I am not dead. Despite the best efforts of Gibion's machine gun fire and being left for dead in an Ann Arbor parking lot, I have survived to share a hospital room with the man who will be forever remembered as the one that stopped a murderous tyrant and saved the world from nuclear war."

When Veronica learned I was awake, she came running into the room. Behind her came her own father and mother. Veronica's mother held a leash and behind her came Elmo.

The hospital room was now packed, but two nurses still were able to squeeze in the room to see what was causing the commotion. Smiling when they saw me awake, one went to get a doctor, and the other tried unsuccessfully to shoo out some of the crowd.

It took a few more days for the doctors to let me go, and in that time I heard the whole story from my parents. They had been up late, and their old friend Sam had surprised them by showing up at their door. He warned them that they had been discovered and were in danger. But before they could do anything the Gib-bots burst through the door. Sam and my father put up an insane fight. The house was smashed and destroyed, but in the end, the Gib-bots were too much. They grabbed my father and mother and left Sam for dead on the floor. Before they could drag my father out, he put the key to his safe in Sam's hand and whispered brief instructions. On the way out the door, one of the Gib-bots stopped and set down a pack of explosives. They posted a Gib-bot outside the house to monitor the explosion. My family laughs to this day about the fact that I was able to sleep through all this. In my defense, my room had thick walls. And I was dreaming about exams.

When Gibion learned that I had escaped, he schemed to use the police to deal with me. He modified police records to give me a long criminal record and a history of blowing things up. From that point forward, every police officer in the country thought I was a deranged murderer who had killed my parents and blown up my house. The police probably would have killed me if given a chance, just like Sam said. As I was falling down the stairs that morning, Gibion was transporting my parents to a warehouse in Northern Michigan, and he had planned on torturing them for information. But after the government bombed the Ann Arbor control center, things got so crazy that he never had time to question them. They stayed locked up until Gibion was killed. On the day that he was killed, one of the guards unlocked the cell door and walked away without saying anything.

So, now you know how the U.S. government fell, nuclear war was abolished forever, and Gibion was thwarted. I probably do not need to tell you the story of how we came to have six nations where there once was one. Everyone knows that story, and the history books actually get it mostly right... with the exception of the founding of the Nation of Texas.

But our story, the story of the foundation of the Great Lakes Republic, is pretty well known so I will not bother to tell it here.

And so, this concludes my story. What was normal back then is no longer normal. The nation I knew is gone. The life I lived is gone. The internet is gone…. Did I discuss the internet not coming back on? Whatever they did to kill the internet lasted. There was no switch to turn it back on. Wires were fried by high voltage? Servers were bombed? Not exactly sure. But no hardware worth using was left. Computers became paperweights. And that is maybe the biggest difference. I know that I sound like an old timer but there was a time when everyone used to sit around on their computers all day. I used to play video games with people from Russia - really. Picture a nice day in the summer. Now picture kids sitting inside watching movies or playing online games. That was perfectly normal back then! That is what it was like. All gone now.

But I don't want to go on on and on. I am sure your parents have told you all of this already. Normality as we knew it…. Is gone. But the new life is not bad.

So… you now have the whole story. If you are going to tell it, tell it properly. No more excuses, folks. You have it in writing from someone that was there. Start to finish.

EPILOGUE

I SAT next to my mother and father and watched as the pastor said the ancient words. I watched as he prayed the ancient prayers. The body of Jacob Burke would be buried in the Great Lakes National Cemetery just outside Ann Arbor. He was given a hero's funeral and the presidents of Greater California, the Rocky Mountain States, and Dixie all came. The president of New England sent his regards. Texas said nothing – typical.

The pastor praised Jacob for his heroism in destroying the control centers. He praised him for his ingenious ability to stay one step ahead of both Gibion and the U.S. government. But when I stood in front of that giant crowd in the sanctuary of St. Andrew's Anglican Church, I did not speak of those things. I spoke of what he taught me.

Jacob was always angry and sullen. But he lived not for himself but for others. He lived for principle above pragmatics. And he never considered life something to be grasped. God gave us life to spend it, not save it. He had spent his life gloriously for me. For Veronica. For humanity.

I finished my eulogy, closed the black folder that held my notes, and stepped away from the podium. Standing on the dais, I looked out at the packed sanctuary. My mother and father were in the front pew with Veronica and her family. I looked past them and saw extended family, politicians, and church leaders. I saw Hoover. I saw Sean. And in the back, I saw Mother Catherine, holding Elmo on a leash. The doors were open, and through them I saw the sunny summer day. I saw the church lawn that led down to Division Street. I saw the school across the street. And then I saw something else. Veronica tells me it was probably just my imagination going crazy due to the funeral and all. But I don't think so.

A huge man dressed all in white. Standing mechanically. Looking at me. Just for a moment. I looked down. And when I looked back up, he was gone.

GRATITUDE

My parents for the reading, correcting, suggesting, rewriting,
illustrating, and encouraging.

My wife for the time and love.

My kids for the inspiration.

Fifth Ave for the chance.

The Great Story Teller for everything.

ABOUT THE AUTHOR

VW Shurtliff loves stories. The more astute reader may have already figured out that VW writes stories. But those who know VW are aware that he also loves reading them. His favorite books appeal to his 13-year-old self. He loves Sherlock Holmes, Treasure Island, Narnia, and The Lord of the Rings. More than anything, VW loves spending time with his family, taking long walks with his shaggy and very smart dog, and spending time at his home in Ann Arbor, the city of his childhood. If you want to know when VW's next book will come out, follow him at:

facebook.com/vwshurtliff
twitter.com/WSurely